THE ORIGINAL ALIBI

A Matt Kile Mystery

By

Best Selling Mystery Author

DAVID BISHOP

THE ORIGINAL ALIBI

Cover Designed by Paradox Book Covers.

David Bishop may be contacted through his Internet site:
http://www.davidbishopbooks.com

ISBN: 978-1-938135-49-1 (eBook)
ISBN: ISBN-13: 978-1534625976
ISBN-10: 1534625976 (Paperback)

Version 10 June 2016

Praise for: ***The Original Alibi, a Matt Kile Mystery***

From Authors and Readers:

There are many very good mystery writers out there, but in my view, Bishop is rapidly moving into the top rank. His work is detailed without being wordy, his plots appropriately twisted, yet subtle, and he is always accurate when it comes to police work. Mystery plots that hold a reader's attention are very difficult to concoct, but Bishop seems to do it in his sleep. *"The Original Alibi,"* is his latest.

Gerald Lane Summers, author of *Mobley's Law, A Mobley Meadows Novel.*

***

This witty novel whisks readers into an expertly plotted story populated by well drawn characters with tantalizing glimpses of danger lurking just beneath the surface. Matt Kile is smart, human and very, very funny; a man with his own rules and sense of honor. Bishop leaves us hungering for the next installment in the Matt Kile mystery series.

Kim Mellen, reader.

***

If you like your coffee black, whiskey straight, and private investigators with a questionable past, you'll love this new release Matt Kile tale, *The Original Alibi*, from David Bishop.

Toby Neal, author of the Lei Crime Series.

Praise for: *Who Murdered Garson Talmadge*, the first Matt Kile Mystery

From Authors and Readers:

Bishop takes you from California to Paris at a non-stop pace and mixes in the dead man's grown children, an ex-wife's bitter sister, international arms dealers and the FBI. All presented from Matt's point-to-view and written with dialogue that's crisp, action that's suspenseful and a plot filled with a few twists you'll never see coming. It makes for a can't put-it-down story you won't want to miss.
Cathi Stoler, author of *Telling Lies.*

***

The dialogue is crisp and distinct, breathing life and sincerity into each of the characters. This was my first foray into David's work and I enjoyed it greatly. I can't wait to read more. Recommended!

***

Bishop does a great job in this murder/mystery, keeping you guessing until the very end. The characters are likeable and the pace is fast. Most importantly the ending is definitive and satisfying, leaving you yearning for what trouble Kile gets himself into next. Fans of JA Konrath, John Locke, and Rick Murcer will find Bishop's style to their liking.
Atul Kumar, author of *Seven Patients.*

***

Five Stars for David Bishop's carefully plotted and beautifully written mystery!

Novels by David Bishop

For current information on new releases visit:

www.davidbishopbooks.com

Novels by David Bishop

For current information on new releases visit:

www.davidbishopbooks.com

Currently Available:

The Beholder, a Maddie Richards Mystery

Who Murdered Garson Talmadge, a Matt Kile Mystery

The Woman, a Linda Darby Novel

The Third Coincidence

The Blackmail Club, a Jack McCall Mystery

The Original Alibi, a Matt Kile Mystery

Money & Murder, a Matt Kile Mystery: A Short Story

Death of a Bankster, a Maddie Richards Mystery

Find My Little Sister, a Matt Kile Mystery

Hometown Secrets, a Linda Darby Novel

The Maltese Pigeon, a Matt Kile Mystery

Judge Snider's Folly, a Matt Kile Mystery

Coming soon.

The 1st Lady's 2nd Man, a Linda Darby Novel

The Schroeder Protocol

The Red Hat Murders, a Maddie Richards Mystery

Murder by Choice

To be notified when each of the above titles are available:
Send your email address to,
david@davidbishopbooks.com

For more information on books and characters visit:
www.davidbishopbooks.com
Each forthcoming novel will have a new list of titles and dates.

Dedication

This novel is dedicated to Jerry and Sue Little, Frank and Linda Evans, Harry and Karen Evans, friends lost on the sea of life. Also other friends no longer seen due to relocations and career changes; including, but not limited to, Paul and Marsha Visage, Bill Wark and his wife, Fred Leetch and his wife, Steve and Jan Shanks, Dan and Jeanne Nelson, Adam and Patsy Bono, John Meng and his wife, Richard and Melanie Houser, Bill and Mary Lee, Loy and Ellie Brooks, Tom and Diane, Richard and Toni Yaskowitz, Jim and Nancy Chapman, Dick Rice and his wife, Roger and Nancy Nelson, Lou and Diane Giordano, Bill Holl and his wife, Jim and Sue Bulgrin, and Judy New among others.

I would also like to acknowledge others who have become an extended family to me: Jennifer and Andy Rose, Hayley, Autumn, and Emma, as well as many others who have found their way into this man's life, enriching me by their presence, goodness, and affection. And last, but certainly not least, this book, as with my others, is dedicated to my sons and my grandchildren, nieces and nephews, my sister Diane Kilby, and brother, Bill Bishop. I would also like to acknowledge all my former Kiwanis brothers in Durango, Colorado, I miss you guys.

My special thanks to the wonderful people who read early drafts and made suggestions which greatly enhanced the story: Martha Paley Francescato, Lynne Holmes, Kim Mellen, and Jerry Summers. Recognition is also due Britt Sylvester who provided technical expertise that was a great help in putting this story together. I appreciate your friendships and your talents.

My special thanks to the wonderful people who read early drafts and made suggestions which unfailingly enhance my stories. Among others, these include:

1. **Martha Paley Francescato, Professor Emerita of Literature, Film, Culture, and Honors** and dear friend whose contributions to my novels are too enormous to measure.
2. **Jody Madden,** my fiancée, capable editor and best friend.
3. **Sandy Hess,** a retired English major and dear friend.
4. **Patti Roberts**, founder of Paradox Promotions, who assisted me in developing the cover for this novel and formatted both the digital eBook and print book editions
5. **Diane Minks,** the founder of Focal Point eSolutions, my webmaster (or is it webmistress?), in either case the genius who created and maintains my website: www.davidbishopbooks.com
6. **Telemachus Press,** including Steve Jackson, Steve Himes, and Terri Himes, whose wonderful skills enhanced my earlier novels.

These fine professionals, dear friends and others have done so much to advance my career as a novelist. Thank you.

Chapter 1

"I believe that's your phone, dear," the woman's husband said. She stopped walking and fished her cell from the pocket of her windbreaker.

"Hello, Mrs. Yarbrough," said a voice into her ear. "I see you are enjoying your first early evening walk on the beach with your new puppy. She's such a cutie. Have you and Mr. Yarbrough named the pooch?"

"Who is this?"

"It doesn't matter. What matters is that you stay on the line after what is about to happen."

"What are you talking about?" Mrs. Yarbrough demanded, "Who are you?"

The leash Mrs. Yarbrough held went limp. Her white poodle slumped to the sand. "Robbie, what happened? Snookie is, I don't know, she's just … down." Mrs. Yarbrough held her cell phone as if she no longer knew she had it in her hand.

Robert, her husband, bent down. His knees displaced the sand next to Snookie. "She's dead, Mel. I think Snookie's been shot."

Melanie Yarbrough began bouncing on her toes, frantically waving her hands. She dropped her phone onto the beach, then bent down next to her husband and touched Snookie. He took her in his arms while she sobbed softly.

Several minutes later, Robert Yarbrough picked up his wife's cell phone, shook off the sand, and had started to close the top when he heard a loud voice. He held the phone to his ear. "Hello?"

"I've been waiting. Sorry about Snookie. It was necessary. You should know I took no pleasure in it."

"Did you do this?" Mr. Yarbrough asked. "Who the hell are you?"

"To your left, near the partially burnt log, I've left a box for you to use to take Snookie home. It's the right size. The inside has a soft new towel. It should do nicely."

"You shot Snookie? Why?"

"Take Snookie home and bury her in your wife's garden. You will hear from me. In the meantime, be glad you were not walking your newest grandson, Bobby, named after you, I presume. Your wife sometimes walks the little tike on a leash just as she walked Snookie today. I will know if you say anything about this, to anyone. If you do, Bobby Junior will be my next target."

"But what do you want? Why us?"

"All that will be made clear. Do not fret needlessly. There will be no more violence if you do as you're told. What will be required of you will not be difficult. It will not cost you any money. And it will be painless, if you follow orders. We'll talk soon."

The phone went dead.

Chapter 2

Eleven Years Later

"Don't forget, boss, we got a ten o'clock appointment. It's eight now." Axel handed me the morning paper, and put down a tray holding a glass of fresh-squeezed orange juice, a carafe of coffee, two cups, and a small plate of buttered English muffins.

It was pleasant enough sitting on the balcony, a little chilly but that's why they made robes.

Axel had been working for me only a couple of weeks, but we'd known each other for years in a very different setting. We were cellmates during my four years in state prison. I looked up. "Isn't that my shirt you're wearing?"

"Yeah."

"And my belt, why are you wearing my belt?"

"You wouldn't want your pants to fall down, would you, boss?"

"No, of course I wouldn't. And before you set up any more of these appointments, let me remind you I write mysteries. I don't handle cases in real life."

"You was a homicide dick and a good one from what I hear. And you got yourself a PI license."

"I wanted to prove I could get the license after the governor pardoned me. I write murder mysteries."

"Aren't you cold out here, boss?" Axel wrapped his arms around himself, gripping his biceps. "You wanna go inside?"

"It's a little nippy, but I'll stick for a while. I do wish they made robes in various lengths. No reason they can't." I'd been six-three since the eleventh grade but over the years robes kept getting shorter.

Axel had been inside close to forty years, during which he became as sweet a senior citizen as you'll ever know. Forty-one years ago, a half-million dollar payroll had been taken by a lone gunman, without violence. The jury had found Axel guilty. Axel had never changed his claim of innocence, but he has sometimes winked at me when the subject came up. The fact they had never found the money is likely why they held onto Axel over the years, while letting out younger hard-asses because of the overpopulation of prisons. For his last five years he had been an administrative assistant for the warden, doing a lot of his online research. Axel was a whiz using computers. I helped his parole along with the promise of a job.

In these first few weeks, his duties included trips to the dry cleaners and doing the home laundry and keeping the place clean. Axel always kept our cell neat, and he carried that forward to caring for my condo. I had to go with him to shop for groceries because Axel wasn't up to speed on driving anymore. He planned to take care of that but hadn't as yet. As you can see, his job description lacked clarity, it would evolve or so we imagined.

Unfortunately, we wore clothes similar enough in size for Axel was an even six feet. For each wearing, he had hand-altered my slacks by rolling up the pant legs. He also adjusted for our different waist measurements. I wear size thirty-eight. I'm guessing his at thirty-six, maybe thirty-four because he had my belt two notches tighter, which meant there would now be his-and-mine cinch marks in the leather.

"Boss, you remember that movie where Jack Nicholson's character said, 'never waste a boner and never trust a fart.' Well, that man was a prophet." Then Axel rushed inside. *The Bucket List* was a wonderful movie, but I didn't like him quoting that line while he was wearing my slacks. I settled back and looked at the newspaper with an eye out for Axel's return.

A few minutes later, Axel came back out. I felt some relief from his still wearing the same pair of my pants. He ran his hand across his mostly hairless head, and then wiped that hand on the backside of my pants.

"You helped save Clarice Talmadge," he said, as if he had never left the conversation. "I kept up with that story before you got me sprung."

I looked over at a gull circling past the balcony just off the railing. "I didn't get you sprung. The parole board was about to release you anyway. You'd been in long enough. I just tossed a job offer in the mix. That's all."

"That's what tipped the scales." Axel looked over at the gull that squawked while making its third pass.

Axel was sort of like a friend you took under your wing after he had spent thirty to forty years in a coma. I knew why the gulls, there were three now, were squawking. Axel sometimes threw pieces of bread out over the rail and, with me out here, he hadn't this morning. Feeding the birds was against building policy. I'd have to speak to him about it, but for now I couldn't refuse him the kind of small pleasures he had been denied for decades.

"You got out because you were no longer a threat to society, maybe to my wardrobe, but not to society."

"Well, that don't change the brilliant way you saved Clarice Talmadge's ass and, from what I've seen in the hallway, I'm glad you did, although from what I hear the woman's not the swiftest card in the deck."

"Now where did you hear that?"

"From Clara Birnbaum down on my floor, the former school teacher, she says Clarice spells Cincinnati with an 's.'"

"That's Clara. She's a good lady but she's jealous of Clarice."

"Anyway, the point is you helped her with her case. So, you still dig investigating stuff."

"That was different. Clarice was a neighbor and a friend accused of killing her husband, Garson Talmadge. I handled the investigation for her defense attorney."

"This case'll be different too, boss," he said while picking up the coffee carafe.

"How many times do I need to tell you to stop calling me boss? It's not necessary."

"Seems right to me, after all I work for you."

"You can't call me Matt, but you can wear my pants?" I held up my empty cup.

"Now you got it, boss." He filled my cup with a smirk on his face.

"The appointment, fill me in."

Axel took a seat and poured himself a little coffee. "Not much yet to tell. This guy, Franklin's his name, Reginald Franklin III, how's that for a handle, he's an attorney with a client who needs your help. He freely admitted his client specified Matthew Kile as the investigator he wanted. Admitting that up front told me he ain't shopping the job, so money's not an issue. I told him it would be a grand for this morning, just to talk and see if you'll handle the case. He understands that money's gone whether or not you join up. He didn't quibble. He's bringing the check."

I expected Axel would be around during the Franklin meeting. Axel didn't really have a set schedule. If I needed him, I told him and he'd be there. Otherwise, he came and went as he pleased and when he wasn't around I fended for myself. Like I said, his duties were evolving. I think Axel saw himself as my Kato or Dr. Watson or some such character. If I had my choice, I'd prefer him to be Archie Goodwin, the able assistant of Nero Wolfe, but then I would fail in comparison to Wolfe. My waistline was likely only half of Wolfe's girth, not to mention my falling well short of his genius.

"So what do you have going today?" I asked.

"After our meeting with Franklin, I've got a few close-by errands then I'll hoof it over and have lunch with the fellas at Mackie's. Don't worry, boss, Franklin won't know I'm around unless you call for me."

"You think Franklin could be the real client?"

"No way, he's fronting for someone. I could tell by his voice. He wasn't uptight. He did tell me it was some old case the cops have tossed aside. The dude's a smoker, so get him out on the balcony if he tries to light up. A pipe, I think. I could hear him inhale and bite down on the stem the way pipers do."

After all those years in the big house, as Axel still called prison, he had mastered reading the tone and pace of people's voices. He can read body language or faces, cons or bulls. All the old timers could do it, at least the ones with an ample helping of brains and judgment.

"The odds say I won't take this new case."

"Why not? You've about done up the book you was working on. And, hey, a grand's nothing to sneeze at. You know?"

Chapter 3

It was the fourth of December, three weeks before Christmas to the day, when I parked my new Ford Expedition in the turnaround in front of the home of General Whittaker, the client of the attorney, Reginald Franklin III. The general's home, an elegant place with a second floor, looked to be about six thousand square feet, and sat on a small cliff south of Long Beach, California, which backed up to the Pacific Ocean.

The door was opened by a man approximately fifty-five years of age. He appeared to be house staff. He wore a white shirt with a starched collar, the rest of his dress being black. He was a stout man, but not fat. His pants were hitched up closer to his neck than his navel. His ears reached out from his head like they were expected to catch fly balls rather than words.

He looked me up and down without disclosing the impression he gleaned from having done so. "Good evening, Mr. Kile. You're expected." Seeing my surprise at being recognized, he added, "Your picture is on the dust covers of your books. My name is Charles, Mr. Kile."

Few people called them dust covers any longer so Charles was a reader and, apparently, one not yet converted to reading eBooks.

"Please follow me." Charles was an average sized man. He looked fit and confident in his ability to do his job. He led me into a wide junction in the hallway, next to a wonderfully decorated Christmas tree, tall enough to grace both the ground floor and the second story which was open overhead. "Please wait here, Mr. Kile, while I let the general know you've arrived."

Noise or movement caused me to step beyond the tree and look up the stairwell to my left. From the balcony, a nubile brunette wearing a black something that aggressively fell within the category of lingerie, said, "You must be Mr. Kile." It wasn't a question. Not the way she said it.

I smiled and nodded. One of the principles I live by is that seeing a woman in skimpy lingerie meant, at the very least, the relationship automatically advanced to a first name basis. I said, "Call me, Matt." We exchanged smiles, only they weren't equal. Hers was framed in red and had a gloss that reflected the top light on the Christmas tree.

"Well, Matt," she said, "Charles sat a tray on the side table when he went to answer the door. Would you be a sweetheart and finish bringing it up?" She added, "Please," while leaning her forearms on the banister, her brown hair sliding around her shoulders. At least I assumed her forearms were on the banister. I wanted to be a good sweetheart so I picked up the tray which held one glass and a decanter of something you and I would guess was alcoholic and started up the stairs.

"This is a lovely home," I said after advancing a short distance.

"Yes it is. During the general's career, toward the end when he was a member of the joint chiefs, this home entertained two U.S. presidents and one pope."

"With you wearing a much different outfit, I'm sure."

"I was living with my mother then, and a little young during those years to wear something like this." She stood straight, bust out, and turned slowly to be certain I understood the full meaning of "something like this."

I actually preferred her enhancing the banister, but if that sounded like a complaint, you know it lacked substance. I had come not expecting to see anyone more attractive than a long-retired general. I was ten steps from her when Charles silently arrived beside me and took the tray. I stopped, wishing that Charles had waited for me at the bottom of the stairs.

"The general will see you now, Mr. Kile. Please follow me back downstairs to the study."

As we turned, she revealed her red, patent leather heels by coming down the stairs far enough to take the tray from Charles. She was old enough to realize that platform heels and skimpy lingerie went together like me and a warm feeling. Had I worn a hat, modesty would have required I hold it in front of myself as she came closer. She glanced down briefly then looked into my eyes. We exchanged one of those smiles that meant the kinds of things that smilers in such situations are never sure about. Then I switched my attention so as not to ruin her first impression by tripping and rolling down the stairs.

Her voice slid around me the way hot fudge slides around cold ice cream. "I hope we can continue getting acquainted some other time." I held the railing and turned to see her again displayed on the banister.

"I'd like that," I said. Then I followed Charles down the stairs. Well, I did after wishing I might one day be reincarnated as a banister, but not just any banister, her banister.

"Matt." I turned back and looked up at her. "Ditch the tie. You can do better." Then she turned her head, tossing her brown hair across her shoulders, and retreated into a room with double doors directly behind where she had stood.

"Charles, who was the lady?"

"Karen Whittaker, sir, the general's daughter. She's thirty-five, in case you're curious about that. The general was a late-season poppa." His tone did not disclose disapproval, but I did detect a slight shake of his head.

"Why, Charles, I understood it was bad form to speak of a woman's age."

"Yes, sir. But not Karen. She's proud of being thirty-five and looking twenty-five. She works at it. Hard." We shared those brief looks that men share. I'd explain, but the guys would kick me out of the club because they know women read my books.

* * *

General Whittaker rose from his chair, slowly, but agile for his age. His body looked slender compared to the pictures I'd seen of him in his robust years, yet he still had a military bearing. A burgundy colored jacket, not exactly a smoking jacket, but not a sport coat either, covered a long-sleeved khaki shirt. The jacket had been tailored to expose a matching measure of shirt cuff on each of his arms which were thin enough that the garment hung as cleanly as it would on a store mannequin. He was well dressed and neat except for a tangled crop of white hair freely growing from his ears. His wrists were frail. The skin on the backs of his hands, mottled. Still, his handshake remained mildly firm, yet cool to the touch.

"Mr. Kile," he said, "as you stated in one of your books, I like people better than principles, and people without principles best of all. From what I've learned, you should be one of my favorites. And I like your tie, but you didn't need to wear one on my account."

So far I had learned that my ties were a matter that could divide families. I agreed with the general, I liked the tie, but I doubted I would ever wear it again. Women who show cleavage don't fully realize the power they possess over mortal men, and please don't tell 'em.

"Are you married, Mr. Kile?"

"Once."

"Divorced?"

I nodded without hiding my irritation at his questions.

"Too bad."

"My ex-wife would disagree with you."

"Kids?"

"With due respect, General, that's enough of that. This isn't a lonely hearts meeting."

He smiled. His face revealed that he did not often smile.

"Before we get started I want to return the check your attorney, Mr. Franklin, gave me yesterday." I put it on his desk. "I can't help you with your case."

He left the check lying there and flicked his wrist a few times as if shooing a fly. I took this as an invitation to sit down; I did. After looking at his pocket watch, likely the one the articles reported he had carried since his youth, he said, "You are on time; I like that, sir."

His study was as elegant as the rest of the house, though more masculine. A massive mahogany desk sat between us, a wall of glass behind him showing off the Pacific Ocean as if it flowed simply to grace his home. The moon glazing the night fog sitting on the horizon gave the sheen of a protective coating. The way the sky looked, we might have another hour of good visibility, depending on the wind. The light in the study had been designed to be soft and indirect. According to the daily column in the newspaper that announces the ages of people they figure the rest of us care to know, the general was eighty-seven. One of the articles on him that I read before coming said he suffered from chronic uveitis, an inflammation of the eye. The condition could explain the subdued lighting.

The sidewall of the general's study closest to his desk was mostly bookcases, with some wall area left for photos from his career, the wall on the other side busy with more photos and plaques. One four-shelf bookcase held only VCR tapes. He noticed my looking and said, "Family events mostly, I've had the older ones originally in film converted."

"I wish I had done more of that. My early family life is mostly in still pictures, but I've got a ton of those."

The general ran a hand through his thin pepper-colored hair, which each day was surrendering more of its territory to salt-colored hair. "Mr. Kile, if you won't help me, why in tarnation did you come?"

"You're a great American, General Whitaker. It would be disrespectful not to tell you in person."

"Call me General. Everybody does, even my daughter. As long as you were kind enough to come, before you leave please do me two favors." Not used to being opposed, he went on without waiting for my decision. "The first, you should find decidedly easy. Drink an Irish on crushed ice with a lemon twist." He picked up a handheld bell and rang it. Charles came through the door instantly with a pewter tray centered by a short frosted glass, apparently filled with the whiskey of my Irish ancestors.

The reports said the general could no longer drink himself, but enjoyed watching others imbibe. If he liked them, he felt he was drinking with them. If he didn't like them, well, they didn't get offered the drink in the first place.

The general gave the impression that being eccentric could be a lot of fun. Of course you had to be somewhat wealthy to be eccentric. If one is poor and unconventional in manner and deed, one is simply considered a bit nutty.

"You said two things, General?"

"That I did. While sipping your Irish, read this letter. It is addressed to you. You will notice it is not opened. The letter is from one of my dearest friends, yours too, Mr. Barton Cowen."

I took the letter gingerly between two fingertips and held it for a moment, feeling like a mouse eyeing trapped cheese. Barton Cowen was the father and husband of the family killed by the thug I shot dead on the courthouse steps to earn my four years inside with Axel. Bart came to see me every week while he relentlessly inspired public opinion until the governor's office granted my pardon. Like the mouse, I could not turn from the trap.

When I finished reading Bart's request that I help the general, I sat motionless, looking, I suspect, like an envelope without a name or address on its face. But I knew I had no real choice.

"General, tell me about the case."

"The older I become," he said, "the more impressed I am with what a man is, rather than what he seems. And I like who you are."

"Were it not for Mr. Cowen I would have spent three more years as a guest of the state before walking out an ex-con rather than a pardoned man. But you knew that, General. You knew I could not refuse you after reading this letter." I dropped it onto his desk.

"What I knew, Mr. Kile … may I call you Matt?"

"I'd prefer you did, General. Please go on."

"What I knew, Matt, was that you were intrigued. Perhaps it was my reputation mixing with your curiosity. Perhaps from the stories, you wished to learn if I would offer you a drink. Then it may have simply been that you are divorced and hoped to meet my celebrated daughter."

"Hmmmm."

"And what does that mean?"

"It means, hmmmm. But to revise and extend my remarks as you regularly heard members of congress say during your years on the Joint Chiefs of Staff, 'I had the pleasure of meeting your daughter on the way in. She is a lovely woman.'"

"Nicely said. A man predisposed to be a fighting man learns to do so. A woman predisposed to being a seductress hones her skills similarly. Both arts designed to control the man before them. My daughter is not an excessively promiscuous woman, but, like her mother, she enjoys men and is an unapologetic tease."

I recalled a quote from Count Tallyrand, *In order to avoid being called a flirt, she always yielded easily.*

The tone in which the general spoke about his daughter suggested he was not stressed in the slightest by her choices or personality. I also guessed he liked the style of woman she had grown to be, or so it seemed from his reference to her mother.

"But, yes," he said, picking back up with what he had been saying before discussing his daughter. "I expected you would come. From your history, I knew you felt a responsibility to set things right. Tell me, Matt, what is your opinion on firing squads?"

"Well, General, they do get the job done. Of course, there are no appeals so one must be certain of the guilt of the person put against the wall."

"You were sure when you took out that crud on the courthouse steps, eleven years ago."

"Yes, General. I was. He deserved it. Now whether it did more good than harm I can't really say."

"That disgusting fellow would have killed more people. Destroyed more families. What you did was the right thing."

"I do think that, General. Yes, I do. Still, it hurt those I love, confused their lives. I didn't really think about that part of it when I should have."

"Now don't backslide, Matt. America has become much too soft. We need more swift justice. There is a certain discipline society surrendered when we gave up the immediate effectiveness of firing squads and public hangings. As for my situation, I knew you were the right man when I read of your helping your houseman, Axel, get his parole. You're a smart, tough guy with a heart and that's exactly what I need."

"What I need is another one of these." I held up my glass. "Then I'd like enough details to determine if I can help. I understand it's an old case."

It has been said that mankind has seven deadly sins. I have eight: curiosity.

The general rang the bell, and again Charles magically appeared with a tray balanced on his hand, the new glass as frosty as the first. The general's troops had been trained and strategically positioned. I had come to show respect to a famous retired general. He had welcomed me similarly to how Sitting Bull had greeted General George Armstrong Custer into the Valley of the Big Horn.

"I am no longer able to project my orders as I once could," he said, raising the bell, his smallest finger restraining the clapper. "I know this bell appears aristocratic, but it is, unfortunately, necessary. Charles understands, don't you, Charles."

Charles nodded and then stood tall. "Will there be anything else, General?"

"Nothing, Charles. As always, thank you for your attentiveness and efficiency. Oh, there is something else. Mr. Kile will be looking into that ugly matter some years back involving my grandson, Eddie. His work will require that he learn a great deal about each of us and the goings on within this family. You are to cooperate fully. Answer his questions whatever they may be. And run interference as necessary to gain him access to the individuals and firms that serve this family. We shall trust Mr. Kile's discretion."

"As you wish, General." A slight bow, then Charles closed the door to the study.

"Charles seems able to read you mind, General?"

"He should. We've been together over thirty-five years. Well, except for about five years, early on, when he pulled some special training and did several ops behind enemy lines for the DOD. He soured on that work and returned to be my right hand. We've been together without separation for the past thirty, both in and out of service."

"I respect his devotion."

"Charles is also my friend and confidant."

I took the first sip of the fresh drink; the general licked his lips.

"You were correct," he began, "it is an old case. Eleven years tomorrow to be exact. Late that night, my grandson Eddie's fiancée, Ileana Corrigan, was murdered. She was expecting my great grandson, a tragedy. I doubt you recall the case; it happened during your first year in prison."

"Tell me about Eddie's parents."

"Eddie's father, Ben … Benjamin, my son, was forty-five when he was killed in Desert Storm. That engagement did not kill many of our boys, but it did my son. His mother, my wife Grace, died from breast cancer when Ben was twenty-four; that was in '70. My grandson Eddie was born to Ben and his wife, Emily, in '79, so Eddie was twelve when his father was killed. Emily never enjoyed motherhood. After Ben died she wanted to leave. I gave her some money, she signed what my attorneys required and Eddie came to live with me. Truth was Eddie had been with me whenever Ben was overseas, which was about half the time. Emily would take off until Ben came back, so I have largely raised Eddie with the help of Charles."

"I'm sorry for your difficulties, General."

"Yes. Well. We all have our troubles. But let's get back to the matter at hand. Sergeant Terrence Fidgery was the homicide detective who handled the murder of Ileana Corrigan, my granddaughter-in-law to be. I understand you and he are great pals."

General Whittaker had launched his attack against Fort Kile with a letter from the one man I could never fully repay, and then closed his entrapment with a reference to the case being one of Fidge's unsolved. In between he served Irish whiskey, and likely arranged for his daughter to extend her, what shall I say, enticing welcome to the family Whittaker. I felt like the deer tied across the hood of a pickup truck. And I didn't yet know jack about the case.

The general smiled. If tonight had been a chess game, this would be the point where I leaned forward and tipped over my king. But I had no king to tip over. Instead, I illustrated my capitulation by leaning forward and picking up the check for the thousand dollars.

Like Axel had said, a grand's nothing to sneeze at.

Chapter 4

The fog had silently come ashore before I left General Whittaker's house, dressing the outdoors in wet. Everything obscured as if veiled in the angel breath that adorned the general's Christmas tree. The time to drive home was twice what it took to get there.

I had lingered an extra fifteen minutes to visit with Charles, mostly just to get his cell number so I could reach him later when I was ready to talk. I quickly learned he was more than the general's houseman. He also served as administrative assistant, with his own assistant, a maid and cook for the pure household duties. He gave me the numbers and names for the general's CPA, banker, and investment broker. Charles agreed to call ahead to clear the runway for me to get in and get answers. The general's attorney, Reginald Franklin III, and I had already met.

Charles also told me about Cliff, who drove for the general. Cliff had been a sniper in the Marine Corps when on duty, and then as now a hard drinking man off duty. One night, off the base, Cliff had gotten into an argument with a superior officer. The confrontation was not Cliff's first altercation over a woman's favors. When it was over Cliff had nearly killed the officer. He spent some time in the brig before being dishonorably discharged.

* * *

I walked in my door at eleven to find Axel waiting up like a nervous mom on the night of her daughter's prom, taking his self-proclaimed duties as case nanny a bit too seriously.

Before Axel got paroled I had considered getting a shell parakeet. They are well known talkers. There are times when I'm so slammed writing a novel that I want to hear a voice other than the characters that live in my head, but a voice that wouldn't demand any more of my time than I cared to give at the moment. A voice I could shut off by simply dropping a dark cloth over its cage. Another advantage, one I hadn't considered previously, the parakeet would not wear my trousers, but then I don't need to clean the bottom of Axel's cage. So, I imagine on balance things had worked out well enough.

Last week, I bought Axel a one-bedroom in my condo building on the floor below mine. In any event, a decent investment as the prices had dropped along with the rest of the ugly real estate market. Axel spent most of his non-sleeping hours in my place, at least those hours he didn't spent in Mackie's, a local bistro and watering hole owned and operated by one of his ex-prison pals. Mackie's prison term had expired the year before I went in, so I had only recently met Mackie. The year after he got out he received a significant inheritance, a portion of which went to buy a seedy bar in a good neighborhood a few blocks from our building. After remodeling, Mackie's opened and immediately became a gathering place for ex-cons. Mostly older ex-cons who had retired from whichever careers had incarcerated them. Mackie and Axel had been inside together for twenty-five years; they were tight.

"I knew you'd take the case, boss. Give me the dirt. All of it."

"This stuff is confidential, Axel. These are real people, not characters in my novels."

"Hey, I'm your assistant. Telling me is like, well, telling yourself."

"Except I'll keep it to myself."

"Who would I tell, boss?"

"Half the ex-cons in Long Beach, that's who, your pals at Mackie's Bistro."

"Hey, there'll be times you'll need my pals. Trust me on that one. There's a lot of talent in Mackie's, people who know how things really go down. The whos of the whats and whens. They'll be cases where—"

"Not cases. This is an exception, one case."

"Talmadge was one case. This here's number two."

"Okay. One more case. But that's it. After this one I'm a writer, period."

"Sure, boss, whatever you say. Still, every professional shares stuff with their staff; I'm your staff. I won't repeat nothin'. Well, nothing touchy anyway. I was never no snitch inside. You know that. The same thing goes on the outside, with your cases." I frowned. Axel revised his comment. "Okay, your case, singular. Just one, now open up."

So I cracked like an egg and gave up what I knew. Maybe I shouldn't have, but Axel had been right. As the poets often write, no man is best alone. Everybody trusts somebody and there's no place you get to know a man better than in a cell. Nothing I ever told Axel came back to me in the yard, so, okay, Axel was my staff, well, sort of. He always said. "Our cell's our home and home stuff don't get repeated in the yard." Our current home was much nicer than the one we had in those days, but that principle seemed one of Axel's core beliefs.

"Actually, I don't know all that much," I began. "I've called Sergeant Fidgery. I'm taking him and his family to lunch tomorrow. He made copies of the relevant police files. We'll get into those at his house in the afternoon. The department is carrying the Whittaker case as an unsolved … for them it's the Ileana Corrigan homicide case, but they haven't done anything with it for more than ten years."

"He's the one you told me all about while we were inside? One of those two guys who came to see you a lot. Fidge, right?"

"Yeah. Ten years we were together."

"So, what do you know at this point?"

"The pregnant fiancée of the general's grandson, Eddie Whittaker, was murdered in a house she rented on the beach up the coast toward Malibu. There were two witnesses. One who claimed he saw Eddie in the house doing the killing. The other said he saw Eddie in the immediate area fifteen or so minutes later. The cops arrested Eddie. A week or so later, witnesses came forward saying they had seen Eddie in a different location. The D.A. dropped the charges and Eddie walked. I'll know more after I talk with Fidge. I'm going to bed. Let yourself out."

"Where are you meeting Fidge?"

"At noon at Red Robin, I'm taking his whole family to lunch. Then we'll go back to his place. He has a great family so it'll be a nice Saturday."

"Okay, boss, but I'll want a full report."

"Maybe. The odds will improve if you're wearing your own pants when I get back."

Chapter 5

Fidge and I had, if anything, grown closer since I left the force. More accurately, since the department tossed me, and the system threw me in prison with Axel. Not that I blame them. I shot a man in plain sight of the cops and the press so I got what I deserved, I suppose. But then so did the guy I shot.

Fidge had never seen a form of exercise he didn't enjoy watching, a meal he couldn't eat, or a beer that didn't meet his standards. He also lusted after his wife, Brenda, a hunger she returned in kind. She was a great mom, a super cook, and a solid friend. I always suspected that in a former life Brenda had been a braless bar wench serving the King's musketeers while wearing a revealing top stretched out over the ends of her bare shoulders. In this life, she was Fidge's Dulcinea. Fidge adored her. For that matter, so did I. Brenda was a man's woman, and a friend's wife, and she knew more naughty jokes and double entendres than anyone I knew.

After we had Red Robin burgers, a stack of onion rings, and milk shakes all around, Fidge and I walked his wife and children to their SUV. Brenda was driving their teens to the homes of their friends. Then she planned to fill her afternoon with errands.

Fidge and I, walking as if we had swallowed single car garages, belched before getting into my Chrysler 300. I drove us to his place where we would hunker down and sift through the fascinating story of the murder of a pregnant woman, and an arrest with a direct eye witness, quickly followed by a dropping of charges and the release of Eddie Whittaker.

Fidge had originally thought Eddie Whittaker guilty. It certainly looked that way. But not after two witnesses independent of one another came forward to say they saw Eddie where he said he had gone. He claimed he spent the hours before, during, and after the murder of his fiancée driving to and from Buellton, California, where he dined in Pea Soup Anderson's Restaurant. It was impossible, short of using a helicopter, to make it from the restaurant to the place of the murder in time to commit it. In the aggregate, the evidence said Eddie was innocent. The way the D.A. told it, he didn't have enough to get a conviction. The charges were dropped and Eddie became a free man. After that the case settled in among the many unsolved in the Long Beach homicide department. A cold case, as they're called on television. In real life, there simply isn't the manpower to work cold cases. They languish in file cabinets waiting for the good fairy of law enforcement to unexpectedly drop new evidence or clues onto the department's lap. Until then, the best the department could do was keep them dry and protected from excessive dust. Which to no great surprise meant the file on the murder of Ileana Corrigan, Eddie's fiancée, had been handled only once in the past ten years. That happened when it was taken from its metal file coffin to a cardboard one in the department's warehouse for old cases that had failed to trip over new inspiration.

"I always wanted to get back to this one," Fidge said. "It was odd, but we had nothing to hang odd on, so it became one of those never-really-forgotten cases that snag on some hook in the dark corner of a cop's mind. Truth is, I haven't thought about it in many years, but it all flooded back when you brought it up. You don't remember it at all?"

"Not a lick."

"Well, it happened about a year after you went brain dead and shot your way into prison."

Fidge had a way of making some things I did sound really stupid. And while I'll admit it to you, but never to Fidge, this was because some of the things I did were really stupid.

"I remember that General Whittaker had a wonderful gun collection from World War II," Fidge said, "including a British Welrod bolt-action silenced assassin's pistol. I'd read about them, but never seen one. His was equipped for a 9mm cartridge, and had a rear set knob that had to be manually rotated to eject a cartridge and then pushed forward to introduce a new cartridge from the magazine into the chamber. I remember that gun like it was here on my kitchen table. It's been reported the British forces carried one into Iraq, for the tradition. A Welrod assassin's pistol has been in every British engagement from WWII forward."

"Did you check all his weapons?"

Fidge nodded. "None of them had been used to kill the Corrigan woman. Oh, yeah, the Welrod assassin's pistol was stolen about two years ago. He came down to the department to report the theft. Nothing else had been taken, so likely some worker or visitor in his home snatched it; it never turned up."

"What's the status on the murder weapon?"

"Never found. Still, it looked open and shut, and you know how much Captain Richard Dickson likes open and shut cases. But right fast it sprung a leak and all the evidence drained out. Our perp walked. No rumors. No talk of anybody being paid off. Nothing backchannel, it just went flat."

"Captain Dick Dickson," I said with a disgusting tone I saved just for him, "the man suffers from delusions of competence."

As you have undoubtedly surmised, I don't like the man and the feeling is mutual. He had been the only detective in the department with a smile on his face when I was arrested for the courthouse shooting. I did Captain Dickson a favor last year that I thought might chip some of the ice off our relationship, but no. One of our few truly private rights the government hasn't infringed upon is our freedom to decide who we don't like and why. The politically correct types would say Two Dicks and I had a personality conflict. But you should know that's hogwash. Dickson has no personality. No cop I ever met liked him. That's why Captain Richard Dickson was known around the department as Captain Two Dicks.

"Well," Fidge said, "you'll be pleased to know Two Dicks has been sick the last couple days. He's hardly been in the station."

"Let's hope it's nothing painless."

Fidge and I shared a few bad and ugly stories about Two Dicks. I know the saying is, "the good, the bad, and the ugly," but there were no good stories about the man.

Fidge had made me a copy of all the documents in the case file so we were looking at the same information while we talked. He recalled the case as if it had happened yesterday instead of eleven years ago. The gist of it went like this: A young fellow hanging out on the beach had looked into Ileana Corrigan's beach house and saw her murdered.

"We got the witness's name?"

"It's all in there," he said, pointing toward the copied file in front of me, "along with a copy of the report on the stolen Welrod assassin's pistol, which came nine years after the murder. Like I said, the Welrod wasn't the murder weapon."

"Where was the eye witness?"

"About a hundred yards or so out from the house, he had binoculars he used to look out to sea before it got dark. He had fallen asleep on the sand and saw the murder after he woke up. He picked Eddie Whittaker out of a group of pictures. The time of the murder, the witness said was 8:45 at night, and that jibed with the M.E.'s report. An attendant working in a gas station also pointed to Eddie's picture as having bought gas a little after nine that same night. The station was an old one with a security camera the owner failed to use. The man working the station alone said Eddie paid cash. He remembered because so few folks used cash. The police picked up Eddie. Both the witness to the murder and the gas jockey picked Eddie out of a lineup.

"Two days later, Eddie was released after the D.A. dropped the charges. Eddie's claim that he had driven up from Long Beach to have dinner in Buellton was substantiated by a man and his wife who had dined at the same restaurant. A retired middle school principal who lived in Buellton also stepped forward to say he saw Eddie in the restaurant between 8:30 and 9:30."

"Did Eddie have a credit card transaction or maybe a debit card he used for the dinner? And what about buying the gas? Oh, you said he paid cash for the gas."

"No dice," Fidge said. "I verified Eddie Whittaker had gotten pissed at his credit card company, cut up his card and closed the account. He had an application pending at a different local bank, his grandfather's bank, to get a new credit card. He didn't have a debit card. They weren't as popular back then as they are now. So, he was using cash for everything during those few days."

"That was convenient. That way there would be no paper trail as to where he was during the critical hours."

"Convenient if he murdered his fiancée. Serendipitous, if he didn't," Fidge said. "Nothing else pointed anywhere then and nothing's come up since. No con or suspect in any other case has offered anything about it to bargain for a better deal. It would seem the murderer has kept his exploits to himself. And you know how rare that is."

It was rare. Thugs often brag to other thugs about their crimes, as if such behavior constituted something to brag about in the first place. And, later, the listening thug trades that knowledge to bargain with the police for a pass on some lesser charge.

"I understand Ileana Corrigan was pregnant when she was killed. Was a determination made that Eddie Whittaker was the father?"

"When I met with General Whittaker, the general insisted we make that determination. DNA testing was still gaining stature, but it was established. We would have anyway, particularly when Eddie quickly became a suspect, as it could have gone to motive. He was the papa."

"Bail?"

"Eddie Whittaker had a clean record so his attorney argued he posed no threat to the community. The issue of special circumstances was questionable and the D.A. decided not to pursue that. The bail was set at one million. The general posted the bond. Eddie Whittaker walked."

Fidge offered another beer but I waved him off, then he said, "Have another, there's something I wanna kick around." I nodded and he pulled us two more, twisted the cap off mine, and passed it over. "You heard Salt ate his gun last weekend?"

"I read the piece in the paper. Did any of you pick up on him getting … I don't know, funny, depressed, like that?"

"No. His partner, Washington, the black guy they call Pepper, had no idea, and if a guy's partner doesn't know"—Fidge interrupted himself with a shrug.

"Salt was divorced wasn't he?" Fidge nodded. "Been a few years, right?"

He nodded again. "About as long as you and Helen. Why?"

"Just trying to get a handle on it."

"Why is it us cops lead the league in divorce, alcoholism, and suicide?"

"Long hours," I said, "lots of stress."

"Hell, hedge fund managers deal with that. Course they make big bucks to salve the shit they handle."

"I think it's that cops deal with the crud all the time," I said. "Lose perspective. Begin to think everybody's a lowlife. Truth is only a couple percent of folks are rotten, but cops deal almost totally within that couple percentage. It starts to look like the whole world's that way. You never get ahead of the cases, hell you never even catch up. You keep locking up the bad guys and the world keeps sending more."

"But I don't feel that way, Matt."

"Course not. You lead the league in happiness."

"Brenda. You know. It's her. Her and the kids, they keep me rooted."

"I don't know why she puts up with you, but I sure hope she stays on the job."

"Everyone said Salt's wife always nagged him to can the job. She hated him being a cop. Wanted him to, I don't know, drive a hack. Be a Wal-Mart greeter. Whatever. He couldn't do it. He loved being a cop. So do I. Why do we love it? It's a crummy job. The scum don't like us. The citizens think we're all on the take or hassling them for no reason. Every time we get into it with some piece of shit, the folks yell police brutality. The attorneys treat us like we're idiots. The rules are tilted in favor of the crooks. Why in the hell do we love the job?"

"For all those reasons," I offered as if I really knew. "Cops like to buck the system. Fight the odds. The thin blue line and all that shit. You hang onto Brenda, she's aces."

"Yeah," Fidge said. Then he shook his head and raised his bottle. "To Salt. Rest in peace."

"To Salt," I repeated. "Let's hope he went somewhere the scum can't get in."

"So, how's the writing business? You got something new coming out soon?"

"In a couple of months. My publisher's bugging me to get through the proof. I shouldn't have taken the job from General Whittaker. I went there planning to turn him down."

"What happened?"

"The old man's a master strategist. He left me standing in the corner holding a wet paintbrush. I don't know. In the end, as a soldier he did a lot for us. It could also be because I'm a dumb fuck. I guess that tells it best."

"Why's your publisher pressing you?"

"The way it works, the publisher pressures my agent. My agent pressures me. Everyone with a piece wants me to get the next book out."

"Deadlines," Fidge says while shaking his head. "Just like at the department, the suits upstairs keep pushing."

"This is the last book I'm doing for him or any of the big name publishers. They're not bad people, it's just the publishing business has left them clinging to a leaky boat. Today's book buyers are asked to pay too much because of all the layers that stand between the author and the reader. I'm going to start self-publishing. I'll use a work-for-hire publisher so I can control the rights to my own books. That way I can set lower prices, make a good living and protect my readers from getting ripped off."

"And you can work at a pace you choose without the suits putting the screws to you. So, how's Helen?"

"How the hell would I know? We're divorced."

"Okay. How's the divorce going?"

"Divorce is … it stinks. Hell. It's shit."

"If it's shit, it would stink," Fidge said. We looked at each other. Then he laughed. I laughed. "Fuck it, Matthew."

We touched bottles. I nodded, and then picked up the pictures from the Corrigan scene. Fidge had made me copies of all the file docs but not the pictures. Other than showing Ileana dead, the photos revealed nothing.

"The place doesn't look tossed. Anything stolen?" I asked.

"Not so's we could tell. And I doubt it. Her jewelry box had some rather expensive pieces. Things I doubt a secretary could afford. Her folks were struggling middle class so the diamonds weren't family presents."

"Where'd she get them?"

"The neighbors spoke of a couple of luxury cars that would be there from time to time. They never saw the drivers. A good guess she had a couple of part-timers besides Eddie Whittaker. The landlord said the rent always came from her. On her salary, the rent would have been a stretch, the diamonds impossible."

"Was she hooking?"

"No arrests. My guess, she did it for the rent and diamonds. She had a straight job and her boss and coworkers spoke well of her."

"What did Eddie Whittaker have to say about all that?"

Fidge took a moment to glance at his case notes in the file. "He said he didn't know of any other men in her life. As for the expensive stuff, he not only claimed he didn't buy it, he said he never saw any of it. I sure remember his jaws being tight when I showed him. A check of his bank account and credit cards didn't show any purchases or cash withdrawals that could cover even one piece of that jewelry."

"Stacks up like a straight gal with at least one sugar daddy?"

"That's how I added it, but I never got no names. Her gal pals at work only knew about Eddie Whittaker. We had some unidentified prints at the scene we could never connect up. They could've been left by Mr. Jewelry Buyer, or the cable guy, or somebody who came to some party she threw."

Fidge and I talked about the case for a while longer, but nothing more worthy of mention. The precise facts were plain and clear, a quick arrest of Eddie followed by his quicker release. Since then, eleven years of wind pudding.

I went out Fidge's back door. My stomach had processed enough of the burger and fries that my bloat had shrunk from the size of a garage to the size of a golf cart. The beers had tasted good, but I expected a coming clash with the banana milk shake I drank with my burger.

I stopped at the supermarket and then gassed up the car. When I got home, Axel was not there. My guess he was still down at Mackie's with his buds. Some nights he went over to Clara Birnbaum's to watch an old movie. After putting the groceries away, I went down the hall to see Clarice Talmadge. Clarice was the widow I had helped when she had been arrested for murdering her husband, Garson, about a year ago. Clarice had been innocent of anything more than an overactive sex life, with the kind of body you see featured on television helping to sell Cadillacs and cosmetics.

Since her husband's murder, I periodically made myself available to Clarice. I also liked her. She's smart, and has a great sense of humor, nearly as bawdy as Fidge's wife. When her husband, Garson, died, with what he left her, she became wealthy. Clarice and I had close to a divorced man's perfect relationship. No strings. No pressure. She enjoyed that and she had no desire to marry again. She also liked to sleep alone so there was no awkwardness about getting up and going home afterwards.

Like I said, Clarice is the perfect set up for a divorced guy, particularly one still stirring hot ashes for his ex-wife. But keep that to yourself.

Around one in the morning, I drifted back down the hall to my place. Axel had returned and was waiting up like Dr. Watson always did for Sherlock Holmes. I spent the next hour bringing my loyal staff man up on what Fidge had told me. The cop's file was cold with no real leads. The file did have the names and addresses for all the witnesses. Those who got Eddie Whittaker arrested, as well as those who got him released. That gave me some places to begin poking around. Hopefully some of the addresses would still be good.

* * *

At six a.m. Fidge woke me. He was at the beach and it was raining, a drizzle more than a rain, but the gusts off the ocean were hearty with a wind chill number he said I wouldn't want to know. He told me to come down. He'd explain then.

When I got there, I saw Fidge wearing a black stocking cap. From the back he looked like a chest of drawers balancing a bowling ball.

The main attraction turned out to be a soggy homicide lying in the surf. The ID pulled from the dead guy's wet wallet identified him as Cory Jackson. After a minute, the name came to me and I knew why Fidge had called me to share the event. People always say, the name rang a bell, but I always thought that was silly. Cory Jackson had been the eyewitness who had seen Eddie Whittaker's fiancée, Ileana Corrigan, murdered in her beach house. Mr. Jackson worked at a restaurant up the beach from where we stood over his body. At least he worked there back on the day he pointed his finger at Eddie Whittaker. The restaurant didn't serve the fishing trade so it would be closed this early. Later in the day, Fidge would check to see if Jackson still worked there. The important point being that while both Jackson and the restaurant had been closed only the restaurant would reopen. The hole in Cory Jackson's forehead was bigger and rougher around the edges than the hole in the back of his head. He had been shot from behind.

There were no tracks, not even Jackson's. The tide had come and gone, smoothing the sand on its way out. This suggested he had been shot sometime last night before the high tide came fully in. His wet clothes seconded that motion. There were no powder burns around the entry wound so the shooter had not been especially close. Neither Fidge nor I mentioned the old Whittaker case, but we were both thinking the same thing. Someone involved in that eleven-year-old case may have chosen to remove the only supposed eyewitness to the killing of Ileana Corrigan. That, or Cory Jackson getting rubbed out the day after I started messing in the case was pure coincidence. In my view, such coincidences were rarely coincidences.

Chapter 6

At seven, with the morning sun tussling with the hang-around fog, Fidge called to say the department had reached the manager of the restaurant at his home. Surprisingly, Cory Jackson still worked there after eleven years. The manager told Fidge the address we had for Jackson was no longer good. The manager had not known the new address by memory but he had it in his office in the back of the restaurant. Fidge would meet the manager there in an hour. He also told him to hang out his help wanted sign. I couldn't tag along, official police business and all. At this point, there was nothing that clearly drew a line between the old Corrigan case and last night's murder of Cory Jackson. My hanging around while Fidge worked this case would do nothing but suggest that line existed.

I decided I'd beat it over to the address the Whittaker case file carried for Cory Jackson and sniff around before the cops shagged the old address, if they ever did. The murder of Cory Jackson would not be a high profile case. Well, not unless it got tied back to the Corrigan murder and by extension to General Whittaker, one of Long Beach's most storied residents.

Jackson's old address was a tired building on the sand along an old road near Seal Beach, south of Long Beach. From the street I could see an opening for a double carport with one vehicle inside. As I approached on foot, a lamp shining through an upstairs window revealed living quarters over the carport which appeared to be that same size. A set of stairs went up the side of the building past a rusty metal mailbox that hung crooked just below a porch light filled with cobwebs, but no bulb. The stairs were gloomy, but the morning sun from the east had already cracked open the new day. The air still felt cold. The fog wet. A gull screeched as I put my foot on the first stair.

According to the restaurant manager, Cory Jackson didn't live here any longer. Of course we knew that to be true. In point of fact, Cory now bunked in the County Coroner's office. But someone was inside. I decided to proceed cautiously and avoid provoking someone who might be an innocent citizen. At least until I knew more.

The door bell didn't work. I flipped on the tape recorder in my jacket pocket and knocked, loudly, which wasn't hard. The screen door, warped from the damp air, and dried by the wind and salt, no longer fit the doorway, so it rattled and banged from a normal knock. My knock exceeded normal.

The upper third of the door was a filthy glass panel shrouded with what had once been a white curtain. After a moment, the silhouette of a man's head blocked some of the faint light that made its way through the smeary coating on the glass.

"Who is it?" the blurry figure said through the door.

"Cory Jackson?"

"He's not here. I don't know the guy. Go away."

For starters, this guy wasn't too bright. He had begun talking before he finished thinking about what he didn't want to say. "I'm not going away," I hollered back. "And your door won't keep me out."

He pulled the door open. I didn't hear any metal, so it had not been locked. He stood on the other side of the screen door wearing a pair of black drawstring sweatpants and a yellow v-neck t-shirt. I couldn't tell if the color was how it came when he bought it, or had yellowed through a devoted avoidance of laundering. He wore dirty white athletic socks and no shoes. The way the sock fabric twisted in front of his toes told me he was right handed. People make hard turns with greater pressure on the more coordinated leg, thus the sock on that foot bunches up and twists more. He looked close to thirty, but beyond it. His left sleeve, rolled up on top of his shoulder, held a pack of smokes.

"Who am I talking to?" I asked.

"Doesn't matter—"

"It does to me," I said interrupting him. "You know Jackson and we're going to talk so don't make this harder on yourself than you need to."

"You the cops?"

"No. And that's the good and bad parts."

"What's good about it?"

"The good part's to my advantage. I don't have to waste time doing things by the book or respecting your rights or any of that crap. That's also the bad part. That part's yours."

I grabbed the little handle on the screen door and rattled it until he slapped the hook out of the eye screw and pushed it out toward me. I walked right at him until he gave ground and backed up into the clearing in the center of the main room. A sort of brown contemporary couch, liberally stained, stood against the far wall, fronted by an early American coffee table. A blue Naugahyde chair sat to the side. The light that had filtered through the window came from a milk glass up-lamp that sat in the corner behind the blue chair. His decorator favored the style of mix-and-match-nothing.

"How do you know Cory Jackson and where is he?"

"I don't know where he is. He don't live here no more. Lives alone in a studio unit a couple blocks from the restaurant he works at."

"You were rooming with Cory back when he testified about seeing Eddie Whittaker kill his fiancée. Let's start with why he lied about that." In fact, I didn't know if they roomed together then or not. I made it a presumptive statement. He didn't disagree so it was true.

"Hey. He saw the dude. Least he said he did. No reason to lie."

"What's your name?"

"Quirt. Quirt Brown."

I walked over to the table and picked up his wallet. His driver's license confirmed his name, Quirt Brown. "Quirt?" I said, with an inflection that asked, where had that come from.

"My parents were John Wayne fans. Quirt was the name of one of his characters."

"Hey," I said while still looking in his wallet. "Look at the bright side. No one gets you confused with anyone else and it's easy to pronounce and spell, well, pronounce anyway." When I turned back he had moved closer and his right hand held a gun.

"Okay, pal. Who the hell are you and why are you here asking about Cory?"

Quirt wasn't a big man but he had big hands with longish fingers, webbed together the way hands come, like linked sausages with transplanted fingernails.

I stuck my thumbs in my waistband. "Now why did ya wanna go and do that? We were having a friendly little chat. No reason to go hostile."

"Now I ask the questions," he said.

"Quirt, a man's got to learn his limits, and when he knows them he's got to live within them."

"I don't wanna hear that shit. Who are you and why are you here?"

"My name's Carson. Kit Carson. I'm working my way through college selling magazine subscriptions. We got whatever you want. Mysteries, sci-fi, erotica, handyman mags, you name a hankering, I got a subscription fer ya."

"Okay, wise guy. Let me see your wallet."

I pulled my left thumb out of my waistband and reached around to the left side of my rump, my right thumb staying cinched in behind my belt. As I brought my wallet around slowly, I dropped it. When he reflectively glanced down, I thrust my right hand out from my waistband with maximum force and jammed the flat of my palm against the finger side of his gun. I also slammed my left hand against the outside of the wrist. The timing resulted in nearly simultaneous blows, each driving against the force of the other. He involuntarily straightened his fingers. The move also drove his hand away from me, which was good in the event he somehow got the trigger pulled. He didn't. His gun was now in my hand.

"Okay. I've got the gun and everything you thought you controlled is now gone, or dripping down your leg."

"What do you want from me?"

"All of it. Why Cory Jackson lied about Eddie Whittaker. And who paid him to tell that lie. That'll do for starters."

He just stared at me. Eventually, stupid fosters its own punishment. "All right," I said. "Let's go outside. Down by the surf."

"I'm not going out there with you."

I poked him in the belly with the barrel end of his gun. It was rude of me, but he brought the gun into our conversation and he might have planned to use it for more than stomach poking.

"If you plan to die defending your home, this place ain't worth it."

"Cory's a friend."

"Would your attitude change if you knew he was dead?"

"Dead?" He turned slowly in a circle, his head shaking, and his hands on his hips when they weren't jabbing the air to punctuate what he said. "I don't believe you. No. I just saw him last night. We had beers. He split around ten." Quirt put his palms together and blew into the crevice between his hands as if they were cold. Then he turned back the other way as if unwinding his first turn. "No. He can't be dead."

I took out my cell phone and brought up the picture of Cory lying in the surf. Wet and cold, only Cory no longer felt the wet or the cold. The hole in his forehead meant nothing good other than the politicians would be leaving him alone because Cory Jackson would not be voting in the next election. I handed Quirt the phone.

He looked at it. His other arm dropped to his side. His chin touched his chest. "We was brothers, man. He's my kid brother, different fathers."

"Sit down, Quirt. I'm sorry to bring the message so hard. I didn't know."

"When?" He sagged down onto one end of the soiled brown couch.

"Last night. He was found early this morning. In the surf, down from the restaurant where he worked, not far from where he claimed he saw Eddie Whittaker kill his woman."

"Why? After all this time. Why?"

I sat in the blue chair to the side of the couch "I assume by 'after all this time,' you meant time after the Whittaker thing. Right?"

Quirt just looked at me. I tried to break his malaise. "Your brother's dead. Whoever framed Eddie Whittaker appears to be sweeping his trail clean. I'm after that son of a bitch. Will you help me or are you going to clam up and help the guy who killed your brother?"

"Cory lied. He didn't see nobody kill that woman."

"First off. Did you or Cory know Eddie Whittaker before all this happened? Ever see him? Have a run in with him? Anything like that?"

"I didn't know the dude from nobody, man."

"What about Cory?"

"Far as I knew, Cory didn't know the guy. I knew everybody Cory knew. If there'd been a hassle between Cory and this Eddie Whittaker, Cory would have filled me in. No. No way. We didn't know him from Adam."

"Okay. So Cory was paid to lie. Who paid him? Who wanted Eddie Whittaker jailed?"

"I got no clue, man. Listen, I need a beer. You want one?"

I nodded and followed him to a white Kelvinator that was old enough to be gaining value as an antique. While we twisted the tops off the beers, I asked, "Who did Cory say paid him?"

"He didn't know. He was sitting on the beach one night. Back then, he did that a lot. On a log that had washed up on shore. He heard a voice that told him if he turned around he'd die. Right there, man, killed for just turning the fuck around."

"Man or woman?"

"Man. Wouldn't be no woman. Would it?"

"You're sure?"

"Hey, I wasn't there. Cory said it was a dude. That's all I know."

"Okay, so what did Cory do?"

"He didn't turn around. I'll tell ya that. The voice told him which house and what time to be there and on what night. That he would see a man kill a woman inside. Shoot her dead. That Cory should go to the cops after he saw the woman's picture in the paper. He told Cory the woman's name, but I don't recall it. He handed Cory a picture of Eddie Whittaker and shined a flashlight over Cory's shoulder so he could see the picture. He told him to study it and remember the man's face. He even pointed out a few facial features that would help Cory remember the dude. He told Cory that his life depended on his doing it right. Then he pulled the picture back."

"Go on."

"He handed Eddie one hundred twenties, that's two thousand bucks for IDing a guy. In those days, Cory was into drugs and always needed money. But Cory's straight now … He was straight … anyway."

"That's nice. To die clean."

"The voice told Cory that if he done it just like he was told there would be another eight thousand. If he didn't, there'd be a bullet. A mercy bullet, the guy said, because he would first cut off each of Cory's toes and fingers. Then he told Cory to count to one hundred by ones before he turned around or he'd get the bullet right then."

"That's it?"

"That's it. Cory did what he was told. He got the rest of the money. Found it in his bedroom, on his bed. Right here, just down the hall. Right down there," he pointed. "How's that for putting the willies in you, right on his fucking bed, man. Cory was mighty happy that someone came forward to save Eddie Whittaker from being put away for something he didn't do."

"What else do you remember?"

"I remember thinking how weird it was the dude gave Cory the rest of the money after Eddie Whittaker got freed up."

We talked some more, but Quirt had nothing more to give. Then he asked for his gun back. I considered tossing it in the ocean, but one gat more or less wasn't going to change the local crime rate. After my pardon the state lacked adequate legal grounds to deny me a PI license, but given my conviction for shooting someone, they were able to deny me a license to carry a weapon. My lawyers are still fighting that. They expect to eventually win the point that a pardoned man has full rights, including obtaining a gun permit. Still, for now, I decided I'd hang onto Quirt Brown's gun for a few days.

"I'll hang onto this for now," I told him, "but one day fairly soon you'll find it in your mailbox."

I must have brought back memories for Quirt. Halfway down the stairs I heard the sound of him engaging the deadbolt.

Chapter 7

At eleven-thirty that afternoon, Axel had walked four blocks toward downtown Long Beach. In the next block, just around the corner, he would arrive at Mackie's. He lunched there most days along with a handful of the city's oldest ex-cons. Men now retired from their life's work. Mackie's had also become a popular lunch spot with the area's white collar workers so he required his former jail pals to meet a certain dress and behavior code. The rules began with no drunk or loud behavior and no planning the kind of jobs that led to them all meeting in the first place. Mackie's served great food, with soft Sinatra and Steve Tyrell in the background mixed in with Linda Ronstadt and Mackie's personal favorite, Julie London. Sure, his music was dated, but so was Mackie. It happens when guys like him and Axel spend decades up the river, as Mackie called prison. They came out wanting their now world to be as much as possible like their then world.

The booths were well padded and the walls coated in hunter green wallpaper with cherry wood wainscoting. An assortment of sports pictures hung around the perimeter along with sexy women dressed in cherry wood frames. The lights were low, but not so much that you couldn't read the menu or see the lovely ladies that waited tables and brought drinks wearing outfits that made you think of Hooters. It was all in good taste. A place you'd take the girl you were going to bring home to meet mother, assuming mother was reasonably hip, as they used to say.

As Axel turned the corner, a block from Mackie's, Axel was approached by one of the street's younger women who worked the world's oldest racket. "Hey Mister, want something different for lunch?"

Axel walked over to the blonde who he sized up as having less crust on her than the other young woman standing beside her. She was taller than five feet, but not by much, and had the smile of an angel wearing too much eye makeup and swap-meet perfume. Axel shushed away the other girl standing near her. "I want two hours of your time, young lady. What'll it cost me?"

"Two hundred … How about one-fifty," she said a moment later, negotiating against herself.

"Anything I want?" Axel said. "No hassle. I'm the boss for my two hours."

"Whatever you say, mister."

"Forget the one-fifty, I'll give you the two hundred, but if you resist whatever I want, the deal is off. Agreed?"

She looked at Axel. "You're the boss."

"Okay. What's your name?"

"They call me Lacey 'cause I wear lots of lacey stuff."

"I didn't ask what they called you. I asked your name. I thought we agreed I was the boss? Now are we ready to start this relationship or end it? It's your call. Makes me no never mind either way."

"My name's Hildegard. My family calls me Hillie."

"Come with me, Hillie. I'm Axel." They walked until they were outside Mackie's where he pulled open the door and pointed his head in a way that said, go in. She did. He followed. Mackie looked up from behind the bar and waved. Several others along the bar and three guys at a far table raised a hand or nodded a head. A few also mumbled something Axel couldn't quite hear.

"Sit down, Hillie." She turned to face Axel with a confused look on her face. "Here's where we're spending our two hours. Order whatever you want from the menu. It's over and above your fee. For two hours we're going to talk. No bullshit. No lies from either of us. You ask me whatever you wish. I'll do the same. Straight talk for two hours. Can you handle this without going all bratty on me?"

"What do you mean, bratty?"

"You know. The attitude you gave your parents before you ran away. Shrugs. Looks at the floor. Pouts. Lies. Telling them they don't know or don't understand. That attitude won't fly with me. If our relationship is gonna work, we'll do it with straight talk. No meanness for meanness sake. We're equals. We'll talk that way. I hold nothing back. You hold nothing back. You game or do you want to skip lunch and hit the streets looking for a guy who only wants to get in your pants or to get you in his? That's not me. I wanna get in your head. Decide now, before we order."

She looked down a moment, then lifted her head and looked directly at Axel. "I'm in."

"No rebellious teenager?"

"I don't think you're a very nice man, Axel. What kind of a name is Axel anyway?"

"Your name is Hildegard and you're judging my name?" Hillie smiled. "Now that's better," Axel said. "And, by the way, my being a nice man was neither part of what you offered on the street nor what I accepted. I'm the boss. That means I can be a nice man or not. You're free to form your own opinion but keep it to yourself. Last warning, if you can't handle it, storm back out onto the street where you'll go hungry, work harder, likely make less, and feel crummy doing it. This here's fish or cut bait time, girly."

Hillie opened her menu. Axel didn't need the menu. He knew it by heart.

After a few minutes, Mackie, an average-sized man of around sixty, with a gut that allowed his belt buckle to live in the shade, came from behind the bar and stopped at their table. "What'll it be, Axel?"

"First, say hello to my new friend. This is Hildegard. Her friends, which she has temporarily allowed me to be, call her Hillie."

"Hi, Hillie. Welcome. My friends call me Mackie and if you're Axel's friend, you're my friend."

"Hi, Mackie. I'm pleased to know you."

"One tip, don't play checkers with this old scruffer. He cheats."

"Axel," Hillie looked shocked. "I'm getting a different impression of you now."

"I wouldn't cheat if Mackie played an honorable game like chess." Hillie perked up when she heard Axel say that. "Do you play?" he asked. She nodded. "You any good?"

"Probably not any more, I used to play with my dad, after school at his office."

"Let me turn that blind some," Mackie said, "get the sun out of your eyes." He walked over to the window.

"Seriously, do you like to play chess?"

"Love it. I used to anyway."

"Wanna play now?"

"It's your two hours, remember? You're the boss," Hillie said, sipping the water Mackie had brought to the table.

"No. Chess is an honorable game. Nobody is forced to play chess. At least they shouldn't be. Only if you want to."

"I'd love to play, Axel. It'd be like old times, but where?"

"Right here. Mackie's got board games." Axel looked over to Mackie who was back behind the bar and wiggled his hand in their form of visual shorthand.

A moment later, he brought over a chessboard and the pieces. "You two gonna order now or wait till after your game?"

"Now," Axel said, "the lady is hungry. We'll get started then finish after we eat."

Hillie ordered a bacon, lettuce and tomato sandwich and Axel ordered a crab louie.

"Do you want your BL&T Axel style or traditional?"

Hillie looked at both men. "What's Axel style?"

"With chunky peanut butter," Mackie said, "rather than mayo or any other spreads." Hillie nodded and smiled. Mackie smiled back and then said, "Sweet tea for both of you?" Hillie looked unsure what that was. Mackie explained. "It's a Southern name for iced tea sweetened."

"Yes, please," Hillie said. Axel nodded. Mackie left.

"Mackie has hard hands, but a big soft smile," Hillie said. "He seems to be a friendly man."

Axel smiled and nodded. "Okay, Hillie," he said. "Our food won't be here for about ten to fifteen minutes. We can get a good start on the game." They set up the pieces and Axel put one pawn of each color in each of his hands while he held them below the table.

Before Hillie picked one to start their game, she asked, "Is there anything you want to say to me before we start our game?"

"You wear way too much eye makeup. It cheapens you and you're too pretty to do that to your eyes." Hillie said nothing, just pointed toward Axel's right hand. He opened it to reveal a white pawn. She moved the center piece from her front line forward one space to start the game.

After eight or ten moves apiece, Mackie brought their food. He looked at the board and smiled. "I see you got yourself in a real match, Axel. I think the little lady has an edge at the moment."

"Whatdaya know, Mack? Get out of here and leave us alone." When he left, Axel turned to Hillie. "While we eat, I want your life history. Where you were born. A fair bit about each of your parents and brothers and sisters. Then why you dropped out of school. Not the reason you told your friends back home, but the reason you kept to yourself. Why you ran away. I figure you're what, seventeen, eighteen?" She nodded when Axel said eighteen. "You got through the eleventh grade maybe?" She nodded again. "You're no dummy, that's obvious. So I want the why. Remember our agreement." Hillie nodded. "Okay, let's have it. Pull no punches. Tell it straight."

Chapter 8

By late afternoon, I was knocking on General Whittaker's front door. Charles opened it and led me into the study. On the way, I glanced up the stairwell. Karen Whittaker was neither favoring the banister nor me. When I entered, the general was watching one of his family VCRs. He pointed out his son, Ben, who had died in the engagement known as Desert Storm, and Eddie as a small boy. He used the remote to turn it off, put the tape back in its container and that onto the shelf.

"Well, you didn't come to watch an old man wallowing in family pictures. Do you have a report for me?"

"General. I lost a good part of today learning a big piece of this story that you didn't bother to tell me. The witnesses against Eddie were paid, so it figures his alibi was also bought. For the alibi, I figure you were the buyer. Wasting my time hurts both of us."

"Sit down. I see you didn't wear a tie today. I like the look."

"Folksy doesn't fit you, General. Why didn't you tell me that you paid someone to get Eddie released?"

"Well, Mr. Kile. You are a resourceful man. The police never learned what you have in the first day."

"Whom did you pay? How much? Why?"

"The why is easy. Eddie's innocent."

"That dog don't hunt, General. To some degree you're questioning his innocence or I wouldn't be here. So, why am I here?"

"Like I told you. I'm coming to the end of my time. I need to know, absolutely know. I always have believed him innocent and nothing has happened to change that belief. But I don't want to meet my maker while I'm still pushing away any doubt at all."

"Okay, that's why, but what about whom?" I repeated, "And how much?"

"The who, I don't know. How much, two million."

"Before or after Eddie was released?"

"After. I refused to pay until she—"

"She?"

"It was a woman who called me to make the offer and arrange the payoff drop. On some level, the voice seemed familiar. I keep rerunning that voice in my mind, but I've never been able to place it. It stays just beyond reach."

"Okay. You were saying?"

"I refused to pay until she proved she could get Eddie released and the charges dropped. She agreed, telling me that Eddie would not live a week if I didn't pay."

"Where and how did you pay?"

"She instructed me to contact my bank immediately after Eddie's release to assure they had time to configure the money the way she demanded. I was to pick it up near closing time on the Friday after Eddie had been released with the charges dropped. I was to speak only with my personal banker and not disclose why I wanted the money. The fact that Eddie had been released had been in all the papers so the bank apparently didn't connect my wanting the money with his predicament. The cash had to be in unmarked bills. She insisted that half of it be in hundreds, the rest in twenties, and nothing smaller, no fifties. I was told that if the bills were marked, Eddie would die. I was instructed to go and get the money alone. Apparently, she didn't want any younger men with me. I still drove then. Not often, but it wasn't a problem."

"And how did you pay it over?"

"I was to bring the cash home. She would call me at her choosing. I was told not to grow concerned if I didn't hear from her for several days, even a week or more, that she would have me under surveillance."

"And did you get the call after you got home?"

"No, before I got home, while I drove the road back here after leaving the bank. From the highway it's about a mile."

"Was it dark by then?"

"Yes. Not fully. But I had turned on the headlights. The call came on my cell phone. The voice said enough for me to know the caller was the woman with whom I made the deal. She ordered me to stop at a certain point in the road and toss the valise over the side. The cliff there drops about thirty yards to the sand. Then she ordered I pull forward another hundred yards and run the car off the road into a ditch and turn off the headlights. About a half mile from the house there's a patch of ice plant on the ocean side of the road. The ditch is on the inland side across from there. I couldn't coax the car out of the ditch so I walked the rest of the way to the house. I hadn't had my cell phone long and I didn't think to just call Cliff. When I got back, Charles sent the chauffeur to deal with the car. He had to call a tow truck to pull it out."

"Since then?"

"Nothing. Eddie was free. The bitch had the two million. Nothing whatsoever since."

"The police department records show that you insisted that paternity tests be run to establish that Ileana's unborn son was your great grandson. Why did you feel that was necessary?"

"Eddie was, is, I think this generation uses the term, a player. Ileana seemed a sweet girl, yet they met in one of those clubs that Eddie frequents. She could have been a player as well. I like to be certain. I learned long ago to reconnoiter."

"And the results of those tests?"

"As you know, they confirmed Eddie was the father. The child would have been my great grandson."

"And why didn't you tell me about the payment for the alibi?"

"You're a detective. You came highly recommended, but I wanted to see for myself if you were any good."

"And?"

"Apparently you are."

"Are we solid now, General? No need for any more games?"

"We're solid, Matt. I'm impressed. Get to the bottom of it. Find out for me." After a moment, he added, "Please." The way he said it, well, it wasn't a comfortable word for him.

"Now that you've observed my bona fides, let's talk about my fee."

"We should've discussed that the first night."

"No, we shouldn't. You wanted first what you have now."

"Your bona fides?"

"Yep."

"State your fee?"

"Two hundred thousand plus expenses."

"Seems hefty."

"I worked my last case pro bono, it averages out. You paid two million to get Eddie free. Seems a dime on the dollar is a reasonable fee to find out whether or not you should have forked over the big money."

"And if he's guilty?"

"That matters to you. Not to me. My fee is for finding out what you said you wanted to know."

"You want it in writing?"

"Give Charles a signed memo and copy me. The fee is due when Eddie or someone else is arrested for the crime of the murder of Ileana Corrigan. Not convicted. Arrested.

The rest is outside my jurisdiction. My fee is payable on an arrest and indictment by a grand jury."

"Agreed. Charles will have a copy for you the next time you come by."

* * *

As I left the general's house, Karen Whittaker met me outside the front door. She had been swimming. If I could've licked her, I'd know if she had swum in their pool or in the ocean. Then she took the fun out of it.

"I just got back from a swim in the ocean. The water was cold." Her brown hair reflected the setting sun to create a nimbus around her head. She shivered and jiggled. "I'll go back if you'll join me." She stood staring at me, her back to the westerly sun. Her eyes were as soft and inviting as a warm pool with steam rising in the cool air, beseeching me to immerse myself and swim into her soul. At least that's how I would have written it in one of my novels.

"Sorry," I said, reluctantly. "No time. I'm on the job. But how about having dinner with me tomorrow night? I've got some questions I'd like to ask you."

"I'm here. You're here. Ask."

"Some of my questions need a chance to grow up a little more. Dinner? Tomorrow night."

"No."

She had been playing up to me so I guess my surprise showed when I stammered, "Why not?"

"Because you're just a writer."

"But I have a really big Bic."

She laughed heartily before running her tongue across the front of her teeth. “On that promise, I’ll pick you up in front of your building at seven.” She turned, went inside and shut the door.

I stood for a moment staring at the airspace her black bikini bottom had just slapped out of her way.

Chapter 9

For now, the cops were working the homicide of Cory Jackson, while I was working what I saw as the Eddie Whittaker case, but in the Long Beach Police Department they had it booked as the homicide of Ileana Corrigan, cold case. My job was to find out who killed her so General Whittaker would absolutely know it wasn't his grandson Eddie, or that it had been Eddie. That would likely kill the old man, but I would do my job.

I anticipated Fidge would drag his feet some to allow me to keep my shrinking lead on the department. But, at some point, Fidge would need to act out discovering the link of Cory Jackson to the Ileana Corrigan case, and my head start would begin to evaporate. To press my temporary advantage I headed for the address in the file for Tommy Montoya, the gas station attendant who claimed he sold Eddie gas a few minutes after someone had permanently ended Ileana Corrigan's problems and pleasures.

The address in the file was no longer good. According to the retired lady who lived in the duplex next to where Tommy Montoya had lived, Tommy had moved about a year ago. She first shared her opinion that Tommy should be spelled Tommie, with an "ie" rather than a "y." Then she did something useful. She dug a crumpled note from the drawer in her small kitchen desk. It had Tommy's new address. We chatted a while longer and she didn't ask for the scrap of paper back, so I left with it. Taking it might allow me to stay ahead of the cops for a few more hours. It wasn't Fidge's job to help me, not officially, but the death of Ileana Corrigan had been a case that lodged in his craw. He couldn't work it, but he knew that case sat on top of my list.

I found Tommy's new address with the help of a little boy with two lanes of glazed snot traveling from his nose to his upper lip, where his tongue came into play. I said Tommy Montoya and the boy pointed with his left hand, using his right hand to hold his hair above his eyes while he looked up at me.

Through the apartment window I saw a man sitting with a blonde. They were on the couch facing the TV, starting to watch a movie. The title on the screen, Debbie Does Dallas, a classic for folks who cotton to that style of entertainment. What looked to be a blank white business card attached to the screen door with a pushpin had his name printed in block letters: Tommy Montoya. The screen was unlatched; I turned on the recorder and walked in.

Tommy was tall and thin with a nose broken often enough to permanently point it toward his ear. I gave my name and extended my hand; he shook it like it wasn't worth the effort. Offsetting these negatives, he had beautiful hair, dark and wavy, with a healthy sheen. He had bluish-green eyes that didn't seem to belong in his face.

The bleached blonde wore a dull look that told me that her bra size exceeded her IQ, which despite her abundance left her not very smart. I said nothing, just stared at the blonde. After a couple of minutes she clearly got uncomfortable, which was my reason for staring. She got up to go, likely disappointed she wasn't going to watch Debbie work her way through Dallas. Tommy patted her backside as she went out. Then he turned his attention to me.

"Who the fuck are you?" His voice didn't go with his look. It went with his nose but not his hair and eyes. His diction was bad and he swore too much.

"I'm your conscience. I'm here to give you a chance to die without that load of guilt you've been carrying around for the past eleven years."

"What the fuck are you talking about? I'm not telling you jack until I know just who the fuck you are."

"Then die with a guilty conscience, your choice." I pulled out Quirt Brown's gun. Tommy responded by sticking both his hands in the air, like we were acting out a stagecoach robbery in a 50s B-western.

"I've got a few questions I need you to answer. If you don't cooperate you have no more value to me than did Cory Jackson." I showed him the picture still in my cell phone of Cory lying in the wet surf with a hole in his forehead. "The picture doesn't do him justice," I said. "You can't see the sea water pooled in the hole." I paused to grin. "Cory didn't tell me shit. But then, from now on he won't be telling anybody anything. So, which way are you going to play it, tough or smart?"

Montoya's eyes kept flittering between my face and the hole in the end of the gun that I held pointed at his heart. It's fun to tell the truth in a way that makes the listener feel he heard something different than what you said. Everything I told Tommy Montoya had been the truth. In listening, he added two and two together to come up with a total that to him meant I had punched Cory's ticket. Being a PI could be so much more fun than playing under cop rules.

"Eleven years ago, you and Cory Jackson consorted to get Eddie Whittaker arrested for killing his woman."

"I never met this Cory guy." He flinched, ducked actually, when I crinkled my lips and angled the gun more toward his face. "Really," he said like that was supposed to make his denial more convincing. "I mean it," he added for even more emphasis. "I never knew him, but I've known the name ever since. He was the dude on the beach who claims he saw the killing."

"Cory's history. Let's stay with you. You lied about Eddie buying gas. Why?"

"For money, man, you know. We all do shit for money. I sold myself as a witness against the guy."

"Who and why?"

"I got no clue who. When I asked why, the man said, 'I wanna fuck up the general.'"

"So, how much money?"

"Ten grand."

"That's what Cory got too, ten big ones. He also got a bullet, but that came eleven years later. Your bullet could arrive any time now."

Again, I said one thing, he heard another.

"You here to kill me?"

"My job is revenge against the man who killed Ileana Corrigan. She was Eddie Whittaker's fiancée. My job is that guy. Cory Jackson played it stupid. He didn't help me. If you help, I might just get the guy before he gets you. If not, don't buy any green bananas."

"I don't know shit. The way it happened I never saw the guy."

"Lay it out for me. First sit down." He did. I remained standing. He sat in a leather Barcalounger that had seen its best days. The rest of his place wasn't worthy of description beyond tawdry and tired. That same description had fit the blonde.

He started talking without further prodding. "One night late, two or three nights before Whittaker's broad bought it, I was closing up. Locking up, you know. I went around back and saw light around the door to the women's can. The gals are always walking out and leaving it on. I have to turn it off every night. If I don't the boss gives me hell. When I pulled the door open the light went off like magic. Then somebody shined a large flashlight in my eyes. I couldn't see shit. A voice told me, 'don't move.' I froze, man, couldn't have moved if I wanted. The dude reached out and stuffed something in my shirt pocket.

"'Here's two grand,' he said. Not those exact words, but something like that. Then he said, 'there'll be eight more if you play ball. If you don't, you die. What's it gonna be?' I said I loved to play ball. He handed me a picture and told me to turn around. Then he shined the flashlight over my shoulder down onto the photograph. 'Study it. Day after tomorrow you'll see this guy in the papers or on TV about a woman being killed. So you'll need to pay close attention to the news.'

"I told him I didn't want nothin' to do with no woman being killed. 'You got no choice on that,' he said. 'She will die. The only thing that's undecided is whether or not you die. You catch my drift?'

"'Yeah,' I said. 'I'm with ya. Just don't pull that trigger.'

"He said, 'When you see him in the news, you're to go to the cops. Tell them that a few minutes past nine the night the woman was killed, this guy bought gas from you at the station. That he paid cash. You don't recall his car, but you remember him because so few people pay cash these days.'

"When I tried to look back over my shoulder, he hit me in the side of the head with his frigging flashlight. 'Eyes front,' he said. 'Study this picture.' He pointed out a slight nick in the side of the dude's ear and his square chin. His hair, you know, stuff to help me remember the guy. 'They'll do a lineup. Pick him out. Then stick to your story. That's it, a piece of cake for ten thousand. Drop the ball and I'll drop you and you won't get up.'

"I did it just that way. I got my other eight thousand and nothing after that until you show up now. I wouldn't be telling you shit if that other witness hadn't gotten iced."

"Do you remember the guy's name that you identified?"

"Sure. Eddie Whittaker. Something like that falls in your lap, you remember, man."

After a few more questions I verified he had not previously known Eddie or Cory Jackson and that he got the rest of his money after Eddie had been released. Pretty much the same story I had gotten from Cory Jackson, secondhand through his half brother, Quirt Brown.

The other three witnesses, the ones who caused Eddie to be released, were more reliable than Cory Jackson and Tommy Montoya. As I recalled, one was a local retired middle school principal and the other two were a husband and wife. He retired from a career as a bank manager, back in the days when bankers were considered respectable. She retired from being a registered nurse. From the D.A.'s viewpoint, three solid citizens trumped a pair of losers so it added up to cutting Eddie Whittaker loose. Right now, things were looking good for the general; his grandson Eddie was coming up clean as a choir boy.

I could see three possibilities, maybe more would come to me later. The first went something like this: Somebody had wanted Ileana dead for their own reasons and felt it would work best if there was a patsy set to take the fall and close the investigation into her death. It could have been one of the sugar daddies who were paying her rent and buying her expensive baubles. Thus the real killer bribed and frightened Jackson and Montoya into falsely setting up Eddie Whittaker as the patsy. The plan soured when three law-abiding citizens just happened to see Eddie dining right where he said he had dined.

Number two spread out this way: The murderer didn't know Eddie or Ileana, using them both as a ruse in a violent confidence game wherein the real target was the general, or, more accurately, the general's bank account. This scenario required the killer have a complex plan that would include the two losers to falsely accuse Eddie, and some citizens with solid credentials to come forward to alibi Eddie off the hot seat. Of course, for the second part to happen, the general would first need to pay the shakedown. If he didn't, Eddie would take the fall. It would also require the illicit cooperation of three people we generally don't think of being the types who take part in this kind of chicanery.

The last but not least scenario was that Eddie did kill his fiancée. But this stacking of the facts would again require the assumption that three good people would falsely testify to get him off the hook. If they were salt of the earth folks as they appeared on the surface, they would not agree to commit perjury in a murder case. Fidge said the D.A. looked into the three of them and they had all come up solid.

I needed to confront Eddie. To get in his face and get a read on him. First, I needed to get the wheels in motion to find out everything I could about the bank manager, the RN, and the retired middle-school principal. That meant bringing Axel on board may have been a really good idea.

Of course he was handicapped because he still hadn't gotten his license to drive.

* * *

It had been a long day, but I wasn't ready to sleep. Not yet. I had planned to talk with Axel, but he had gone downstairs to his place by the time I got back. We'd talk in the morning. I took off my day clothes, down to my shorts, pulled on a t-shirt and my too-short robe. Then turned on some Miles Davis and cracked the slider to the patio so the sounds of Mr. Davis could follow me outside. I got a snifter of Irish for sipping, and tugged on my Dodgers' cap with a sweat ring obvious even in the ambient light.

Sitting in the patio recliner reminded me of late nights in prison. Just the quiet, after Axel had fallen asleep on the upper bunk. I'd think about whatever and leave my senses to snag on sounds and stray light. Out here on the patio, I didn't have all the sounds and sightings down pat. Not yet, but I would. There was a greater variety of sounds here than in prison. Inside it mostly came down to differentiating between the steps of the various guards. Other sounds were mostly the farts, snores, coughs, and sometimes muffled sobs of inmates. Newer cons usually paced their cells, but that generally ended in a few weeks. Once in a while, a light would slide silently through the lockup when a guard opened a distant door. Lights and sounds were the only things that really escaped from anywhere inside stir.

My life had become much different from what I expected while growing up. It started for me, like it may have started for you. Mom could make any hurt go away. Dad could fix anything. The nuns who taught at the Catholic school weren't gods; they just demanded to be treated as such. But we learned. We had to, our lives depended on our doing so. None of this mushy treatment kids get today in the public schools.

When my age rolled into double figures I started to see the world differently. Mom and dad weren't perfect. They didn't have all the answers. By the teen years, my head was where most teens' were, angry at my folks for letting me down. For not deserving to be on the pedestal I had put them on, a pedestal I now realize they never claimed they deserved. At that point, in ever growing gobs, I turned to the real source of knowledge, other teenagers. My pals became the center of my universe. Along about that same time the girls started sticking their noses under the boys' tent and things changed again. Tits. Legs. I still don't understand how the girls all seemed to instinctively know how to look from the corner of their eyes, or turn to display the profiles of their breasts. Billy Bataglia, my tightest bud, said the girls learned it watching the vamps in the movies. That was about the time the girls started riding the cotton pony a few days each month, while we struggled to learn that women had two personalities when one was more than we were ready to handle. That last point, still hasn't changed all that much.

Life kept advancing. I no longer carried my Hopalong Cassidy lunchbox. I spent mornings watching the clock in the classroom, urging it to move quicker. When lunchtime finally came, I dashed to the cafeteria and sat near Marilyn who had just transferred into our school from who knows where—heaven would have been my guess. She wore tight sweaters. Tight enough that rumors claimed the school had once called her mother to come and take her home to change clothes. One of the boys who happened to be in the office at the time said Marilyn's mother had bigger bazooms and wore a tighter sweater than her daughter. That boy, who had been sent to the vice principal's office for a paddling, likely smiled all the way through it.

By the age of sixteen, Mom and Dad's image was totally tarnished, and Hoppy was out of my life except for watching him on TV when no one else was home. Life had lost its black or white clarity. I started knocking ever bigger hunks out of my childhood ideas about good and evil, reshaping it all into what I somehow concluded was reality. When I got confused my friends had the answers. The world of teens is the world where the blind arrogantly lead the blind, feeling smarter while the whole bunch of them stumble through puberty.

In those years, the only thing I ever did without my buddies was devise a plan to get hired to wash Marilyn's mom's car and mow her lawn. I longed to find out firsthand how accurate the one boy's description of Marilyn's mom had been. Fortunately, for me at least, Marilyn's parents were divorced so her mom needed help with those chores. To me, their divorce spelled opportunity. My price was the lowest, lunch with them at their outside table after I had cleaned it and swept off the patio. It was here that I learned even more about the *gray* in life. Marilyn spent one weekend a month with her father and when she did, her mom fleshed out the things that had theretofore lived only in my private fantasies. This expanded my circle of teaching adults from Mom and Dad and the nuns at school, to Marilyn's mom who took charge of teaching me the extracurricular stuff. I knew it was bad, maybe more bad for Marilyn's mom than for me. I had the semi-excuse of being young, an excuse I would eventually grow out of so I wanted to use it to full advantage as long as I could.

I never told my buddies what went on at Marilyn's. I just quietly prayed for summer when the grass grew faster. And, believe me, keeping my trap shut about what Marilyn's mother taught me was really hard.

Don't get me wrong. I grew up knowing, and still know, what good is. It's that, for me, getting good done has become more important than how I get it done. At least that's the way I see it. And I don't have a lot of patience with the rest.

Chapter 10

I spent the early hunk of the morning getting Axel familiar with the three good witnesses whose testimony provided Eddie with his real-life get-out-of-jail free card. I had prepared a bit of a dossier on them the night before from what had been in the police file. I had asked Axel to put together a team in the likely event I needed someone followed. He put up a thumb, "all set, boss." The day shift would be comprised of him and Buddha, with the night shift staffed by another of the ex-cons who hung at Mackie's. Buddha had been a full-time cabbie in New York, with a part-time side job of driving getaway cars for pros, no thugs. "Buddha has ethics," Axel said. Buddha was also Axel's driver's education teacher. Axel said he could add more men if they were needed. At this point I hadn't even decided if it would be Cliff, or Eddie, or perhaps one of the solid-citizen witnesses who would need following. Axel had the effort poised to launch. I also promised Axel a tenth of my two-hundred grand fee if we got someone arrested; he understood it had to be a legit pinch.

Axel would do the Internet search stuff himself, generally following the procedure he used inside to search people the warden wanted looked into without going through state personnel. Often this would be new guards, screws or bulls in Axel's language, but sometimes guests of the state who were checking in. The big names mostly, high profile crooks usually had scads of background stuff. This group included the white collar criminals who used brains and smiles to grease their Ponzi schemes and other swindles as they fleeced overly trusting seniors and others out of their life savings. Those fellas liked to think of themselves as businessmen, not crooks. Yeah, right.

I called Fidge, who told me the department had made the connection between Cory Jackson and the Ileana Corrigan homicide. Still, they had nothing with any meat on it that hooked Jackson's death with the eleven-year old Corrigan homicide. Their take was that Cory bought it as a result of his drug activities, or money he owed his bookie for NFL games in which the players had not sufficiently met Cory's expectations.

The day became one of those that flittered away without being productive, beyond learning that certain alleys were dead ends. Finding that out did had value; it just didn't feel like it did. A lot of the time consumed in discussing articles and rumors Axel had found on the Internet about the general, Eddie, and also Ileana Corrigan. A few of those led to phone calls and one to my taking a trip across town. In the end, all of it went nowhere and meant less.

* * *

Over dinner that night, Karen told me she came to live with her father and her nephew, Eddie, about a year and a half before Ileana Corrigan was murdered. At that time, she had two more years to go at University of California at Los Angeles, where she was majoring in finance. She and her mother weren't getting along. From the general's house, she would drive farther to school, but she had structured her schedule of classes into three days a week. She knew the general thought of Eddie as his son, rather than his grandson, putting her, the daughter, in second position for his largess. The general had raised Eddie for most of his life after Eddie's father had died in Desert Storm in 1991. During her college years, Karen admitted she preferred being with her father. He left her to live her own life and didn't interfere as much as her mother had.

"How do you feel about that, now I mean?" I asked her. "Eddie is the general's grandson while you're his daughter."

"That's true," she said, "in an official kind of way. But in a life kind of way, Eddie is the general's son. I'm the daughter he really didn't know all that well until I was a grown woman. It's different. Besides, the general is a sexist. I don't mean that nasty like, he just is. He's a man of his times."

She said she hadn't seen the will. That a copy had been mailed to her a couple of years ago by Mr. Franklin, the general's attorney, but she hadn't opened it. The general had sat her down and explained that his estate was his to do with as he wished. That she would be provided for, but the lion's share would go to Eddie. The general told her he was leaving two million to Charles, and a half million to Cliff. That she would get two and a half million and the rest, about fifteen million, would go to Eddie who would also get the house. To me, it seemed everyone in the general's circle patiently or eagerly awaited the inevitable reading of the will.

"You didn't open the will?"

"No. I didn't go to him, the general came to me. I don't figure he'd do that to tell me lies. The general has always been straight with me. Everyone knows his word is good. Would I rather have Eddie's cut than mine? Sure. But, hey, Mom and I struggled some, financially, so from my perspective two and a half million seems like all the money in the world. I'm cool with it."

"The general's wealthy," I said, "very wealthy, so your mother should have gotten a fat marital settlement."

"The general's wealth came from his parents who died the year after mom and he divorced in '78. Their marriage had lasted only three years. After his inheritance, the general stepped up and paid Mom more than she was entitled to under the divorce. So, I guess I'd say our struggles were somewhat comfortable. The general paid for all my schooling and bought me a car when I started college. He still sends mom something now and again when she gets in a bind. He's really been there above and beyond. But let me not leave an incorrect impression. While the general inherited a lot of money from his parents, he has more than doubled his net worth since his inheritance. He has a shrewd head for investments."

"Have you helped him with his investments? You majored in finance."

"I help some, but the truth is for most of the years he didn't need my help. I do some company specific research for him. We kick stuff around. The last few years I've been more involved in helping him keep up with all of it."

"And still you're okay with the lion's share of his estate going to your nephew Eddie?"

"Eddie and I don't think of ourselves as aunt and nephew. I mean, I'm thirty-five and he's thirty-two. But, no, Mr. Kile, if you're looking for bad blood between Eddie and me over this, there is none."

"Does Eddie think the setup's fair?"

"It's not up to Eddie or me, the money is the general's and he can do with it as he chooses. I've already explained how I feel about that. Besides, if need be, I've got the qualities to hook a man who has even more than the general. If I ever decide I need to go that route. I don't see why I'll need to. Did that sound conceited? I didn't mean it that way. Everybody ought to have an honest talk with themselves about their strengths and weaknesses and then strive to improve their weaknesses. I've done that and I continue to do it."

I couldn't argue with her assessment. She played ladies golf and tennis at UCLA. She was educated in a wealthy man's subject, has a good sense of humor, and is conversant. She enjoys visually tempting men while still coming across as classy, and from what I know, men enjoy being visually tempted.

"I've gathered that nephew Eddie is a player. That true?"

"Did I mention Eddie likes the ladies and he enjoys his trips to Vegas."

The waiter stopped to tell us about their tempting dessert specials. We said no, but ordered a second bottle of the Krupp Brothers Cabernet Sauvignon we had enjoyed with dinner. When he left to get the wine I asked, "Seriously, what gets Eddie's attention? Career, charities, what?"

"Eddie likes the ladies and he enjoys his trips to Vegas."

We laughed before I asked, "What other women has he been serious about? Before or after Ileana."

The waiter brought and opened the second bottle of wine. I put my hand up for him to leave the bottle to breathe and I would pour when we were ready.

"None that I know of and I would know," Karen said. "We talk pretty openly. Ileana was the only one that made him think about settling down, about getting serious about life and what to do with his. But no dice. Eddie seems a fellow content with the superficial." She laughed. "Look at me, like I should talk."

"You and Ileana were friends, right?"

"For a while, before she and Eddie became an item."

Karen knew of no jealous boyfriend or sugar daddy. She also said Eddie didn't buy the expensive jewelry found in Ileana's house.

"Eddie couldn't afford that kind of stuff," Karen said. "None of us knew she had it. I agree the jewelry suggests she had a man bringing her gifts. But, if she did, I doubt that man killed her." When I raised my eyebrows, she said, "If he had, why wouldn't he take back the diamonds he had bought for her?"

While I had listened, I poured our wine. "Could be, then again, if he did kill her and the cops ever put his name with their suspicions, the fact the jewelry hadn't been taken could argue against him being the killer."

"Or, if he did take it, it might have suggested a killing during a robbery. Somebody could have seen her wearing it and followed her home to take it by force."

"You have a point," I said. "Such is the grist of investigating homicides. The possible theories, winnowing them down, and then finding or not finding support for each."

She nodded. "Apparently, the robbery theory lacks support as the jewelry remained. The sugar daddy theory has support in that it is the best argument for how the jewelry came to exist in the first place, yet the police could never identify him."

"Fidge, ah, the department never found where the jewelry had been bought. So it could have been hot, but they found no record of stolen jewelry that matched up. Ileana seems to have liked bikers. Did she have a thing for bad boys? Maybe one of them could have heisted the jewels and gave them to her?"

"She had sort of run through her bad boy thing. It ended after she met Eddie."

"But she had a sugar daddy, so perhaps her bad boy thing just morphed into married wealthy sugar daddy bad boys, sort of."

"Could be, but then maybe she got the jewelry from one of the bikers before she met Eddie and there was no sugar daddy."

"No. Not likely. Two different neighbors reported seeing luxury cars in her driveway now and again. She had at least one wealthy fella; one who could get his hands on quality jewelry that couldn't be traced."

"I just don't figure Ileana that way. I thought she was sold on Eddie. She loved him, and he would eventually be rich. Why blow that for a necklace or two? Ileana was smart. And she really did love Eddie."

"Could Ileana have had a sugar mommy?"

"Not Ileana. She liked the real deal."

"Okay, enough on that, what about you? Career or charity?"

"I won't have enough money to do much for charity, not like Eddie will, but then his favorite charity is his ladies. As for me, I'd like to get into investment banking or something like that. But not now, I'm content being there for the general."

"You love him, don't you?"

"He's a great man. A real man. When I think about how my life would have been. How my mother's life would have been, would still be, if it weren't for the general. Well, I figure I owe him. It won't be long now. I mean I hope it is, but the doctors say no. He knows that. That's why he brought you in now. We talked about it. He wants to know and he could no longer push off his doubts."

"Could Eddie have killed Ileana?"

"He was in Buellton so it's really impossible."

"I'm not asking could he in a procedural sense. I meant emotionally. Could Eddie kill?"

"Millions of people in our armed forces over hundreds of years, not to mention the armed forces of the rest of the world, have killed. Cops sometimes must kill, also executioners who work for various governments. On that level, with an aura of external justification, I guess many, even most, could kill. The dicey part is one finding the justification alone, inside, you know. On that level, I'd say no. Eddie couldn't."

When dinner was over I asked her to come home with me.

"Do you think that's a good idea?" She put her hand over mine, palm up, and kneaded me with her knuckles.

"You're damn right I do." She smiled when I said that. "I got the idea from you," I added as if that should cinch the deal.

"When did I give you that idea?"

"That first night. When we met. You were leaning on the banister."

"Oh. That was lust, Mr. Kile."

"Every relationship has to start somewhere. Lust seems as good a starting point as any other."

"You have to promise me you're not going to get all gooey in the morning and start talking about love or something."

"You don't believe in love?" I asked.

"I just don't understand it. Don't know if I'd recognize it. And if I did, whether I could get into it."

"I can help you along if you get stuck."

"No. You get too serious, we're history. I've never seen love work, certainly not between my mom and the general. Both good people, but it just withered and died. And not between my mom and all the men she's tried on for size to replace the general."

* * *

I woke Karen gently before setting the bed tray over her thighs. Axel had prepared mimosas, coffee, and buttered English muffins with fresh strawberries dipped in chocolate. He left a note on the kitchen counter saying he saw this in a movie. Axel was working out just fine. The talking parrot I considering getting instead would have left beak marks in the strawberries.

Karen and I had enjoyed a wonderful evening of food and drink before we came back to my place. In a lot of ways she reminded me of Clarice Talmadge, only Karen liked the idea of staying the whole night. I suppose it's a good thing that not all women enjoyed entertaining and seducing a man as much as these two ladies. If those two were the norm, the life expectancy for us men would be shorter, but then more of us would die with a smile on our face. And that's not all bad either. When Helen, my ex, and I got married we were quite young and during our years together I imagined that other than hookers and in the movies, there were not all that many women who were so enthusiastic about sex. Man, was I wrong. And man, am I happy I was wrong.

Karen left about an hour later. Both of us fed, watered, and satisfied. She said she had things to do and I needed some time to sift through and process what I learned from her during dinner. I was meeting Charles for lunch, so after the strawberries and mimosas, I only wanted coffee.

Chapter 11

Charles picked me up in front of my condo building at noon. He looked more relaxed away from the Whittaker house, his smile easier. I took him to Mackie's where we chose a quiet corner booth. Axel was sitting at the end of the bar, around the curve, from where he could watch Charles. I hadn't planned that, but apparently Axel had, which was okay. He had a good feel for people so a second opinion might be helpful.

"Thank you for meeting me, Charles. I trust you won't be uncomfortable with my asking questions about the general and the family."

"The general's instruction were that I should answer your questions and that we would trust your integrity, Mr. Kile, so you may ask whatever you wish."

I first asked a series of questions that confirmed his recollections matched what the general had told me about his trip to the bank, and the cell call he had received before tossing the bag with the two million over the side of the road. Charles also confirmed the general had walked the rest of the way to the house, and that he, Charles, had found Cliff working out in his gym over the garage and sent him back to get the general's car out of the ditch.

"Did the general look over the edge where he had dropped the satchel with the money?"

"No, but I did. I walked back to the car with Cliff."

"Did you see anything?"

"No. It's really dark in that section. That spot's about a hundred yards back from where the car had been driven into the ditch. The light from the road is shaded by the edge; erosion has torn hunks out of the sandstone cliff face all along that section of the beach. The general had to have it reinforced in a few places to secure the road. But, no, I saw no one. I couldn't even see the satchel. By then I doubt it was still there. I'm sure whoever had called the general to drop it, had picked it up right away and left before the general got back to house, let alone before Cliff and I got back there. Later, after I got back to the house, I got a large flashlight, went down the stairs and walked back there in the sand. I saw no satchel and there were too many tracks in the sand to learn anything."

"Why didn't the general call for you and Cliff?"

"He said he just wanted to walk some. The ordeal had ended. The car wasn't going anywhere. It was one of the few times I've ever seen the general out of sorts, if I can say so, sir. He had just been ordered to throw two million dollars over a cliff." Charles grinned and shook his head. "I suspect that would rattle anyone."

"Did he say the call was from a man or woman?"

"Woman."

"A woman's voice, okay, but what I'm asking is whether the caller was a man or a woman?"

"Women's voices come from women, Mr. Kile. I don't understand."

"For legitimate or personal reasons as well as illegitimate reasons people can learn to speak as a member of the opposite sex. With a modest amount of practicc, a woman can learn to speak in a masculine tone from lower in her throat, below the Adam's apple. Conversely, a man can speak like a woman by projecting his voice from above the Adam's apple. By keeping your finger on your throat you get feedback as to the level on which your voice begins. The doing isn't all that hard, but it takes practice to make it sound easy and natural."

"That's beyond me, Mr. Kile. The general said a woman. That's all I know."

"Yes. That's what the general told me when I asked him the same thing."

We took time to look at the menus and ordered beef dips and a draft beer; Charles ordered a side of horseradish sauce. Then I asked Charles how long he had known General Whittaker.

"When he first made general, I was assigned to his staff as his driver. Other than a few years when I was otherwise assigned, I've been with him ever since."

"You know you can call me Matt."

"I'm comfortable sir, if you are."

"Why have you stayed with him all these years?"

"In the beginning, in the army, he was a father figure I suppose. I had joined the army after growing up in foster homes. I enlisted at the youngest age I could. Since getting out, well, a man must work. The general pays well and with room and board included it provides a healthy income that allows me to make modest investments. I should also say that over the years a deep friendship evolved. I understand my place, of course, at my insistence more than the general's."

"And then there's the inheritance. You being provided for in his will."

"Yes, Mr. Kile, if you're angling to learn if I know about that. I do. However, I have no doubts that if I were to leave, the general would not change my place in his will. I believe he sees providing for me therein as for services rendered, not to be rendered. No, sir, I stay because it is my home. I have no other family and I am devoted to the general, also for services rendered, to reuse the phrase."

"I guess you know the general better than anyone. What are his strengths and weaknesses? I'm not needlessly prying, Charles, I need to know how he will handle himself depending on where my investigation takes me. Please speak candidly."

Our meals came before Charles began to answer. I glanced up at Axel who had taken a position to far away to hear, but sufficient to study the face of my lunch guest.

"The general has so many high qualities I don't know where to begin or how to summarize, but I shall try. He is an old-fashioned man. He believes in honor, duty, and integrity. If he gives you his word, you may safely rest your life upon it. He demands loyalty from those near him and gives a full measure in return. If he has a fault it could be his intense commitment to those qualities. At times it keeps him rigid. But in the end, I'll take his kind every time."

"His greatest trial? Most trying, I mean."

"Certainly the death of his first wife, Grace, in 1970, she died of breast cancer. Then there was his failed marriage to Karen's mother, Mary. With those exceptions, the general rarely achieved less than he set out to achieve. Mary, his second wife, was a smart woman and beautiful. Frankly Karen is much like her mother in looks and style. Mary could not countenance the military life. She demanded the general choose between her and his army. He did. But he always loved her. And he always provided for her and Karen. He saw them a few times each year and always attended special events in Karen's life as she grew into a woman. I had the pleasure of accompanying the general to many, probably most, of those events. Karen and Mary squabbled like many mothers and daughters. That's what led Karen to come live with us while still in college."

"So you like him, don't you, Charles?"

"Above all others, Mr. Kile. General Whittaker is my employer and, as I said, we maintain that relationship. We are also friends for life and he has never wavered in that commitment."

"How is he doing? His health I mean. Is he able to keep up some of his favorite activities and hobbies?"

Mackie came out from around the bar and started toward our table. I held up my hand, palm out. He did an about face and headed back behind the bar. I also noticed he had been staying away from Axel. In prison you learn to be aware of who is watching who, before deciding whether or not to approach. Mackie knew Axel was watching Charles and me, so he stayed at the end of the bar away from Axel.

"The general's condition is deteriorating rather quickly now. The last six months he has been forced to curtail pretty much all his activities. The last to go was his target rifle shooting. He loved that and used to shoot regularly with Karen and Eddie and Cliff. Sometimes I would participate as well."

"Who is the best shot?"

"In the old days, before Cliff joined us, the general. Cliff had been a Marine sniper so he shot rings around the rest of us. Karen nearly always finished next, although she preferred handguns, followed by Eddie. Well, except for when I joined in, then I would come in behind Karen and ahead of Eddie. Along that time, Eddie lost interest and no longer tried all that much. In my five years of service away from the general I became quite a marksman, but that's one of those skills you use or you lose. We haven't had a family shooting competition in nearly a year, but just the other day the general mentioned we needed to do it again. However, I doubt he will try to do so."

"Your thoughts on Karen?"

"What specifically do you wish to know, Mr. Kile?"

"Whatever comes to mind. Again, please be candid."

"Conventions don't control her actions. In that way she is like her mother. I see a pleasure in the general whenever she is near. I should add that Karen got straight A's in college and is quite disciplined in her intellectual pursuits. My comments were more on her personal side."

"Do they spend much time together, she and the general?"

"Karen dines with the general, whatever he is eating, most nights. Eddie joins them perhaps once a week. She spends in the aggregate about a day a week with him on his investments. They play chess a couple times a week. She swims with him whenever he wishes, which has been seldom these past months." Charles smiled and I asked what brought it on. "When she beats him at chess, the general is conflicted. He remains very competitive and fancies himself an excellent chess player. Yet, at the same time, he is tickled and proud of her for having beaten him. He will talk about it to me off and on for days."

I dunked my last bite of my beef dip and asked, "What about Eddie? Is he capable of having killed Ileana Corrigan? I know this is not easy, but no one knows the characters in this drama as well as you. I value your opinion."

"The characters in this drama, a little of your novelist side, Mr. Kile?" We shared a chuckle before Charles began to answer. "Eddie has lived a soft life. Everything paid by the general, including a liberal spending allowance. He was a strong young man, good high school athlete. The general did not want him to go into the military, not after he lost Eddie's father in Desert Storm. Eddie has never really worked. In my day, we would call him a playboy, a womanizer. Then he met Ileana. It would seem she tamed him. They became engaged. She turned up pregnant. Then, well, you know."

I motioned to Mackie to bring us two more drafts before asking, "I don't see the general as the kind of man who would raise a boy soft. Why did he?"

"The general raised his son, Eddie's father, Ben, quite differently. He required Ben take a part time job in high school. Ben was raised around military people and talk, and wanted nothing more than to follow in his father's footsteps. Ben joined the army and had reached the rank of captain when he was killed in Desert Storm. The general anguished over whether he contributed to his son dying in '91 by bringing up the boy to be rugged and encouraging him toward the military. My guess is that doubt led to his handling Eddie exactly the opposite. The general has never said that to me in so many words, but I believe it to be correct."

"You spoke earlier of your great fondness for the general. Do you like Eddie?"

"Not particularly. He's spoiled, of course. And he does not speak to or of the general in the manner he should. He has so far squandered the advantages of his life. I suppose his life is what men often say would be the ideal: enough money, no work, lots of liquor and women. Truth is most of us would not want that life. Eddie has it and seems to like it. I find life without an absolute dedication or clear purpose shallow and superficial. Men should be committed to something above all else."

Mackie brought our fresh beers and took our plates and empty glasses.

"I ask again, could Eddie have killed Ileana?"

"I don't think so, Mr. Kile. He seems never to be out of control, never to be angry. Everyone likes him, not much respect, but he has polished his social graces. Until Ileana's death and his arrest, Eddie had never dealt with anything tough or hard or demanding in his life. I have to think killing someone would be all of that. No. I don't think so. The general has never believed Eddie guilty, and I know no better judge of men."

"Does the general like Eddie?"

"Ah. That's a hard one. The general is disappointed in the choices Eddie has made. He has waited for Eddie to take his life in some direction. When he was a boy, we hoped he might become a doctor, an engineer, whatever. In college, he drifted, took quite a few legal classes and psychology. Whatever happened to interest him without concern for a degree or career. For years, the general has encouraged Eddie to contribute his time to some worthy cause, but none of that has taken hold. Eddie is happy being Eddie. Things have always gone as Eddie wanted them to go. Well, except for the devastation of losing his fiancée. He loved Ileana and needed treatment for depression for nearly a year."

"When did Cliff join the staff?"

"About thirteen years ago, something like that. Karen came to live with us first. Her coming was part of the general's reason for increasing the size of the staff. My duties also expanded to helping the general with some of his non-investment business matters. This made me less available as a driver and the general had become less capable of driving himself."

"I've only seen Cliff once from a distance. He looks around fifty. How was he chosen?"

"That requires a bit of back story. First, Cliff is forty-five, but you're correct, in the face he looks older. He's a hard drinker but exercises vigorously. His focus is on his legs and gut and stamina, like a boxer trains. For years, the general had covered the costs of keeping five old soldiers, badly disabled men from his command, in a home. When the last one died, the general assigned me to find Cliff, the last soldier's son. He had gotten into drugs and started running with a motorcycle gang. The general put him in rehab, with Cliff's consent of course. After that Cliff continued weekly therapy for some time. He's the general's driver and takes care of the five vehicles used by the family and myself. He also cares for the pool and spa and oversees the work done by the landscaping service."

Charles also told me the best time to catch Cliff at the house without his expecting me would be tomorrow midday. That Cliff had to take one of the cars into the dealer in the morning, but should be back by around noon. As for Eddie, he was a wisp of smoke that drifted in and out, but Charles agreed to call me when Eddie was home and looking like he wasn't headed out.

"So," I asked, "what's your opinion? Who killed Ileana Corrigan?"

"The wisest thing I can say is that the general has a good man on that job, so I expect we shall finally find out."

Chapter 12

I started the morning at the home of Robert and Melanie Yarbrough, the retired couple who had reported seeing Eddie Whittaker at Pea Soup Anderson's restaurant in Buellton on the night of his fiancée's murder. She was taller than her husband. Robert was stockier. Melanie had more hair, but they were tied as to who had more gray hair. I got to their house a few minutes after nine-thirty.

I would have arrived earlier except Axel wanted to talk about the case and be brought up to speed on what I had learned from Charles during our lunch at Mackie's. And I wanted his read from watching Charles. That took about an hour. While we talked, I gave Axel another assignment. He had done a lot of computer work for the Warden and developed quite a reputation in prison as a computer guy, not so much as a technician, but a researcher for the warden. His assignment: dig into the retired middle school principal who also claimed to have seen Eddie in the restaurant. I told him for now to restrict his inquiries to the Internet. Later, based on what he learned or didn't we'd decide how to proceed. I was hoping he'd find that former Principal Flaherty had some nasty habit which could have been used to leverage him into lying about seeing Eddie.

Robert and Melanie Yarbrough were each dressed in warm robes, sitting on their front porch, having coffee and sharing the newspaper. Their home faced east so they were enjoying the warmth provided by the morning sun. I introduced myself and we exchanged Merry Christmas greetings, and then I told them I was working on the death of Ileana Corrigan. The moment I mentioned her name, Melanie Yarbrough's eyes got big, and she grasped the front of her robe as if it a cold breeze had sneaked inside. They had not forgotten the incident in the slightest. After a few more pleasantries I won't bore you with, I dove into the water, so to speak. Well, my entry was more like a cannonball than a dive. I wanted to measure the size of their emotional splash.

"It's been eleven years, folks. I know you lied about seeing Eddie Whittaker in Buellton. I just don't know why you did. You are lawful citizens, honorable people. Why would you cheat justice and possibly help a murderer go free?"

"We saw him, Mr. Kile," Robert Yarbrough said. "Just as we swore we did." After he said it, he looked at his wife.

"We saw him, Mr. Kile. Just as my husband said."

"The murder of this young woman, Ileana Corrigan remains unsolved. The murder of her unborn child remains unsolved. Neither mother nor child will rest easy until their killer is brought to justice. Folks, please, consider how you would feel if Ileana were your daughter and you were approaching yet another Christmas without knowing what happened."

Neither of them said a word, but their body language screamed their discomfort. That and the numerous glances each made toward the other. Had they been telling the truth they would have resented what I said. Instead, it made them nervous and uncomfortable.

"Perhaps I should come back later and bring Ileana's parents with me, the grandparents of the unborn child."

They were ready to crack, but for now were holding firm. Their eyes flittered, their gazes everywhere but upon my eyes. Their claws dug into the lie that had lived for so long, hanging on desperately.

"Look at me! Damn it!" I hollered. "Look me in the eyes." I sat still until they each had. "You are both grandparents. You have a grandson named Bobby. Can you imagine, just for a moment, enduring Bobby being murdered and the killer not being found for over eleven years. Imagine your living with that grief. That wound open. Come on!"

Melanie Yarbrough broke first. She covered her eyes and cried. Her husband slid his chair close so he could reach over and hold her. Her sobs temporarily drowned out by the scrape of the metal legs of his chair against the concrete porch. "Robbie, I can't do this. I can't do it any longer. This lie … I can't. I just can't. I'm sorry. We must tell the truth. Please?"

Robert Yarbrough patted the top of his wife's hand. With his open palm against her face, his thumb gently wiped the stream of tears staining her cheek. "You're right, Mel. The time has come. It should have come long ago." They clutched each other's hands and turned toward me, their eyes now on mine, looking for understanding, for forgiveness. Robert cut the core out of their lie.

"We never saw Eddie Whittaker in Buellton. We were told to drive up there and have dinner in that restaurant. We were to be there at nine at night and to stop and buy gas for the car on the outskirts of town as we left. Once we heard of the arrest, we were to go to the police and swear we dined in the Pea Soup, leaving around nine-thirty. And that we had seen Eddie Whittaker in the restaurant when we left."

"We were to use a credit card to pay for the dinner," Mrs. Yarbrough said, "and for the gas on our way out of town." Robert nodded as if he had just recalled that part of their charade.

"And that's what you did?"

"Yes," she said while her husband nodded his head, his lips drawn tight; his eyes down.

"Why? How much money were you paid?"

"No, no. We received no money. We would not do such a thing for money, Mr. Kile."

Until then I had been standing up. I leaned back against their wooden porch railing. "Then why?"

"Can we go inside?" Mrs. Yarbrough asked. "I'm getting chilled sitting here. It's probably just the stress. Please?"

Mr. Yarbrough stood up. "Of course dear, Mr. Kile, please come inside. There is more you need to know."

Their home was pleasant. Clean, neat, and big enough for two, and nicely furnished.

"Have a seat, Mr. Kile," Mrs. Yarbrough said while fidgeting with her hands. Then she began to cry again. They sat on the couch. Mr. Yarbrough held her.

"How long have you folks been married?" I asked.

"Thirty-five years. A wonderful life together, except for this terrible thing. We are so ashamed."

"Mr. and Mrs. Yarbrough, why did you lie?"

They had clearly lost their will to continue as they had for so long. The wrong of it had eaten through their resolve. Over the next half hour they told me of the morning when they walked their new puppy at the beach. The phone call Melanie received on her cell phone, the shot that had killed Snookie, and finally about the threat that stopped their hearts. "Do what you are told or my next shot will kill your grandson, Bobby."

Robert continued to hold his wife, but now he also swiped at tears of his own. Then I asked, "A man? A woman?"

"A man," Mrs. Yarbrough said, "a cold, heartless man, without feelings. How can anyone speak of killing a little infant, barely able to walk?"

"There are such people. Fortunately, they are few." I didn't tell them that the number of such people seemed to be increasing every year. Or maybe saying that would only have revealed my cynicism which had grown with time, and my knowledge of too many such people. I also recalled the general's words about America losing its taste for swift and final justice.

"I know what I am about to ask you will not be easy. But believe me, it is necessary. Will you repeat everything you have told me into a tape recorder? I will not take it to the authorities without your permission." After some resistance, they came to accept they had crossed a bridge this morning. That they could not put what they told me back into the darkness. They needed to do what they could to make amends for the pain and emptiness that filled the hearts of the parents of Ileana Corrigan.

I went out to my car and brought back the tape recorder. They asked if they could record it as well. I agreed. With two tapes running, Mr. Robert Yarbrough and his wife Melanie retold the horror of their morning eleven years ago, and the tribulations they had endured since. When they finished it was clear, they had never seen Eddie Whittaker anywhere except in the newspaper and on the news eleven years ago.

I drove back to Long Beach searching for the answer to the meaning of what I had learned. Someone had eliminated Cory Jackson, the only witness who had claimed seeing Eddie Whittaker at the scene of the crime. Oh, sure, Tommy Montoya could testify he was bribed to say he sold Eddie gas. But that only proved, especially with Cory Jackson dead, that no one knew where Eddie had been the night of the murder of his fiancée. The Yarbrough confession argued only that they had not seen Eddie in Buellton, not that he had not been there. Eddie says he went up there and nothing I had proved he hadn't.

Fact: Someone had coerced Mr. and Mrs. Yarbrough into claiming they had seen Eddie in Buellton. *Fact:* Someone had bribed and threatened Cory Jackson and Tommy Montoya into providing the original evidence that led to Eddie's arrest. *Fact:* Someone had sold that alibi to the general for two million dollars. Lies told by others, along with an unknown party bribing and threatening Mr. and Mrs. Yarbrough to tell those lies did not prove Eddie did anything. Not that he had dinner in Buellton. Not that he didn't have dinner in Buellton. Not that he killed his fiancée. Not that he didn't kill his fiancée. The rest was conjecture that could fit various theories. One being that Eddie killed his fiancée and then extorted money from his grandfather. Was he capable of such a bold and diabolical plan, including arranging for his own arrest and release? Could someone else have murdered Ileana and crafted both events as part of a plan to shake down the general?

We still had Principal Flaherty who claimed he also saw Eddie in the Pea Soup Andersen's restaurant in Buellton. Maybe Axel had found something on Flaherty. If Flaherty, like the Yarbroughs, admitted not having seen Eddie in Buellton, I was still in the same position. Eddie either went to Buellton for dinner or he did not. At worst, that meant he lied about where he was. Not that he murdered Ileana. He could have been in bed with a married woman and lied to protect her secret. People lie about their whereabouts for many reasons, rarely to cover up having committed murder.

I needed to get in Eddie Whittaker's face. Get a read on the guy. In a normal murder investigation, the immediate parties are among the very first to be interviewed. However, the case of the murder of Ileana Corrigan was eleven-years old. Eddie had been interviewed, and later interrogated after his arrest, so his opinions and reactions were a matter of record. I had read them in the police file. I had intentionally held off confronting the general's grandson until I had immersed myself in the case and all the other players. For a little longer, I would leave Eddie to stew in his own juice. He knew I was coming. He just didn't know when, or where, or what I might learn before I got him nose to nose.

* * *

My next stop was at the home of Ileana's parents, Betty and Willard Corrigan. They lived modestly in San Fernando Valley. Their home appeared to be about twenty years old, with blue siding and a block and iron rail wall around the property. The pride of their front yard, a queen palm whose fronds rose above the composition roof.

I introduced myself at their door and they warmly greeted me into their home. Mr. and Mrs. Corrigan were recently retired, although Betty still worked some in real estate, sitting open houses for other agents. We chatted for a couple of hours.

When I asked how long they had been married, their memories included the general giving them an all-expense paid two-week cruise from Long Beach to Hawaii, roundtrip, for their last anniversary. "They don't make men like the general anymore," Mr. Corrigan said.

Mr. and Mrs. Corrigan did not recall their daughter having an old boyfriend who became incensed when Ileana chose Eddie Whittaker. That didn't mean there was no such boyfriend. Only that after all these years, if there had been one, the Corrigan's didn't remember. Parents are often the last to know much about a daughter's lovers. I asked the Corrigans about the expensive jewelry found where their daughter lived. They didn't even know she had it. Faded memories are always a major problem when working old cases. That and real or possible witnesses having moved away or died, which I s'pose constituted faded memories to the max. Ileana's parents did remember how their daughter had met Eddie Whittaker. Ileana had been out with one of her girlfriends, Karen Whittaker, and the two of them were with a group of bikers. They admitted that in those years Ileana was struggling with maturing and often took up with bad boys, like the bikers. That was why they were so pleased when she took up with a respectable boy like Eddie Whittaker. One of the bikers, the one who had introduced Ileana to Eddie Whittaker had been identified as General Whittaker's chauffeur; Mrs. Corrigan said it like show-fer. They had remembered Cliff because, as a young man, Mr. Corrigan had been in the army and knew of General Whittaker.

* * *

I drove back to Long Beach wondering what role, if any, Cliff played in all this. Perhaps, the chauffeur's connection to Eddie went beyond being the family driver. While I drove, I called Charles at the Whittaker home. He told me that back then Cliff had taught Eddie to ride a motorcycle and the two of them had hung around some. "Partying, they called it." Charles further recalled that Eddie had trouble keeping his balance and eventually lost interest in his motorcycle.

"You have to understand, Mr. Kile, Eddie was very coordinated and most things physical came to him easily when he applied the effort. When something didn't come easily he'd sour-grapes it and walk away."

I asked Charles if the two men were still close.

"The only thing the two had in common was riding motorcycles, so once Eddie tired of that, as he eventually did nearly everything, he sold his motorcycle and they quit palling around."

"How long ago did Eddie sell his motorcycle?"

"Right after Ileana died. Cliff found the buyer."

Charles also said that Cliff still arrived each day on his motorcycle and while on duty kept it in the Whittaker garage. Charles explained that Cliff had an apartment in town, in addition to a small sleeping room upstairs over the garage.

I thanked Charles and hung up. So, Eddie and Cliff had been pals, but no longer. I needed someone to poke around and see what could be learned about Cliff's dad and the other four old soldiers the general had taken care of in the assisted living facility. I called Axel. There would be lots of hits about the general on the Internet: his life and philanthropic activities, so maybe something would come up on his providing the care for those soldiers. I also needed someone with at least solid bookkeeping skills to go through the records to see how many years and how much the general had spent to care for the five men. I wasn't certain if doing that would mean anything, but I wanted to have the information in the event I chose to follow it.

All this was likely a dead end, but so far the game only had the general, Eddie, Karen, Charles, and Cliff. I couldn't shake the feeling that I was playing poker with an empty chair at the table, a chair for a player who had yet to join the game.

Chapter 13

Axel wanted me to join him and a young lady friend for dinner tomorrow night. He said their relationship was not romantic. They had met outside Mackie's and he had invited her to join him for lunch. "She's young enough to be my daughter," he said, "my granddaughter even. For Christ's sake."

He asked me to go along for two reasons: so she and I could meet, and because he hadn't yet gotten a driver's license. I had gone through this kind of thing with my daughters when they first started dating so I suppose I had a feel for it. But Axel was in his sixties and from what he told me the young lady was still looking up at twenty. It would be weird, but he said it was no date. "I'm no pervert," is how Axel put it.

Axel also said she had some skills I might make use of. Although, when he told me how he met Hildegard it left me somewhat unsure to which skills he had referred. Then he told me her father had been an accountant, and that she had worked with him summers and weekends for several years. Before she left home she had planned to become a CPA like her father.

"She can handle going through the records about the five old soldiers the general helped," Axel said. "She can use the money, boss."

I understood, but promised nothing.

Cars had changed enormously since Axel went to prison over thirty-five years ago, not to mention changes in the roads and the traffic lights. Yesterday he had begun driver training. His teacher was Buddha, one of the ex-cons who hung out in Mackie's. The cars Axel drove before going inside featured split front windshields, bench seats, bigger steering wheels, and stick shifts to mention just a few of the differences. The roads in those days had fewer lanes and not many designated for turns. In prison he had gotten more than comfortable with computers, but he found nearly everything else on the outside new and a bit strange. So far I had only identified a few changes he found agreeable: big-flat-screen color television, and women's shorter skirts along with the improved engineering of brassieres.

* * *

At nine I stopped for a quick meal in Hof's Hut on Long Beach Blvd in the Bixby Knolls area. I took in the department's homicide file on Ileana Corrigan and went over it again while I ate. There was nothing in the file about

Cliff and Eddie being pals around the time of the murder. I hadn't expected there would be, but I recalled the report mentioning guns at the Whittaker residence. The general had approved Fidge taking and testing any guns he wished. Fidge had taken a few possibles to determine if they had recently been fired. Ileana Corrigan had been shot twice, first in her throat and then a make-sure bullet in her head. The department ran tests, but none of the weapons had been fired recently enough, and in the opinion of their experts the bullet wounds had not come from shots fired by those guns. The shots that killed Ileana had been through-and-throughs from a powerful handgun. The evidence team had found no casings or bullets at the scene. Whoever had murdered Eddie's fiancée had been calm and knew not to leave behind anything that ballistics might use.

After getting in my car, I called Charles's cell phone to see if Cliff was still around. The chauffeur had left. Charles reminded me Cliff had a small place he kept in town to use sometimes. That he had gone there for the night and gave me that address. I started to head for his apartment on the off chance I might catch him there.

* * *

"Cliffy? Cliffy?"

Cliff Branch heard his name being spoken softly. It was after ten and he had just turned off his television. He knew the voice, but had not heard it spoken just that way in nearly a year.

"Hello," he said after opening his door. "What brings you here?"

"I need someone to talk to and you're the only one who really understands me."

Karen Whittaker walked in wearing a loose extra large man's tee shirt and red high heels. He could tell she wore no underwear and the way she moved without it could have been a commercial for a pediatrician. He wore only the jockey shorts he always slept in.

"I just don't know what to make of this Matt Kile nosing into our family's business. I'm not sure it's good for Eddie."

"Why not? The general believes Eddie didn't kill Ileana. He's hired Kile to prove that."

"But what if Eddie did do it?"

"Well, from what you said a while back you'd get a much bigger slice of your dad's dough."

"I guess that's true. If so, I'd be set up, that's for sure. Then you and I could pick back up where we were years ago. You'd like that, wouldn't you? I mean, I still see you watching me. Can I sit down, Cliff?" He nodded and headed toward the couch to move some clutter off it. "Oh, don't bother. I'll just sit here on the bed."

"Do you think Eddie did kill her?"

"No. No, of course I don't, Cliffy. We both know Eddie couldn't do anything like that, that violent. Still, I wish he'd just beat the crap out of Kile and make him go away. But Eddie isn't man enough to do that."

"Heck. Why not let Kile try. If he proves Eddie did it, the general may just knock him out of his will and you'll wake up in clover."

"But," Karen said, "if he proves Eddie didn't do it, any chance I have of the general deciding to give me a bigger cut goes down the drain. It is only the general's doubt, tiny as it may be, that Eddie is innocent that might cause the general to reconsider how he'll split it up between Eddie and me. So, no, things would be better with the general having his doubts. I wish he had never hired Matt Kile."

"I don't know, Karen. I mean, I want whatever you want. You know?"

"What I want is for you to come over here. Lie down. It's been too long, Cliffy."

After Cliff sat on the bed, he felt Karen's hand on his naked thigh. He looked over at her. She put her hand on his cheek and pushed him back until he was lying beside her. She kissed him on the lips, his neck, and then on his chest. From there she worked her way down until she took him into her mouth and controlled him.

Chapter 14

Last night I stopped short of going to Cliff Branch's house to confront General Whittaker's chauffeur. Instead, I had gone home and put in a couple of hours reading the proof of my next novel that my publisher had attached to his email two days ago.

Today would start with me in Cliff's face. He could have been the male voice that had threatened Cory Jackson and Tommie Montoya eleven years ago as well as Robert and Melanie Yarbrough. None of them would recognize his voice. From what Charles said, he had the skill with a rifle to have shot the Yarbrough's little dog, Snookie. He had also been tight with Eddie in those days, introducing him to Ileana. I also figured that as the general's chauffeur he had been an unofficial observer of the Whittaker family for more than a decade. And he had undoubtedly spent time ogling Karen. I understood this completely because I had known her only a few days and I had already spent time doing my own ogling. I had even earned my more-than-ogle merit badge. Maybe Cliff and I were also lodge brothers in that regard.

Charles came out the front door to meet me. I had called ahead to be sure Cliff was there.

"Good morning, Mr. Kile. The general is feeling poorly and won't be using Cliff today. I saw him head down the stairs to the beach about ten minutes ago. He was in his trunks so he might have gone in for a swim. There's hardly ever anyone in that stretch of the beach except coming down from our house."

I wasn't wearing a swimsuit, but I had dressed in a pair of casual slacks, a polo shirt and tennis shoes. They would be good on the wooden stairs; Charles had said there were one-hundred and eleven steps down to the beach.

There were landings about every ten-to-fifteen stairs. When I got near the bottom, a man I recognized to be the general's chauffeur stepped up toward me. "I'm Cliff, you're Matt Kile, right?"

I reached out to shake his hand and he hit me square in the jaw. I went down backwards onto the stairs behind me. He stood there waiting for me like an umpire waiting for Tommy Lasorda. His hands up, all Marquis of Queensberry like. I obliged him and stood. When I did, he took another swing at the other side of my jaw. It was my right to turn the other cheek, not his to do it for me. I blocked his blow and hit him in the stomach, then in his face, coming up under his chin. It was his turn to fall back. He did, stumbling down two steps before falling onto the sand.

"What's your problem, Cliff? I wanna talk, not fight." After I had my say, I stood back, waiting for him to get up. He didn't keep me waiting long.

It was an old-fashioned fight. No weapons, just fists. It was the way men used to fight before every punk decided he needed a gun or at least a knife. We smiled, more like smirked, at each other as we moved slowly. His bare feet scarred the sand while my tennis shoes made strange imprints that filled with water, and then went dry.

"Why don't you get lost, Kile?" He punctuated his question with a controlled left hook. I blocked it. Then he said, "Leave this family alone."

I let my hands sag to my sides, and then brought my right up into his stomach. My left followed. He took the two blows to his gut well. I could feel its hardness.

"You're all sweaty, Cliff. You been running on the beach?"

"Karen and me run a couple times a week." He then dropped to one knee and hit me on my inside thigh. I staggered but stayed upright. He knew how to hurt somebody, but he had chosen not to hit the inside of my knee. He let me have a moment. I wasn't sure whether he wanted to fight or talk. He kept doing both. "I want you to stay away from the Whittakers."

It's hard to say much when you're getting slugged so I kept it short. "That's the general's decision." I got up off my one knee and drove hard toward him. My head hit him flush and slid off the side of his chest. I wrapped my arms around his back and drove with my legs. We moved toward the surf and didn't stop until I could see the darker, wetter sand below our feet. "I've got … questions," I said, having to take a breath in the middle.

"Like what?" He grabbed me with his arms down under my chest, and groaned as he tried to lift and throw me off. He wasn't able to lift me off but he cancelled my ability to drive him farther. Then he leveraged me sideways. I gave up my hold on his midsection and we went back to circling, our feet tearing the harder sand.

He hit me on the side of the forehead with a left cross, then a right to the nose, and two quick blows to my belly. Whomp. Whomp. He was good. He knew how to hit and how to do it in combinations.

I stepped back. "You're a bit rusty? That combo should have put me down. Hey, let's sit and talk." He stood back, smiled and lowered his hands. When I relaxed, he lunged forward and hit me with the same combination leading first with the other hand.

I spat blood on the sand.

I left myself open a bit, inviting him to lead with his right. He did. I punched him in the armpit with my left, then brought that same fist up and around and hit him in the face. Then after faking a tired right cross, I used the flat edge of my open left hand to chop him hard in the throat. He was hurt. He was tough. He dropped to his knees. I dropped to mine and hit him two more times. Once with each fist, my left found his chin, my right caught him high on his opposite cheekbone. I figured he was about done in. I was wrong.

While we were still on our knees, he hit me in the stomach, again and then again. Then two times in the face.

I could no longer keep count. It was all I could do to return as good as I took. His blows that landed weren't hurting as much. I guessed mine had also turned feeble. We were both near the end of our endurance, no longer able to hold our hands up in any semblance of a defense. We were each taking blows and delivering them back, just two hard heads too ornery, too stupid, and too stubborn to do what we both longed to do—collapse onto the sand.

Then I heard voices. Cliff turned toward them. Over the crash of the surf, I couldn't understand the words, but I saw the people yelling: Karen and Charles were hollering at us to stop fighting, that much was clear. We ignored their words and watched Karen running toward us. The uneven sand made her body do things that made us forget our fight.

"A draw, Mr. Kile?" Cliff extended his hand. I took it, stood and pulled up, helping him stand. Did that make me the winner? I won't go there. We had fought to a draw. Cliff was a tough guy. It was a good old-fashioned fight, the kind that hurt like hell while feeling good on some level.

"Cliff," Charles said, "the general will hear about this. The last time he bailed you out, he said no more fighting or you're gone."

"Whoa, Charles," I said. "This wasn't Cliff's doing. We got talking about his time in the military, mine in the department. How we both missed getting in the ring with our buds. I asked him if we could go a couple rounds down here in the sand. He said he couldn't. He had promised the general. I told him the general said the staff was to fully cooperate with me. I talked him into it and told him I'd take responsibility."

Karen put her hand on my neck. The shoulder seam of my black polo shirt was torn. I looked at Cliff. It was obvious he didn't like her fawning over me, but he stayed quiet. I put my hand out. "Thanks, Cliff. I appreciate you helping me. I'll let the general know you were dead set against it."

"Thank you, Mr. Kile. To tell you the truth, it was fun. You said you had some questions you wanted to ask me. I can be free in about an hour. Can you stick around?"

"Take the time you need," Charles said, "whenever Mr. Kile wishes to talk with you."

"An hour's fine," I said, "I'll come out to the garage. Okay?" Cliff nodded and the four of us turned our backs to the surf. I've always hated elevators, they make me mushy inside, but as we approached the hundred and eleven stairs up to the Whittaker estate, for the first time ever I would have preferred an elevator.

Chapter 15

Back at the Whittaker house I ran my hands over my clothes and arms trying to knock off any remaining loose sand. Karen took me by the hand up the stairs into her room and then into her private bath where she handed me a towel and matching washcloth before stepping out and closing the door. I stripped down and took a shower, then got back into my sweaty clothes. I walked into her bedroom still running the towel over my head and finger combed my hair, still damp enough to take some form. Karen was lying across the bed sideways, facing me, wearing a white halter top that seemed even whiter against her tan.

"There's a little caveman in all of you men, isn't there? I mean you're all alike, just with different faces so us girls can tell you apart."

"At least Cliff was straightforward." I draped the towel back over my shoulder. "Why'd you put him up to it?"

“Me?” she said, propping herself up onto her elbows, her biceps running firmly along the sides of her breasts.

“Did you learn how to manipulate men from your mother?”

Karen swung her legs around, got up, and walked over to me. Her eyes big, white and wet, like jawbreakers after they’ve been sucked a while. “How dare you?” She slapped my face.

I figured the slap was for the remark linking her to her mother, not my thought that her eyes made me think of sucked jawbreakers. The slap stung, but she hadn’t put all she could into it.

“I’m investigating a murder. I dare anything. Your cleavage might turn Cliff to mush, but it has no effect on me.”

Karen disrobed to the waist. I immediately noticed her tan covered her completely from the waist up. I actually prefer the light and dark contrast from a woman having developed her tan wearing a bikini. You understand this comment could never graduate to a complaint.

Her disrobing had called my bluff and I’m sure my face showed she held the winning hand. “So,” she said, “what makes you think I had anything to do with you and Cliffy doing your Neanderthal dance?”

“If the general wanted me gone, he’d tell me or have Charles do it. I haven’t met Eddie yet, but my guess is he’d try to order me off the case. As for Cliff, I don’t think he gives a shit one way or the other. Why did you manipulate him into that fight down there?”

Karen put the fingernail of her middle finger in her mouth, between her teeth and bit down easily. She lowered her head, her eyes angling toward where my gaze roosted. Then her look moved up, slowly, with a grin, like the screen vamps in the 50s.

By the way, if you're thinking me rude for brazenly gazing at Karen's breasts instead of glancing, the rule changes when a woman purposely bares herself in front of a man. When a woman shows a small portion of her abundance a man should take a small look, a glance in that instance is a compliment while a gaze rude. However, when a woman intentionally bares herself in front of a man, a glance would be rude and a gaze a compliment. I know it's confusing. Things like this have slowed the evolution of the male species.

"I didn't mean for you two to fight. Cliff and I run on the beach. We see each other now and then. I mentioned to him that the general was less calm, and Eddie a basket case. I think I said something along the lines of wishing you had never gotten involved, that I'd prefer it if you just went away. Apparently, Cliff processed that all wrong. I never told him to run you off, and certainly not to hit you."

"You're good. You're very good. The way you turn all coquettish. Teasing and flaunting at the same time, a very sexy pose, a carefully worded suggestion. With a guy like Cliff you're not fighting fair."

"Oh, Matt, I don't want you to think badly of me. Sometimes I can be a little … men like me. You like me, don't you, Matt?"

"Yeah, I like you. But I don't know any better. I collect blondes and brunettes."

She stepped a bit closer, her breasts coming to a halt after the rest of her. "What else do you collect?"

"Bottles of Irish whiskey, full ones. I trade them in for empties. It's a hobby a man has to work at."

"Do you enjoy drinking that much?"

"It doesn't matter if I like it. It's a family tradition. An obligation passed down from my ancestors. Now why don't you stop picking on Cliff? Choose somebody who can fight back."

"Can you fight back, Matt?" She brought her black sweat shorts closer, her arms crossed below the feature of the day. Then she hugged me. Her hair tickled my face while her perfume played its way into my lungs.

"You just don't quit, do you? You just keep coming."

"I like to come, Matt." She put her open palm on my chest. "Don't you? But I know that already, don't I. I'm guessing you'd like to come with me again."

I backed away a few steps. "I'm supposed to go meet Cliff, remember?"

"I could come by your place later." I didn't respond. "Like the other night after we had dinner. This time I can bring the chocolate-dipped strawberries. I'll also bring the container in case you'd like to drizzle some on me." She took the bath towel from over my shoulder, walked into the bathroom and hung it on the rod. Then she walked back toward me, slowly, parts of her in constant motion, teasing me with each step.

"Ten o'clock," she said.

"Perfect."

I know. I sold out, but somehow I couldn't place what would come my way at ten tonight anywhere in the realm of punishment.

Chapter 16

I found Cliff in the garage. He had showered and changed clothes but likely had done so without the rain forest shower head, the plush bath towel, and the eye candy that had accompanied my clean up in Karen's boudoir. Life is good.

"You're a tough son of a bitch, Kile."

"Make it Matt. I'll be sore for a week." We shook hands. Yeah. This was like the old days when men could fight and find friendship, at least respect.

"So, you represent the general in this?" Cliff asked.

"I represent myself. It's a tough world out there. For now, working for the general is in my best interest." I had been cagey because I don't like suspects being too certain of my motives or ethics.

"I got a couple of beers in the fridge in the corner?" I nodded and he got them. We screwed off the caps and took a pull before I spoke.

"I mean no disrespect, but I know Karen manipulated you into what just went down. You must know she enjoys pushing your buttons."

He sat on a stool that faced a small workbench below a wall of tools, mostly for cars, not gardening. "Yeah. I gotta get over her, but it ain't easy. If fucking were an Olympic sport, Karen would bring home the gold."

I laughed. "She's jobbing ya. Getting you to do something I doubt is in your best interest."

He just lowered his head, shook it some and looked up with a smile. Then he nodded. "Beer okay?"

"Good and cold. Thanks. Look. You know why I'm poking around in the Whittaker family closet. I also figure you do a bit of watching and a lot of listening while you're driving them here and there. You introduced Eddie to Ileana, didn't you?"

"Yeah. Back then, Eddie and me rode our Harleys together. He'd never done that and needed an experienced rider along. For him it was a new toy. He sold it some years ago and I went back to just being the general's driver."

I went over and opened the passenger door of a black 1950 Mercury with wheel-cover skirts, it's lines as sleek as Karen's hips. I left the door open and sat with my feet on the sill, facing Cliff. "Tell me about Ileana."

"Hot chick. She loved it like Karen, only Illy didn't use her talents to tease. She dug Eddie, but I think she also saw him as a ticket to the good life."

"You ever hear her say that?"

Cliff came over and got in the driver's side. I swung my legs around and we became just two fellas talking in a car, a guy thing if ever there was one.

"Never heard any scuttlebutt, just my take on it. Illy was gorgeous. I went after her once. Did it right, flowers, met her folks, the whole deal. But I had nothing material to offer her. We became friends. That was it."

"Could that be why you think she saw Eddie as a meal ticket?"

He hunched up his nose like he'd detected a foul odor. "Could be, I s'pose. Who knows? But Illy was good. Nice, you know, funny. Didn't seem to take herself too seriously. But she wanted more than her folks had. Guys' eyes followed her. She always smiled at them. Not flirty. I think she liked being noticed. And I can tell you, the guys liked noticing her."

"Was Eddie a player or the kind who wanted to settle down?"

"He's always liked playing around, no doubt of that. But then why not, he was a young man and he had a generous allowance. He lived good, didn't need to marry for a second income to pay the bills. But the man was nuts about Illy. Her death broke 'im, man. He was down a long time. I used to drive him to therapy. In those days he didn't even care to drive his Mustang. On the way, he'd just sit quiet. Three times a week. Silent. Just sit there. Like a year, man. I was worried about the dude."

"But he came out of it?"

"Yeah. A year I guess. How long can a guy be in the dumps? Hormones keep getting produced. Tail talent keeps swishing by. Life goes on, you know. But for years, I could tell. There's a point out there where he and Illy used to sit and look at the ocean for hours. Just talk. Laugh. You know. He still goes out there some. Sits. I don't think he's full over her yet."

Cliff got out and brought back two more beers. When he got back in, I turned on the seat to face him. "Cliff, did Eddie kill her?"

His eyebrows went up, but his answer came fast. "No way. He loved her. Even if he didn't, Eddie doesn't have killer in him. Few guys do. Eddie spends most of his nights looking for a new place to hide his dick. No. Somebody tried to frame 'im. It couldn't just be a random killing. The papers said nothing was taken. She wasn't raped. And a random killer wouldn't have known about Eddie, or not enough to try and frame him. Somebody wanted Eddie to go down for it."

"Who?"

He just shrugged.

"I hear you taught Eddie how to shoot?"

"Not long after I started working here, Eddie would have me take him out and we'd practice. Every once in a while he'd get in a groove and shoot the shit out of the target, like a sniper, man. But then he'd go back to missing the barn, you know what I mean? He'd go extra alone and practice. Next time I went with him, he'd be about the same, no better. Eddie just couldn't consistently stop jerking when he pulled the trigger."

"Why'd he want to learn in the first place?"

“The general used to have family shoots, him and Eddie and Karen, usually me and sometimes Charles. The general wanted Eddie to get better. Now Karen, she was a different story. That gal could shoot the light off a candle, particularly with a handgun. She actually did that once while we were shooting, just the two of us.”

“But Eddie never got it going?”

“Not consistent like, no. Just them spurts when he couldn’t miss. After some months, he gave it up, dropped it flat and quit participating in the family shoots. That’s Eddie. When mastering something doesn’t come easy, he drops it.”

“Before you came to work for the general, didn’t Charles drive for him?”

“Sure. But in those years a lot of the time the general drove himself.”

“But since you were hired about twelve years ago, you always do the driving?”

“I’m the general’s driver. Sometimes Karen drives when she takes the general into town for lunch now and again. Charles drives when it’s my day off, but the general schedules his stuff for my days, you know, because Charles is pretty busy. Charles goes along when the general is seeing his attorney. Karen goes along when the general is going to his accountant or broker. But I do the driving; it’s my job. That’s about it, except for when I was driving Eddie to see his shrink, but that hasn’t been for some years now.”

“The general’s dying, we all know that. What’re your plans after that?”

"Eddie has told me he will keep me on. I hope he does. This is a good gig. Easy, you know."

Chapter 17

It was mid-afternoon and Charles confirmed that Eddie was still at home. The general was in bed upstairs. Charles told me to go into the study, and he'd bring Eddie to me.

From the doorway, Eddie Whittaker said, "Mr. Kile, how do you do. I've been looking forward to our meeting." He walked in as if his shorts were too tight. "So, you're a private eye as you fellows are called?"

"Yes."

"I didn't think they existed anymore, other than in seedy books and second-rate movies."

"No. We're for real. Correspondence school, you know. Study at home. All that."

He grinned, but not a friendly grin. His nose was a little wide, much like looking at a double barreled shotgun, but he was a handsome man. He had nice eyes and hair, and his wallet would be getting fatter soon.

"Then you know what you're doing, I take it."

"Oh, absolutely, I finished the course and passed the mail-in exam. Proud to say, top of my class, first out of all five of us. So, what can I do for you, Eddie?"

"You asked to see me, Matt. What is it I can do for you?"

"You said, 'I've been looking forward to our meeting.' Why is that?"

"Well, I've heard you have taken on the task of proving once and for all that I was in no way culpable in the death of my fiancée. For me, that is good news. I will help any way I can."

"That's good to hear, Eddie. May I call you Eddie?"

"Please, Matt, I agree first names are friendlier, more personal." He sat in the general's chair, at his desk as if it was Eddie's desk, or he anticipated it being his. He motioned me to take a seat. I sat in the same visitor chair I used during my meetings with the general.

"Tell me about what happened eleven years ago."

"We had a nice Christmas; the summer was hot that year."

"Let me warn you, Eddie, Chapter six of the Apex detective correspondence course taught how to strong arm recalcitrant witnesses."

"Oooh, recalcitrant, that correspondence school must have really been good."

"It was. Chapter seven taught how to deal with smartass punks and spoiled, pampered brats who don't deserve the treatment in Chapter six."

He squirmed a bit. What I said had stung.

"I thought you had some questions for me, Matt. Why don't you go ahead ask a few?"

"Sure. Let's get right to it. Did you kill Ileana?"

"You do get right to the point, don't you, Matt?"

"Yes. Did you?"

"No."

"You figure you deserve to sit in the general's chair? That you can fill it?"

He grinned, leaned back and intertwined his fingers with his elbows on the arms of the chair. "The general, my grandfather, was a great man. But I'm not exactly chopped liver."

"The general served his nation. Helped his friends. Raised his grandson. Gives to charity. Is concerned with justice for the family Corrigan. What do you figure elevates you above chopped liver, to use your phrase?"

"I have a bachelor's degree in psychology, I'm a member of Mensa, and I lost my father in defense of this country. You don't like me, do you Matt?"

"Alexander Dumas would have called you a fop. Baroness Orczy would have used the word popinjay. But me, I'd just say you're a waste. And, I'd also not say your grandfather *was* a great man, as you characterized him. I'd say the general *is* a great man. Sounds like you already are thinking of him as dead."

"He doesn't have long now."

"Before you get too eager, let me warn you. You might think you can fill his shoes, but you couldn't even wear his yesterday's socks."

Charles knocked softly and entered. "Would you like the usual, Mr. Kile?"

"No thank you, Charles, nothing for me." Eddie looked toward Charles and screwed up his face while shaking his head. Charles left.

"I love my grandfather," he said in a tone about a buck short of having real value. "He is more important to me than you could know. You believe me, don't you?"

"Oh, sure, I believe you. Millions wouldn't, but then I'm a sucker for sincerity, even when it isn't sincere."

"I don't like your manners, Mr. Kile."

"I don't like them either, Eddie. On lonely nights I worry about them. Not all that much. Not enough to work at changing them, but I do worry."

"You can't get in my head, Kile."

"I was in your head before you walked in this room."

"That's enough of your sarcasm, Kile. If this desk wasn't between us, I'd kick your ass."

I smiled. "Please feel free to follow me outside when I leave. Now tell me, I'm curious. You were engaged to marry Ileana, with the engagement coming after you learned she was pregnant. What if I said, she got pregnant to trap you. Saw you as her meal ticket out of the middle class. When you figured out she was doing the Madonna material girl bit, you killed her."

"You're full of shit. We were in love. Planned to marry and grow old together."

"In over eleven years you have found no other woman to replace her."

"That's correct. She was the one, my one. There can be no replacement. I am destined to live alone with her memory. As for your accusation, the court found me innocent."

"Not so. The court ruled the state had not made its case even sufficiently to have you arrested. The D.A. had no real choice but to drop the charges. Those charges can be reinstated. You were not tried and found not guilty. So don't rest all that easily."

"I am innocent, Matt." *So we were back to first names.* "I did not kill Ileana. I loved her. And I want you to find whoever did kill her. I'm sure the general has agreed to compensate you well for proving my innocence. I want you to earn that money. I hope you do."

There was nothing more to be gained by continuing. Eddie Whittaker likely had very little confrontation in his life. I had given him a heaping serving and he had handled it well. I had scrambled his composure, but he had recovered and held it together. The man was smart and cool under pressure, perhaps an inherited trait, perhaps just a cocksure confidence that he believed himself to be the smartest guy in any room.

I left. Eddie didn't follow me outside.

Chapter 18

On the way out, Charles stepped around the Christmas tree near where I had first seen Karen. "The general would like to see you, Mr. Kile." I felt confused. Charles noticed and cleared that up. "The general is feeling much better. He asks that you come to his small private study off his bedroom. He occupies the west wing at the top of the stairs; I'll take you up."

Karen's room had been to the east at the top of the stairs. There was also a door to the right, past her suite, which she had said was Eddie's room.

The general's small study was about twelve feet by fifteen, not all that small, with thick carpeting. Low music played in the background, music similar to what Mackie played in his bistro. The temperature was a bit warmer than downstairs and the general was in shirtsleeves, again khaki. He insisted on standing to greet me. We shook hands. His shake seemed weaker than it had been only a few days before. His eyes a bit more hooded.

"Popinjay?" He laughed, and then coughed. "Fop? That was a bit thick, don't you think? Even for a writer?"

I looked at him. He grinned. "Oh. I heard the whole thing. You didn't see him at all during the first several days of your investigation, left him to wonder, then a full frontal attack. Great strategy. May I ask if you learned anything from it?" When I continued to look at him, knowing he had somehow overheard, he explained. "This room is directly above the main study. I had it fixed so that I can listen or not to whatever is going on in there. I arranged for it while building the house. No one else is aware, so I ask you to keep it under wraps. Over time I have fashioned the study into the place where family members gather to talk seriously. However, there are other rooms that afford me this same … access, shall I say?"

"General, I certainly hope, when our country again finds itself engaged in combat that the defense department will invite you to participate."

The general laughed. "There are advantages to being an old man. Not many mind you, but a few. Young people, even those well into middle-age, have this notion that we curmudgeons have minds which deteriorate in direct proportion to the wasting of our bodies. Their self-indulgence on this point can easily be played against them."

"So, you simply come up to this room and it becomes spy central."

"It is helpful to know what people say when you are not about. How that confirms or contrasts with what they say when you are with them. Dozing in a chair after dinner or toward the end of a family meeting can briefly allow similar access. We old folks are assumed to be unreliable, even as to being awake. Ten minutes of strategic dozing is often more informative than hours spent as an active participant in conversation."

"Don't you feel a bit guilty using such tactics on your own family?"

With some effort, the general crossed his legs. "No more than they should feel using the tactics of waiting until they think I can't hear to say what they really think."

I reached out and touched his arm and smiled. "I see your point, General. You put this in place some years ago, then, while the house was still under construction?"

"Some plans are for near term use. Others have a longer horizon and are refined as time passes."

I looked toward a slight knock on the door. Then Charles came in carrying a tray with what I knew had to be some Irish on crushed ice. The general smiled. "Would you indulge me, Matt? Please enjoy that for the both of us." After I nodded, he said, "Now tell me, did your getting in my grandson's face tell you anything?"

"You heard it all, General. What do you think?"

"Yes, the question in answer to a question. However, I heard only Eddie's words. You saw his face, perhaps smelled his sweat. I could do neither."

"No, General. I don't think my bracing of your grandson told me any more than I knew before. Except for learning he is smart and handles pressure well. He may be made of sterner stuff than even he knows. Of course, that has nothing to do with whether or not he killed Ileana Corrigan."

"That was my read as well," the general said. "And thank you for sticking up for me. Eddie is smooth, but for reasons known only to Eddie, he remains confident he is superior to all others. Feeling so, showing respect is not easy for him. Nonetheless, he feigns it well in the company of outsiders. I know of no one who does not find him affable and courteous. Still, you got his goat a bit. I don't recall ever having heard him threaten to pummel another man."

"I did have him out of sorts for a moment. But he quickly recovered his composure. That's when I knew he would not open up. General, in light of it being eleven plus years since the death of Ileana Corrigan and in light of your clandestine method for overhearing, what have you learned? Did Eddie kill your unborn great grandson?"

"If I knew that answer, I would not have needed you. The investigation would have been over and we would have advanced to the penalty phase."

I asked the general if I could step out and use the men's room. He offered me the use of his which sat between his bedroom and the adjoining study we were in. I had hoped he would. After using it for the justifying reason, I took a few plastic storage baggies from my pocket and collected a significant wad of hair from his brush. I put two cotton swabs from his waste basket, each soiled with ear wax into a second bag. Several used facial tissues went in a third. After that I flushed, washed my hands, and went back to the study to rejoin the general.

"I understand your daughter spends more time with you than does your grandson. Is this true?"

"Karen is very attentive and strives to be a companion and a help. Eddie avoids everything beyond token appearances. And, may I add, Karen displays that same attitude and interest in this old war horse whether I am with her or as far as she knows, not around. I'm guessing you wonder why I'm leaving so much more to my grandson than to my daughter."

"That's none of my business, General."

"I appreciate that, Matt. Go on, now." He motioned with his fingers, raising them in an upward manner. "Enjoy your drink. Would you like another?"

"Would we, General?" After he nodded, he smiled and pressed a button on the desktop. Within less than a minute, Charles entered with the tray on his outstretched hand, the drink obviously made before the general summoned it. The general and Charles worked together like a priest and his acolyte.

"As I was saying, I appreciate that, Matt, but you know more about this family now than anyone outside it so I think an explanation is in order. I have thought about being more generous with Karen. I continue to think on it, but in the end I'm afraid I'm a hopeless chauvinist, unable to think of substantial wealth going to a woman. I do have a meeting with my attorney this afternoon. Reginald Franklin, you remember him. He came to your office to arrange your first visit."

I grinned, “Reginald Franklin, the third, as I recall.” I took a large portion of my fresh drink. The general stayed quiet while I did so.

“I know. I know,” the general said. “He’s a bit stuffy, pretentious, but he is an excellent attorney and a quite honorable man. After Charles, Reggie is my longest and most loyal ally. I think I am the only person alive who calls him Reggie. I think he likes it, but would never confess it. His wife calls him Reginald.”

“I’m glad you told me of your eavesdropping system, General.”

“As I told Charles, we shall trust your integrity, Matt. I wanted you to know in the event you wished to make use of it in some manner. My only concern is that you don’t alter what you say or how you say it in deference to my feelings. I want you to handle things without concern for my possibly hearing them. Agreed?”

“Agreed, General.” I finished my last drink.

The general licked his lips.

I walked out.

Chapter 19

I left the general's home without being certain if I was mixed up with a normal family or one that was completely dysfunctional. Part of that confusion is I'm not all that sure what constitutes a normal family. Are you? What I knew was I liked the general, lusted for his daughter, and neither liked nor respected his grandson. But that did not mean Eddie was guilty of anything more than being a popinjay. I also suspected I didn't have much time if I was going to find the answer for the general while he was still able to hear it.

I had alerted Charles that I would be sending someone by to look at the records on the five old soldiers whose care the general had paid for until they each passed away. I asked him to compile what he had, also to prepare a letter of introduction to the assisted living facility and nursing home where they had resided. The general had donated enough to the facility that concern for the access rules under HIPAA regulations were not mentioned; the patients were all deceased. My representative would be allowed to speak to the administrator and look over their records. I didn't yet know who I would send or the significance of doing this. This plan constituted little more than what the attorneys object to as a fishing trip into records looking for God knows what.

I had been on the case for only a few days and, as yet, had picked up no bones that had meat on them. Met some people and learned some secrets, but nothing that pointed me anywhere in particular. I needed to pick up the pace, multiply my efforts. Have more people sift through more haystacks in the hope that one of us might find the proverbial needle.

I got home late in the afternoon and immediately labeled and secured the three baggies I had filled in the general's bathroom together with some items, secretions, if you must know, that Karen had left at my place the night we had our sleepover. I also had a piece of gum she had chewed and a measure of my dental floss she had used in the morning.

I also assigned Axel to follow Eddie. I wanted the general's grandson shadowed twenty-four-seven with pictures taken of everyplace he went and everyone with whom he came in contact. Twenty minutes later he said it was all arranged. Buddha, his driver's ed teacher would handle the driving while Axel handled the picture taking. Using Buddha had a strange feel to it, but then a former wheelman for the mob should be able to keep up with a popinjay. So, I decided to feel guardedly optimistic. Axel had not yet identified who he would use for the graveyard shift, but he expected to have that arranged by the time it was needed.

"Can Buddha still handle the driving?"

"Boss, that's a silly question."

"Well, can he?"

"Can Kellogg's still make corn flakes?"

I repeated to myself about feeling guardedly optimistic.

"You'll have to pay these guys, boss. But don't worry, I'll set it up. They're good men. I won't be able to be here at all hours like I've been. Can you handle things at the house without me?"

Axel had already become the indispensable man, at least in his mind.

* * *

We met Axel's friend, Hildegard, in front of an apartment building several blocks from our condo on the opposite side of Mackie's. She was around five feet, a little taller perhaps, with a medium build and a smile that could melt butter or men's hearts. Her blond hair was bleached, the roots brown.

Hillie, as I was told she preferred over her full name, had turned eighteen since leaving home. I didn't ask what she was doing in Long Beach. I had an idea, given where Axel said he first met Hillie. If she chose to share that information I would know, officially. If not, it was no business of mine. Hillie appeared to trust Axel, yet she remained wary.

Over the next two hours, we ate and talked at Morton's Steakhouse in Anaheim, a short drive south from Long Beach. I mostly let Axel and Hillie talk; they were developing a great rapport. It always amazes me how much more one can learn by listening, rather than talking, beyond asking stimulating questions in a non-probing manner.

Hillie had grown up in Gridley, California, a small, mostly farming town north of Sacramento and south of the twin cities of Marysville-Yuba City. Her father was a certified public accountant and she spoke proudly of having worked for him all the way through high school. Her job had been to help him prepare financial statements and tax returns for his small business clients, which included several ranches and farms. Her goal had been to follow in her father's footsteps. She had planned to join her father's firm after going to college to major in accounting. Her mother was a different story. Of course, we were getting only the young lady's opinion of her mother. Hillie saw her mother as an intolerable shrew. When she could stand no more, she left home. Hillie and her father stay in touch with the understanding he not ask her where she is or when she will be coming home. They talk Mondays, late in the afternoon while he is still at his office. She said Monday afternoon was a slow time in the work she was doing here in Long Beach. She didn't put a label on her job. And like I said, I didn't ask.

Axel had already told her he had been in prison for a very long time, along with Mackie whom she had met. He had also disclosed the story of my having shot the thug on the steps outside the courthouse, and that we had spent four years together inside. That I had been pardoned and Axel paroled. She seemed unconcerned by any of that. I liked her. But then I expected I would. In prison, Axel always sized up the new cons and new bulls right off and he rarely pegged them wrong. He had made a good choice in befriending Hillie.

By the time dinner was finished I had employed Hillie to go to the Whittaker's and meet with Charles to go through the information on the old soldiers. I had a hard time explaining to her what I wanted her to look for. Without being sure it would prove true, I told her the old standby adage: you'll recognize it when you find it. When it came time for her to meet with the nursing home administrator, Axel would go along. I felt certain she could handle it if the people there gave her an even break. Given her youth, I couldn't be certain she'd be viewed as an adult, so Axel would ease that part of it. Axel also told me that for those few hours Buddha alone could handle keeping an eye on Eddie.

After we got home from dinner, I called Fidge to see if I could meet with him for coffee in the morning. We agreed on eight. I suggested a coffee shop not far from his house. Fidge suggested his kitchen table. By eight-fifteen his two teens would have left for school.

Chapter 20

The morning began at seven with my expanded plan in full blossom. Axel and Buddha were in position ready to tail Eddie Whittaker. I called Charles prepared to apologize for waking him, but it turned out the general had experienced a difficult night and they had both been awake since four. He said the doctor had just left and at the bottom of the stairs had shaken his head and said, "maybe a week, maybe."

I told Charles that Hillie would be there at ten. Then I called Hillie to get her on her way. She seemed excited for the opportunity to do something akin to what she used to do for her father. I would be meeting with Fidge in a little over an hour to fan the flames on another idea.

* * *

By eight-fifteen, Fidge's children were off to school and by eight-thirty I had shared pleasantries with his wife, Brenda. I love that woman. Not in the I-wish-she-were-my-wife kind of way, but in the, I'm-glad-she's-my-best-friend's-wife kind of way. She wasn't gorgeous, but she was sensuous and she loved that big galoot. Fidge had the largest feet of any man I'd ever known. He wore fifteen double EE shoes.

I've often told him that when he walks he should use those red flags that trucks hang when hauling long loads. His other distinguishing characteristic was a pencil-thin mustache, the kind worn by Boston Blackie, the fictional jewel thief and safecracker who became a private detective in books, movies and a television series. Blackie got a renewed dose of fame in a Jimmy Buffett song, "*Oh I Wish I Had a Pencil-thin Mustache, the Boston Blackie kind, then I could solve some mysteries too.*" I doubt it was because of his mustache, but Fidge had solved some mysteries too.

While Fidge and I slathered a couple of bagels that Brenda put on the table, he confirmed that Chris Timmons, known in police circles as Chunky, still ran the outside lab the department sometimes used for overflow DNA testing. I could have found that out without going to see Fidge, but I thought we should touch base on his investigation into the murder of Cory Jackson and mine into Ileana Corrigan, the law's hook into my Eddie Whittaker assignment.

"Yeah," Fidge said, "the department made the connection between the dead Cory Jackson and his past role in being the claimed eyewitness to the murder of Ileana Corrigan. We just don't see a link there. Jackson was discredited over ten years ago as a witness against Eddie Whittaker. If somebody out there had gotten pissed about that, they would have put Jackson down a long time ago. I mean, he's been right here in plain sight all these years."

He got up and kissed Brenda, then got the coffee pot and two cups from the cupboard and came back to the table, while asking, "You agree, don't you?"

"I guess. According to his half brother, Jackson does have some history with drugs."

"Also gambling, small change stuff, but we confirmed he owed the bookies some money. Nothing much, more likely kneecaps, not kill-ya money. Still, you can never be certain about that stuff. The bookie could have rubbed him out to make the point to a bigger better with a bigger past due balance. The Jackson homicide is going through the motions, but we've found nothing and even the effort's fading."

"Shouldn't be that way," I said, "but with the case load you guys carry it happens."

I went on to tell Fidge about the two million dollar shakedown of General Whittaker to buy Eddie's original alibi. Fidge hadn't known it, but he had always wondered about the synchronized timing of the witnesses against Eddie. His arrest, quickly followed by three witnesses who stepped up a few days later to put Eddie in that restaurant, out of the range of the murder, all followed neatly by his subsequent release.

Fidge stroked his chin like he always had while sifting information. I had forgotten about him doing that, but surviving over time is what makes something a habit. "Could Jackson and Tommie Montoya have cooked this up on their own to shake down the general? If so, Montoya might have dropped Jackson to get the entire take for himself, and to eliminate the only person who could rat him out?"

"On paper that could work, but no, I've spent time with Montoya, he's definitely not bright enough to develop the shakedown, likely Cory Jackson isn't either. If these two guys had raked in two million in cash, there's no way they could have sat on it and stayed in their dead-end lives for the past eleven years."

Fidge nodded. "I remember Cory Jackson from back when he claimed he saw Eddie kill the Corrigan woman. That dunce was incapable of brainstorming a fast food dinner, let along that kinda shakedown. He had a taste for drugs then and owed the bookies now. He couldn't sit on that size bundle for eleven days let alone years."

"I still feel like someone's missing from the game, but I can't put anyone in the empty chair."

"You still picturing mystical poker games with empty chairs?"

"It's a way of saying there may be a player we haven't identified."

"So, whatdaya got for Chunky?" Fidge asked, while Brenda put her hand on his shoulder to lean in and refill our cups. Talking cases in front of Brenda was nothing new, as a homicide cop's wife she knew to keep quiet about what she heard.

"You got me to thinking when you said the department ran a paternity test to be sure Eddie was the father of Ileana Corrigan's unborn son. It got me wondering if the general is his daughter's poppa."

"Really? You got anything saying he isn't?"

"Nope. Just trying to match up my thises and thats. You know the dance. To be the poppa, the general would have procreated late in life—"

Brenda interrupted to ask how old the general would have been.

"Mid fifties," I answered.

"No problem," Brenda said, again proving that when it comes to anything related to giving birth, women know more than us guys. At least they think so. And they're likely right.

"Still," I said, "I want to nail it. In those years, the general's ex-wife had a rep for being a frisky woman, by the general's own description. I think he'd know. Trying to sneak anything past that old soldier is like trying to sneak a fresh chicken egg past a possum."

"You got what you need for the tests?"

"I think so. When I researched modern DNA testing for a novel last year, I read that they can do them within a day now. True?"

"Yeah. Chunky charges extra for quick results. If he gets it before noon, next day end of business is about as fast as it can be done."

* * *

After stopping to see Chunky, which first required we share a cup of coffee and some reminiscing, he committed to having the DNA done by the time he closed tomorrow. I told him I'd be back then at five.

From the car, I called Axel. He and Hillie were at the Sea Breeze Manor assisted living facility. The place also had a convalescing wing which had been built while the five old soldiers had still been living in the assisted living section. The general had contributed enough that the wing was named The Whittaker Building.

Axel had checked out the Sea Breeze and the place had a top reputation. All their rooms were rented and they had a waiting list. It was an independent operation run by the owner. I'm guessing the families of the residents liked being able to go directly to the owner. Axel put Hillie on the phone when I asked how it was going.

"Hi, Mr. Kile."

"How's it coming, Hillie? Are you able to work with their records okay?"

"Oh, sure. My dad had so many different small business clients that I think I'm familiar with about all the popular accounting software programs. This one's a snap. Mr. Morrissey, the owner, had his bookkeeper up and quit on him last Friday. It's actually easier not having someone looking over my shoulder explaining things I don't need explained."

"Is it all … checking out?"

"Yeah. I spent a couple hours looking at the records Charles put together at the Whittaker house. Man, that's some house, Mr. Kile."

"You were saying, Hillie?"

"It's all like what you expected, Mr. Kile. The general paid everything. No one else paid anything."

"What about visitors for those men, any records identifying them?"

"I don't know. I'm just into the financial records. But I know Axel's been chatting it up in the restaurant with the staff and other residents. The owner here thinks the world of the general so after Charles called him, Mr. Morrissey is letting us see whatever we want. The restaurant's in the assisted living wing. It's the biggest part of the place. Axel walked over here to tell me you were on his phone. Maybe he knows something. I'm about done. I'm taking notes. Two of the five died about six years ago. One died three years ago, then another about two years back. After that, Mr. William Branch, the last of the five died about a year ago. I hope you're not expecting me to bring you anything of importance cause I'm not finding any of that. You wanna talk with Axel? He's still here."

Hillie must've handed him the phone. "Hey, boss."

"You finding out anything?"

"Two of the five old soldiers never had visitors. The other three did. Two of those three had only infrequent visitors from out of town. There were two regular visitors, the general and his chauffeur, a man named Clifford Branch, the son of the last man to die. The general used to come every other week to have lunch with his men, as Mr. Morrissey said the general called them. They have a private dining room here and Mr. Morrissey always set that up for them to use. When he came, Clifford Branch came with him. Drove him here I'd guess and joined them for lunch. Clifford Branch also came the in-between weeks to have lunch with the group in the main dining room. Is General Whittaker as good a man as everybody says he is?"

"Yes. He's a pip, as my grandmother would say. I'll bet he was a hell of a field commander. But, back to business, are you finding anything we can use? Any friction among the five men or animosity toward the general?"

"Gosh, no. From what the staff remembers, the few I've talked to who were here back then, the old soldiers all swore by the general. Of course, if someone's paying all your bills, you tend to think that person's pretty swell. You know?"

"Sure. By the way, how did you get out there? Buddha drive you?"

"Buddha's on the job. We took a cab."

* * *

At home, with Axel still with Hillie, I picked up the mail and right away tore open an envelope from the Law Office of Reginald Franklin III. Inside was a copy of the general's will with a hand written note from the attorney, dated two days ago.

"The general instructed me to provide you a copy of his last will and testament. If there are any questions I shall be available."

I sat down and read it finding nothing I didn't already know. He would leave a half million to Clifford Branch, the chauffeur, two million to Charles and two and a half to Karen. Another million was designated for Ileana Corrigan's parents. Stocks and bonds were to be sold as chosen by his personal representative in sufficient value to increase cash funds to cover those bequests. All remaining assets, real and personal, tangible and intangible, net of any remaining liabilities inured to the benefit of Edward Whittaker, the general's grandson.

There was one other clause addressing the disposition of the general's assets in the event of any of the legatees dying before the general. If Charles or Cliff or either one or both Mr. and Mrs. Corrigan died before the general, their shares would be divided equally between Eddie and Karen. In the event that either Karen or Eddie predeceased the general, the bequest for that heir would go to the other. In the event both Eddie and Karen predeceased the general, their inheritances would be combined and a foundation created, administered by Charles Bickers, to provide scholarships to the children of soldiers killed during their term of duty.

I had already known about all of it except for providing for Mr. and Mrs. Corrigan. The only other new piece of information, the personal representative was Reginald Franklin and in the event he couldn't serve, his daughter Karen would serve in that capacity. There was the usual language that the personal representative would serve without bond and, in the absence of gross negligence, without liability for acts performed in good faith as personal representative. And, further, that no conflict shall be claimed by others should Karen serve, given that she would be a legatee in addition to her official role. And a proviso that should anyone named in the will challenge its content or division of assets, that person would be removed and his/her portion divided equally between Edward and Karen Whittaker.

Chapter 21

I had taken last night off to have dinner with my ex-wife and our two daughters. That event had been scheduled before I took the assignment for General Whittaker. Back when we set it up, last night had been the only night both our daughters would be home from college and had nothing else they had to do. Rose and Amy, were adults, but of the ages when parents were scheduled in amongst gal pals and love interests.

The evening with them had been pleasant, but not altogether a good night. Don't misunderstand, seeing my daughters had been an absolute joy. Still, when we are all together things seem, I don't know, off center, somehow. It had been that way since the divorce and my getting out of prison. Not the easy way it had always been when we lived together as a real family. We all knew those days were behind us. Our daughters wanted Helen and me to be together again. At least that was my read of their feelings on the matter. Yet my ex just couldn't get over the hump. What I did, shooting the guy, going to prison for it, well, she feels I deserted her, abandoned our family. My pardon meant the state had forgiven me. Helen had not. I understood, sort of.

I'm not sorry I shot the scum. I wish my doing it could be explained with John Wayne's line: a man's gotta do what a man's gotta do. But I doubted Helen would take advice from The Duke. The thug had killed children and their mother, after raping her, and walked out of court free on a technicality. I'm sorry for the impact my flushing that waste had on my family. He deserved to die. About that I'm not sorry. Life is complicated.

After getting home, I sat out on the patio and had an Irish, several actually, but then I stopped. Drinking doesn't drown your problems, it teaches them to swim.

* * *

I awoke at seven to find Axel had already left to meet up with Buddha and get on the trail of Eddie Whittaker. They had to relieve the graveyard man at eight. When Axel had asked if I could get along without him around in the mornings, I had looked at him like, "are you kidding me?" He had only been with me a short while, but here I am missing his having made coffee. Don't tell him that. It's amazing how quickly we become spoiled. I thought about going to see Clarice at the end of the hall. She would have coffee on, but that woman is a major distraction. I would have stuck around for more than coffee and I needed to get back on the job.

My first stop was a convenience market a few blocks from our condo building. I got a big cup of black coffee and before I got back on the road I had taken my first sip. It hurt, too hot. My mouth protested against it not being Axel's coffee. A block and two sips later, my stomach voted with my mouth. While stopped at the next intersection, I opened my door and poured it on the pavement. The empty cup went into the dashboard holder until I could find a place for its permanent interment.

Some days you're the pigeon, some days you're the statue. So far, today I was a statue. Chunky wouldn't have the DNA results until the end of the day. I saw the DNA bit as an effort designed to support my claim that I had followed up on even the remote.

I jumped on the interstate and headed toward Buellton to find Michael Flaherty, the retired middle-school principal who had testified seeing Eddie Whittaker in the Pea Soup restaurant in Buellton. He and the Yarbroughs, but the Yarbroughs had rescinded their testimony. I needed to know if this would be true as well for Principal Flaherty.

Through online snooping, Axel had found very little on Michael Flaherty. The man was divorced and lived alone in a tract home with a backyard swimming pool. He was sixty-four, having taken retirement two years earlier with a twenty-year school system pension and reduced Social Security benefits. He had paid enough into Social Security during the years before being employed by the school.

I found Flaherty's address without difficulty, and guessed the man drove the blue Ford Taurus which sat partway back in the driveway next to a side door, the kind which, on this vintage house usually accessed the kitchen. His car, I figured, because visitors usually parked on the street, as I did, or in the driveway nearer the front of the house. The driveway went all the way back to a detached garage. As I got closer I saw a St. Louis Rams decal in the rear window of his car. The Rams had left Los Angeles many years ago and moved to St. Louis. Flaherty appeared to be a man with a sense of loyalty. I knocked on the front door.

"Can I help you?"

"You Michael Flaherty?"

"That's me. What do ya need?"

Flaherty would be my countryman, speaking ancestrally, but like me he had no accent. Two Irishmen unknowingly brought to America through the emigration of prior generations. I wondered if he had remained loyal to his homeland in some manner, perhaps, like myself, by favoring Irish whiskey. He could not drink scotch, not while claiming to be a respectable Irishman.

"My name is Matt Kile. I'm a PI, ah, private investigator. I'm working an eleven-year old murder, Ileana Corrigan. Do you recall that killing?"

"Please come in." He held the screen open. "I've never met a private detective before. How do I figure in this?"

I studied his face, his eyes, and then said, "Eddie Whittaker." He remembered that name. "You testified seeing him in a restaurant here in town."

"Yeah, in Pea Soup Anderson's, late dinnertime. I don't recall much more than that. It's been a good while, ya know." He motioned toward the couch and sat in an upright recliner across from me.

"How can you be sure, now? After eleven years, I wouldn't remember having seen some stranger. Heck, I might not remember after eleven minutes."

"I saw his picture in the paper a couple days after the murder. He had been arrested. As for remembering, it's not every day a guy gets involved in a murder investigation, ya know?" I nodded. "I had to speak up. As it turned out, Whittaker did me a good turn."

"A good turn?"

"That whole thing led to my divorce the following year. This last ten years have been the happiest of my life, well, the happiest since before the old lady and I got hitched."

"I don't see the connection," I said while looking up at a bar type mirror on the side wall that featured the logo for Jameson's Irish.

"My old lady said, 'Don't get involved.' I told her she wasn't, I was. I'm the only one who saw Whittaker. But she liked controlling everything and she said, 'stay out of it, Michael.' She always called me Michael when she was ticked about anything. Bitch."

Flaherty and I were both Irish, both drank our nation's whiskey, and both divorced. Apparently, we felt differently about our ex-wives. These kinds of similarities can only carry so far.

"So, you ignored Mrs. Flaherty and came forward?"

"Had to. You know someone is innocent of a crime you can't just sit back and let them go to prison for it. No, sir, I had no choice. That's how I saw it." I nodded.

"Mr. Kile, I had just finished making a sandwich when you rang the doorbell. Can I make you one?" I politely said no. "Well, come along while I get mine. We can sit out back by the pool. Can I interest you in a beer?" I politely said yes. We walked through the kitchen and out back to a table and four chairs under a shading umbrella near the deep end of the pool.

"A few days ago, in the paper, I saw a small story about a guy found shot dead on the beach by the name of Cory Jackson. As I recall, he was somehow involved in that Whittaker matter. You stopping to see me got anything to do with this Jackson guy getting put down?"

"Cory Jackson was the fellow who claimed he saw Eddie Whittaker kill Ileana Corrigan. Then another guy, who worked at a gas station a few miles away from the murder scene, said he sold Eddie gas. It was your testimony and that of Mr. and Mrs. Yarbrough which resulted in Eddie being released from the charge of murder."

"I remember now," Flaherty said. "Was this Jackson killed because of having testified? Am I in any jeopardy as well?"

"The police don't draw a connection behind Jackson's death the other night and his testimony eleven years ago. His testimony against Eddie was muted so I don't rightly see how someone could be angry enough about that to wait eleven years and then kill him. If he, and you for that matter, were in any danger because of that, it would have come calling much sooner. People who are intense enough to kill rarely wait eleven years to act on their anger. An exception might be if that someone was in prison for those years, but no one went to prison. The death of Ileana Corrigan remains unsolved."

Over his sandwich and our beers we talked about the case for another hour. He didn't remember the name Tommie Montoya, and did not recall ever having heard about Cliff the chauffeur. He did remember Fidge, describing him as a very large man, not overly fat, just big, with a tiny mustache. Of course he knew of the general, but then so did most of America's citizens who weren't brain dead.

I kept leaving the case and talking about whatever, he also had two daughters and no son, and then abruptly returning to the case. I asked him various questions separated by other discussion to see if his answers matched up. They did and Flaherty remained at ease through the whole thing. A CIA counterterrorist expert in deep cover might have pulled off such an act, but not a retired middle school principal. It was my judgment that Michael Flaherty had either seen Eddie Whittaker or truly believed he had.

Driving out of Buellton, I admitted that if Flaherty had really seen Eddie Whittaker as he believed, then Eddie had to be innocent of the murder of Ileana Corrigan. So, the unanswerable question of the day became, did Michael Flaherty really see Eddie Whittaker in the Buellton restaurant, or did he simply mistake him for someone else he did see?

* * *

It was five of five when I pulled into the lot in front of the building where Chunky had his testing lab. A lady working in the lab said Chunky had left to deliver something, but that there was an envelope for me in case I came in before he got back. Back in my car I pulled it open to find several pages paper clipped behind a hand written note from Chunky, both were attached to one of my books. "It was good to see you again, Matt. Don't be a stranger." Then a P.S. "Forgot to tell you, my wife loves your novels. When I told her you were coming by, she insisted I bring this one down and ask you to autograph it."

Right then, I heard a knock on the rear fender of my car. It was Chunky. He had just pulled in after making his delivery. I motioned him around to the passenger door. He got in.

"I see you got the book. I'll get no sweet time for a month if you don't sign that thing."

"Well," I smiled and nodded, "we can't be letting that happen can we?" I got her name and wrote an inscription to her, signed it, and gave it to Chunky.

"I owe you, Matthew."

"What's this Matthew stuff? You been talking to Fidge?" He laughed. "Seriously, it's my pleasure. I appreciate your wife reading my books. It is I who owe her."

* * *

Two hours later, back at home, I went out to sit on the patio with some Irish and Chunky's report on the DNA samples I had obtained from Karen Whittaker's sleepover, and from General Whittaker's bathroom.

Chapter 22

Fidge called to say the department had officially drawn the conclusion that the murder of Cory Jackson was not connected to the Ileana Corrigan case eleven years before. As soon as I hung up, my oldest daughter, Rose, called to say her mother had cried after I left following dinner at their home.

I wanted to call Helen, tell her I hoped she had not cried because of me. I didn't want to be the reason for her being sad, but I guess I was. When in hell will that woman forgive me? After pouring a cup of coffee, I dumped it in the sink, turned off the pot, tossed Chunky's still unread report on the counter and went out. I was hungry and didn't feel like preparing anything at home, there wasn't much to prepare even if I did. The truth was my daughter's call had rattled my cage and I couldn't sit still.

It would have been a good morning to have Axel around. Many nights he had indulged me in our cell while I talked about Helen. Why she had never come to see me, whether some day she might. It would appear the governor's pardon had no impact on the sentence she had given me. She would keep me emotionally incarcerated as long as she felt it appropriate. I doubted she knew any more than I how long that might be.

In the lobby I ran into Clara Birnbaum, an old maid retired elementary schoolteacher with dried crust on her personality. She lived three doors down from Axel's small condo on the floor below mine. We were both there to pick up our mail. Axel had been doing some grocery shopping for her. When he picked up our mail, he got hers as well and dropped it off at her condo. This morning he left before the mail carrier arrived so Clara and I both made our own mail runs. Maybe Axel was becoming indispensable, certainly Clara would say so. In return, Clara had promised Axel she would bake us a pie every other week, whatever kind we wanted on condition Axel bought the fixings.

I explained why Axel didn't get her mail. Clara replied, "Then why didn't you pick it up for me, Mr. Matthew Kile?"

"Well, I don't know, Clara. I just didn't think about it I guess, Axel not being here and all. Besides, Axel offered to get the mail for you, I didn't."

"In return I baked an apple pie and promised to bake a pie every other week, apple, cherry or cream. Did you eat part of the apple pie and do you plan on eating some of the future pies, Matthew?"

"Well, yes, ma'am, I do."

"Then if you're sharing in the spoils, you need to do your part. From now on, you pick up my mail when you've sent Axel away so he can't. Do we understand each other, Matthew?"

I felt like one of her students claiming my dog had eaten my homework. "Yes, ma'am, I guess I do. Your pies are very good. So, yes, we understand each other. How about banana cream this week?"

"Your choice, Matthew. I'll have it ready the day after I get the fixings. When will Axel be going to the store for me, or will you be going this time?"

"Let me get with Axel and he'll let you know. Would you like me to escort you back to your unit, Clara?"

"I'm not feeble, Matthew. I can get my own self upstairs and inside. Besides, then you'd want to come in and it's time for my stories."

"Of course, Clara, I meant no disrespect. Goodbye."

* * *

"Buddha," Axel said, "it looks like this Eddie Whittaker is doing a Bill Murray Groundhog Day. His routine's the same as yesterday: breakfast out, go by his stockbrokers, and after lunch the handball club, yesterday the golf course. That's no real difference. Then he puts on glad rags and has dinner with some fox. Last night a blonde, tonight a blackhead; I don't like that word, it makes her sound like something you'd squeeze."

"I'd like to squeeze her," Buddha said.

Axel frowned while shifting his eyes toward his big driving teacher.

"Both nights when he takes them home he goes in for an hour or so," Buddha said. "This prick knows how to live. Sure different than before we did our time, when we was younger."

"He turned south toward the docks."

"What the fuck's this about?" Buddha asked.

"That's what we're here to find out. Stay with him."

"No sweat." Buddha kept his distance as he eased into the same turn. "He'll lose his wallet before he loses me."

After a while, Buddha turned into a chainlink fenced yard in front of one of the industrial buildings, swung around and came out through a different gate. The traffic was light enough that he could still see Eddie Whittaker's Lexus about a quarter mile ahead. "I did that to give him a change in the pattern of headlights behind him."

Five minutes later, Buddha pulled to the curb. "He's going into the lot for that biker bar. What's an uptown swell like him doing going in that kinda joint?"

"The boss says Eddie used to have a Harley and ride with the general's chauffeur who has one. That they used to hang sometimes with the rough bike crowd. That's how he met his fiancée, this Ileana Corrigan woman who got murdered over ten years ago. Eddie got arrested for it, then released a few days later."

"How'd that happen?" Buddha asked. "The cops don't go around arresting people for murder until they're pretty sure they got 'em by the short hairs."

"They thought they had him cold. Then some citizens came out of the woodwork. Solid folks whose testimony trumped the couple of witnesses they had who claimed having seen Eddie murder his woman. Well, one claimed he saw the murder. The other placed him nearby." Axel shrugged. "So, Eddie walked."

"And the case now?"

"An unsolved cold case."

"So, is Mr. Kile trying to nail him for it again?"

"Not particularly. The boss wants to find who did the broad in. Doesn't care whether it's Eddie or someone else." Buddha opened his driver's door. "Where do you think you're going?" Axel asked.

"Check the place out. Make sure Eddie Whittaker didn't go out the back door. Maybe get me a beer."

"No drinking and driving. You stay put. You're not exactly someone who looks like a lot of other folks. If Whittaker sees you, he'll remember. That'll put the kibosh on our following him on foot should the need arise."

* * *

I was turning onto the ramp for the underground parking below my condo building when my cell rang. I pulled to a stop before entering and backed out to the street to be sure I held the signal.

"Mr. Kile, the general wishes to see you. Now. Tonight."

"Charles, it's nearly ten-thirty. I mean, I don't mind, but is he in shape to do this?"

I knew what Charles would say. Whether he was in shape for it or not, that decision had been made before Charles dialed my number. I left for the general's home and arrived a few minutes before eleven.

"Charles, are you sure this is a good idea? It's almost eleven."

"I know, Mr. Kile, but the general is the general. When it's time to do something, he wants to get it done. He's waiting in his private study. You know the way. Go ahead up. He's already ordered your Irish. I'll bring it in right off."

I patted Charles on the shoulder. "You're a good man."

"The general's standing order whenever you are here, only this time he ordered two." I looked at Charles. The question on my mind must have been on my face. Charles shrugged.

I took the stairs two at a time and walked into the private study. "Hello, General. You wanted to see me? If you prefer, I can come back in the morning."

"Sit down, Matt. We're wasting time. Let's talk."

A small brass lamp with a black shade sat lit on the side table, the only light in the room. I took a seat and gave him some body language for you called the meeting. You start.

"What about this murder of Cory Jackson? It must tie in somehow."

"Seems like it should, doesn't it? Do you have any thoughts on it, General?"

"I'm afraid it points at Eddie. That he killed Ileana. Had I just stayed out of it in the beginning justice would have likely been done and this Jackson fellow would still be alive."

"Now hold on, General. You might be rushing out ahead of your troops."

Right then the expected two light knocks on the door followed by Charles entering. As usual he carried the pewter tray, but this time it held two short frosted glasses. I took one. Charles stood straight and looked at the general who motioned him impatiently. Charles went to the general who took the other glass. Charles glanced toward me, and then left the room.

"General, why?"

"For the past year I've been watching you and a few others drink, enjoying it vicariously. I'm sure Charles told you that the doctor estimates I've got maybe a week, give or take. So what the hell is drinking this going to do? Drink up, Matt. Let's have one together."

The general leaned forward, his glass in hand. I got up and leaned across his desk to clink our glasses together. Man's ritual, born in ancient times and shared since without change other than an evolution from ceramic or pewter mugs to modern glass. I sat back down and watched him take in a modest sip. You could see it ease down his withered throat. His eyes closed. Then he smiled and uttered a slight, "ah," the two expressions so close I couldn't tell which preceded the other. Both expressed joy. A moment later, he opened his eyes and took a second sip, this time without the ritual.

"Now, as I was saying. The death of Cory Jackson argues that Eddie killed Ileana. He had to. My grandson knew I hired you to begin mucking about. You met with him. He saw in you a capable man who would be relentless. His killing Jackson eliminated the only person who saw him kill Ileana. There was no other evidence or witnesses who could connect him."

"Yes, General, I've toyed with that thought myself. Still, there are a couple things arguing against it."

"Such as?"

"Cory Jackson had already sworn to seeing Eddie. When the D.A. dismissed Jackson's claim, in reliance on the testimony of Mr. and Mrs. Yarbrough and the retired school principal, Jackson's eyewitness account was nullified. Jackson was no longer a significant threat."

"What about those three witnesses? Have you talked with them? Confronted them?"

"Yes. The Yarbroughs admitted lying. They were coerced with threats of violence against other members of their family."

"What? By whom?"

"They don't know."

"What about Flaherty?" the general asked while excitedly ringing his bell.

"Flaherty is solid. He is certain he saw Eddie in Buellton that night, just as he told Sergeant Fidgery eleven years ago. With Flaherty in his corner, Eddie should never again find the cops on his porch."

"What's your read on this Flaherty?"

"He was straight with me. He saw Eddie or believes he did. And if nothing has shaken that belief in eleven years, I don't see him ever changing his mind."

Two more light knocks preceded Charles entering with two more glasses. I took mine. Charles paused without stepping toward the general. “Damn, it, Charles, bring me my drink.”

Charles stepped toward him and leaned in, the tray just above the desktop. The general took the glass, licking some of the frost from the outside before taking a sip. His eyes were closed in pleasure as Charles latched the door shut. I waited until the general finished savoring the swallow, then he spoke.

“When the Yarbroughs recanted, it became Flaherty against Jackson and this Montoya fellow who claims he sold my grandson gas right after Ileana’s murder. No. It figures now that Eddie removed the only direct danger, the eyewitness.”

“General, you’re pulling a milk wagon with a race horse. Slow it down. The police see no connection between the murder of Ileana Corrigan and the killing of Cory Jackson. Jackson has a history of drug arrests, including one for selling. It appears he had cleaned up his addiction to drugs, but not to gambling. When he was killed he owed some bookies. Conjecture says it’s more likely those activities caused his death, totally unrelated to the murder of Ileana.”

“Are you telling me you think my grandson is innocent?”

“I’m not saying that either, General. Eddie could well be guilty. Eddie could well be innocent. I don’t know yet. Give it more time. Okay, General?”

After that I gave him more details about how the witnesses had been bribed to get Eddie arrested, and how the Yarbrough were set up to alibi Eddie, after the general paid the two million for the alibi.

The general didn't speak, but he nodded, a new dose of hope showing in his eyes.

I got up to leave. With my hand on the doorknob, I turned back. "General, I'd like you to be around at the finish line. If you'd like to be, knock off the drinking."

Chapter 23

Reginald Franklin the third had an office in one of those high rise buildings all dressed up in glass and concrete. The kind that said step lightly, be respectful, I'll be here long after the world has consumed your bones.

I leaned into the shiny, L-shaped chrome handle pushing open the glass door and entered the two-story lobby. From there I walked on a tan terrazzo floor to the bank of four elevators across from the gift shop. The directory on the wall before the elevators showed Franklin's office to be on the seventh floor. Elevators spooked me, but I was running late so I decided to face my fear. I pressed the button for seven, then for four after being asked to do so by a young lady wearing a black and white polka dot dress with red heels and purse. Her hair looked like she had come to the building directly from her hairdresser. Her lipstick matched her purse and heels. She could have been a secretary, a wife, a professional in her own right, or a high-end hooker making an office call. I couldn't tell. She looked over and casually wet her lips. Her tongue, several shades lighter than her lipstick, appeared bumpy along the side I could see. She wore no wedding ring. I couldn't tell her age closer than early thirties maybe. The modern woman could be asked if she was wearing a bra, but it remained tacky to ask her age, so my guess would have to do. I considered telling her I was a writer, not telling her I had been in prison, and asking for a lunch date. At the fourth floor, she got out before glancing back. I fumbled in my pocket, and then extended my hand holding one of my business cards. My arm aborted the door's effort to close our relationship before it opened. She took the card, looked at it, then at me, then again at the card, then the elevator door closed on her smile. I had no idea how to reach her. It would be up to her whether this had been one of life's vignettes or the start of something big.

I like women who make the first move, although this strategy, if it can be called a strategy, can result in long periods of celibacy.

Franklin's office was no less grand than the building lobby except it lacked the two-story ceiling. The built-in front counter and desk combination was backed up by a lady with her hair stacked on top of her head and held there by a couple of those things that look like chopsticks. She was no less pretty than the lady in the elevator. Her outfit held no polka dots, but she did have cleavage. You know me well enough by now to realize that I would trade polka dots for cleavage any day. What man wouldn't? I mean, I like Polka dots, but it's no contest. After four years in a prison of men, I no longer took my appreciation for the female form for granted, honoring it at every sighting. I gave her my name and took a seat in the lobby hoping that Franklin and I would become great friends so I would have a reason to frequently visit this building. There are so many lovely ladies assaulting your senses at every turn. It's like wanting an apple and waking in an orchard.

After a few minutes, Franklin came out to get me. I recognized him. He recognized me, although Charles had made that easier by calling ahead to remind the attorney that the general wanted everyone to fully cooperate with me. Keep no secrets from good old Uncle Matthew, especially anything you know that might shed light on who murdered Ileana Corrigan.

After chatting back and forth about everything and nothing, we took coffee in china cups brought in by the cleavage from the front counter. Styrofoam in this office would be a crime punishable by banishment from the ranks of the employed.

"Mr. Franklin, other than the general's will, what legal matters do you handle for him?"

"I do the legal end of all his business dealings. Look over limited partnership agreements he might be considering investing in. The leases he uses for a small apartment building he owns near the Long Beach traffic circle. He sometimes buys or sells real estate and a few times he has invested in a couple of small businesses. The last six months or so, he's divested himself of many of those holdings."

"Getting his estate in order?"

"Something like that, yes." After a pause he added, "The general's instructions were that I was to give you a copy of his latest will. It has been mailed to you."

I nodded while mouthing the words, "I got it."

"The general asked that I cooperate with you. What is it you'd like to know?"

"Has he recently changed his will?"

"No. We prepared the current will about five years ago, perhaps a little farther back than that."

"I'd like a copy of the former will, the one he changed from, also the one in effect at the time of the murder of Ileana Corrigan."

"I don't know, Mr. Kile. The general said to give you a copy of his will. Then again, the general said to cooperate fully with whatever you wanted to know. All right, his former will dates back fifteen years so that would have been before the Corrigan woman's death. Do you want anything farther back than that? I think we had one, but it involved Benjamin, his son, before his death."

"Skip that one. The one I have and the former one executed fifteen years ago will be fine."

Franklin buzzed his receptionist, told her what he wanted and we chatted about the L.A. Lakers until she brought it in. I left a few minutes later, resisting a desire to approach Franklin's receptionist. At this point it seemed a little too strong a mix of business and pleasure. The polka dot dress in the elevator was still in play, although what might come from that would be up to her.

Chapter 24

Whomp. Whomp. Whomp. I opened my eyes to see a guy in a ski mask slamming his fist into my navel; it didn't fit. The blows had somehow brought me around. I hadn't felt anything before that, but the way his chest was heaving he had been working hard on me long enough for sweat moons to have formed under his arms. I knew I had taken more than three blows. My feet were off the ground, my hands tied above my head. That allowed me to swing back and forth a bit with each blow. He timed his punches so I would swing forward to meet each of them.

The last thing I remembered, I walked out of Russell's restaurant on Atlantic Avenue just north of Carson Street. I had parked in the back lot along the alley. Then I remembered my head being hit, after that I remember only now, now with nothing in between.

I was trussed up like a carcass from a hunt, and that's likely how my friend in the ski mask saw me. My hands were tied, but they didn't feel super tight. I fought against the binds without progress. A blow struck the left of my jaw. Thump. Then just below my right ear. Schwap. The meaty part of my face came into play for a while. After that, he zoned in just below the eye where body design forgot to leave any padding. Crunk. Crunk. The internal sounds of blows to the face varied according to bone density and tissue thickness. He was an equal opportunity thug as he worked one side of my head and then the other. The man was nasty and clearly enjoyed his work. I did not.

I thought about how I would enjoy returning his kindness, should events give me that opportunity. I looked around the room and saw no vise. I had always wondered how well a man would hold up with his testicles in a vise, his in particular.

Then he left the room. I was alone. I tried to take inventory. It appeared I was in an industrial building. One light was on, a lamp sitting on a metal bookcase against the wall near the single door through which my keeper had exited. There was also a big door, a loading type that had a chain pulley next to it for raising and lowering. The ceiling was dotted with hooks, big hooks. Meat hooks, or ones that looked like meat hooks, spaced evenly along a chain belt likely controlled by a switch somewhere that moved the entire row around the room. The whole set up looked like the thing on which your local dry cleaner hangs clothes. Only, if this had been a conveyor belt for a dry cleaner, it took some serious steroids. More like hooks which might move hanging car fenders through a paint booth, and I was suspended on one of them. The walls appeared to be metal, the floor concrete. I swung my legs up enough to see there was duct tape around my ankles, likely from the same roll used to tape my mouth. I wrenched my head back and saw that my hands were bound at the wrist with a white cord that had been looped above the hook.

Screeeeech, the metal door dragged on the cement floor. My keeper had come back. The only good thing, he still wore the ski mask. It was warm. He would be uncomfortable. If he planned to use me as a punching bag until I no longer offered entertainment, and then kill me, he would have left the mask off and gone for comfort. I imagined him ugly, as in if I had a dog that ugly I would shave his butt and teach him to walk backwards.

Thump. Thump. This visit he came to work on my stomach, chest, and kidneys. At least that's where he started. Thump. Thwack. That last one landed on my chest, those sound different. More hollow. At least they do on the inside. Thump, the stomach. Thump again, then twice more. Thwack. Thwack. These two absorbed by the other side of my chest. Whatever he was being paid, he was earning it. Normally I respect a man who takes pride in his work, but not so much when I'm the work. The number of blows disappeared within the pain which had quit ebbing and flowing between blows and became a constant with periodic highlights. The repetition would have been monotonous, if not for the hurt. Instead, I focused on keeping count of the seconds my host spent with me. The last time we had been together a little over 800 seconds.

Thwack. I felt it immediately. That thwack. I knew that feeling. I had felt that feeling before. A broken rib, cracked at the very least. It had to happen. With my feet off the floor I was stretched out. My body's ability to absorb the blows diminished. Damn.

My personal skier was panting. He was tired. If he had the tape off my mouth I could have suggested we change places for a while so he could rest. Then he switched to my face. He had fast hands. He threw good combinations.

Seven hundred and fifty seconds and counting.

The inside of my mouth was getting mushy from repeatedly being slammed against my teeth, particularly after I became too tired to hold my lower jaw up against my upper teeth. My right eye was cut. I felt the blood worm trailing down the side of my face, tasted it in my mouth.

My head dropped down, my chin held there by my chest. Blood flavored saliva trailed out the corner of my mouth.

After standing back for a moment, admiring his work, he quit. His chest heaved as he turned to close the door.

Eight hundred forty seven seconds.

Both visits had lasted about fourteen minutes. I had also counted the seconds between his visits with me. They ran closer to nine hundred. I had roughly fifteen minutes to try and reset the table or our next meeting would go much like the last two.

Chapter 25

It would only get worse after he came back to deliver another pummeling. I took the first minute to hang free, my weight fully on my wrists, willing the rest of my body to relax. The hook I hung on had to look like the others. The hook itself was the curved bottom end of a rod that extended up until it became part of the conveyor system that ran across the ceiling.

I swung back and forth a bit, and with the momentum I tucked and lifted much like a gymnast pulling up chest high on an overhead bar. Of course, the gymnasts didn't do it with a broken rib. Then again, the gymnasts weren't motivated to prevent another beating.

On the third swing I was able to lurch my hands upward to grasp the upper part of the rod rather than simply having the cord that tied my wrists suspend me from the hook. With that hold I swung higher, tucking my knees on the forward swings, and my hips when swinging backward.

The tape on my mouth suppressed my groans from the pulsing rib pain. After a half dozen swings I got the necessary height and tried to loop one heel through the slope of the hook in front of me. Missed. The hook swung away and I went back to regaining the momentum I needed for a second try. Missed. A third. Missed. On the fourth, my right heel seated into the hook and I twisted my foot to put my toes behind the rod above that hook.

The heel of my left foot had been gouged as it cut across the hook which had seeded between my feet. I resembled a fighter plane with one wing sheared off. Still, much of my weight was off my hands. That had been the idea. The next move was critical. I needed to leverage enough of my weight onto my stirruped foot to allow me to pull my hands away fast enough that the cord tying my hands would not slide down to again snag onto the hook. If I succeeded I would fall to the floor. I hoped to land on my feet, but I had no idea how I would accomplish it. That would require a flip I was wholly incapable of doing, first starting toward the floor with my head and then flipping to my feet. Yeah. Right. Still, I had very few, make that no, options at this point. I pushed down with my right heel while releasing my hands from the rod. Almost simultaneously, I violently yanked my hands back and away from hook. The floor was about seven feet from where my nearly horizontal body began the fall.

I hit the concrete. The impact absorbed by the side of my buttocks and my upper arm. The pain from my rib was piercing. The tape across my mouth was all that kept me from crying out. I lay there stunned, knowing I had to get moving or the fall to the floor would have been endured for nothing. I was free from the hook. That alone meant only that my personal skier would need to rehang me should he come in before I was ready to receive him.

Before my bad gymnastics bit, while I was just hanging around, I had put together a plan for overpowering my jailer, a plan which might kill him. Ask me if I cared about that. Fortunately, he had tied my hands in front before lifting me high enough to impale me on hook number eight. Yes, they all had numbers. My foot had been suspended on hook seven.

I needed more time. I needed more luck. I needed my plan to work.

After rolling over a few times I got to the sidewall. There, I leveraged myself into a standing position by inching my body up the wall. The first thing I did was to pull the tape from my mouth. Next, I picked up a spare hook from the floor and wriggled my way over to a metal chair. There, sitting, I held the loose hook in my hands and poked and tore at the cord around my wrist until the hook had weakened it sufficiently for me to pull my hands free.

I hadn't been able to keep count of the seconds due to the effort and concentration of getting off the hook and onto the floor. If my jailer stayed on his prior schedule, I might be ready. I had to be ready. I didn't want to again play punching bag to his Joe Palooka. I needed a couple more minutes to get things set up the way I wanted. In case he returned before I was ready, my hands were free and I still held the spare hook. But I wanted it to go the way I had it planned.

My feet were still bound so I stayed in the chair and worked the tape until I got them free. I could move faster now. I took down the lamp and unplugged it. Next I yanked the cord out of the lamp. That got me a bare wire, two wires actually, holding each I pulled them away from one another stripping the wires from the insulation that had been around them.

The lamp cord was about eight feet long and I had stripped back about six of those feet, using my teeth to bite and pull off the wrapping so I had exposed wire. I wrapped one of the two wires around the metal handle of the all metal door and the other end around the pin that protruded about a half an inch above the lower hinge. Then I put the chair near the wall socket, held the plug in one hand and the loose hook as a weapon in the other, and waited.

* * *

Axel and Buddha had only been watching Eddie's car for about three minutes when he came out of the biker bar, got into his car and drove away. Forty minutes later, Eddie pulled into the general's driveway. He parked in garage four of the Whittaker's five-car garage, giving the impression he had roosted for the night.

* * *

After what seemed five minutes, the metal knob on the steel door into the room where I waited turned and the door dragged along the concrete as it swung in. When I saw clearly that it was my jailer with his hand still on the metal knob, I slid the plug into the wall socket. While I did this he noticed I was no longer impaled on the hook. But his realization lagged behind my plug in. The lamp stayed dark, but the jailer, his body now part of the circuit, went onto his toes and seemed to shimmy there. I was enjoying watching his wattage dance, but after a minute or so I pulled the plug back out.

He dropped to the cement floor. Not moving. I pulled out the plug, then removed a gun from his waistband and went out to look into the outer room. There was no one else. I went back inside.

For good measure or perhaps just for sheer joy, I folded the metal chair closed and slammed it into his head, then I did it two more times. I had seen this done on televised wrestling matches and it always looked to be such fun.

He wasn't dead, but I doubted he would give me much in the way of trouble. I put the spare hook I had used to tear my hands free into his hand and wrapped some fresh tape from the roll he had left on top the file cabinet, around both his hands. Next, I pulled the metal door over near his body and spun him around so I could raise his hands far enough to suspend the metal hook over the metal doorknob. This kept him part of my makeshift circuit, allowing me to plug him back in should he give me reason to do so. I admit to hoping he would. It wouldn't take much.

I went through his pockets and found a wallet and a few hundred dollars. I took the cash to tip waitresses or whatever. Hey, I took a beating from this guy. I earned it and still felt underpaid. I reopened the chair. It was bent, but it worked well enough.

I pulled off his ski mask. He had the face of a bully, nasty, the grown up face of a lunch money thief from the seventh grade.

I sat down to go through his wallet. The end of the cord over my leg in case he needed to be plugged back in or in case I just felt like plugging him back in. His driver's license showed his name to be Ernest Podkin. He looked like a Podkin. I say this having no idea what a Podkin should look like. For me, from this day forward, a Podkin would look like Ernie who lay on the ground before me, the front of his Levis wet from his waist to his knees.

Podkin was about my size, an inch shorter and a couple pounds heavier. He had huge hands with big knuckles, but his palms looked soft except for the calluses on his fingers where he would grip the handlebars on a motorcycle. Like his jacket suggested, he was a biker, maybe a friend of Cliff's.

After finding a box of old invoices on the floor from the company who had apparently occupied the building before vacating it, I stepped outside to find the address on the building. It matched the invoice. I called Fidge at his home, gave him the address, and asked him if he could please get down here as fast as possible. He said it would take him about thirty minutes. Podkin wasn't going anywhere. We'd wait.

Podkin eventually came around and opened his eyes, maybe ten minutes later. "Don't move, I said. I have you wired to be plugged back in." He cranked his head around and saw how I had him *connected.* He nodded. He understood.

"I've got some questions. If you answer them to my satisfaction, I'll let you get up and leave. If you lie or take too long I'll put this plug in." I held it up for him to see. "Then wait until you come around again, if that next time doesn't kill you, then I'll repeat my questions. We'll continue like that until I get my answers or you drop out of the game, permanent like. Understand?"

He nodded. His eyes followed the hook he held up to the metal doorknob and the wire from the wall to the hinge bolt.

"Who paid you to work me over and what were your orders?"

"I was to work you over hard. Keep you here two or three days. Then let you go. Hurt enough that you'd be down the rest of the week."

"Who?"

"I have no idea."

I motioned toward the wall with the plug. "No!" he screamed. "No. I don't know. I swear I don't know. I never saw the dude."

"Tell me all about it."

"He came up on me while I slept in my bed at home. I live alone. He kept a fucking flashlight in my face and showed me your picture. Said you'd be at that office building downtown today in the afternoon. I was to follow you and take you somewheres else. He wanted you out of commission for a week, but not killed. I don't do murder."

The general and his family knew I was going to the attorney Franklin's office so it could have been any of them.

"Sure. You're the sensitive type. Go on. I want it all."

"He dropped a wad of hundreds on my chest and said, 'If you don't take him out of commission today, I'll return and kill you in your sleep.' He warned he knew me and my hangouts and he knew where I lived. He promised me eight thousand more if you were out of it for at least a week. Then he walked out of my room with the flashlight still on my kisser. After he left, I flipped on the light and counted the money. There were ten hundreds, with a promise of eight more big to come. Nine thousand for a beating, that's good money, man. Hey, it's not like I know you. You know?"

"I just went through your wallet, Ernest. You had four hundred, where's the other six?"

"I had some bills man. Stuff I had to pay, you know."

Ernest was telling the truth. He had been hired by the same guy who eleven years ago had paid Cory Jackson and Tommie Montoya, using the same method. The difference being that with the economy in a tough stretch right now, Ernest would have ended up with only nine thousand when Jackson and Montoya each got ten thousand. I felt like the blue light special at K-Mart.

I put the plug back in just long enough to make Ernest spasm. I wanted to leave it in and walk away, but Fidge would be here soon and I didn't want him looking at me for some grade of murder. He might agree it was justifiable homicide, but I didn't want to put him on the spot because it wouldn't be. My killing him would not be to save myself or anyone else so the *justifiable* part would be too much of a stretch.

Five minutes later Fidge came through the outer door. I went out and told him what happened, speaking low so we wouldn't be overheard. Then I took him back to meet Ernest Podkin who had kicked free the end of the wire wrapped around the hinge pin, disconnecting the circuit. His hands remained taped.

"Ernest, may I introduce Sergeant Terrence Fidgery." Fidge showed him his badge. "The sergeant has confirmed I can file a complaint for kidnapping, and assault and battery. Are you interested in avoiding the arrest?" Podkin nodded his head. "Okay, here's how we'll do it. If you don't go along I'll go down and see the sergeant and file the complaint."

Fidge said, "After speaking with Mr. Kile by phone, I pulled your sheet. I'd recommend you avoid this if at all possible."

Podkin looked at me. "What do you want from me?"

"I keep your jacket and your hat, and you leave town. Right now, from here without speaking to anyone, even by phone. Don't return until next month."

"What about my other eight thousand?"

"Ernest. Ernest. You told me he promised you the rest if you kept me out of commission for a week. You didn't do that. You also said he promised you a bullet if you didn't get it done. Seems to me you've earned the bullet. I'd recommend you leave town rather than wait around for a bullet from a stranger. You wouldn't see it coming. Only feel it. Briefly"

"This guy's bought other beatings this same way, on the cheap." Fidge lied. "He's never paid any of the others. He wouldn't pay you, even if you had earned it."

"Podkin," I said, "these are your choices. Take this deal, or the sergeant here hauls your ass downtown."

"With an added charge of attempted murder," Fidge threw in for good measure.

"Why do you want my jacket?"

"Podkin, we've talked all we're going to. Do you take what's behind door number one or behind door number two?"

Podkin stared at me; his face blank.

I simplified it. "Jail or leave town. What'll it be?"

"I'll split man. Lemme go."

I cut the tape from around his wrists. He took off his jacket, put it over the seat of the bent chair, dropped his hat on top, and walked out. We followed him to the door and watched him drive away in the van he must have used to bring me here from behind Russell's restaurant.

Chapter 26

Fidge drove me back to the lot behind Russell's on Atlantic. The slight movements associated with leaning as he turned corners leveraged my rib cage, delivering the trauma of each bump home to the damaged area. It hurt like hell is what I'm trying to say. On the way I explained to Fidge a little more of my plan and how it might, just might, help close his unsolved Ileana Corrigan murder case.

In my own car, I hung over my steering wheel for a few minutes trying to find a way to breathe that didn't make me want to stop breathing. Driving my car felt better. The holding of the steering wheel while turning made it easier. I drove slowly. I wouldn't say life was good, but it had gotten better.

Axel had gone back to his place, or he could've been at Mackie's, or with Hillie, or a movie maybe. He had become a big fan of movies during his years in stir. In any event, he wasn't home. I wanted to go to bed and sleep until the twelfth of never, but first I needed to try to figure who had employed Ernest to work me over. The one thing I knew, whoever it had been would fail at keeping me off the job. I'd be after his ass in the morning.

With some Irish straight in a short glass I went out on the patio. Yeooow. Irish may be good for cleansing a wound, but in a half raw mouth it stung like riding through hell on a splintered board. I swished it around before swallowing. After a few drinks it calmed. As I saw it, or chose to see it, that addressed my need for immediate medical care. In the morning, I'd go see Doc Medford, one of my loyal readers, to learn if my rib was broken or whatever. I was hoping for the whatever.

The person who had hired Podkin knew the doctor had given the general about a week to live, that's why he or she wanted me off my feet for that long. The quest for who killed Ileana Corrigan was the general's private passion. Once he died, the personal representative for the estate could be expected to leave the cold case of the murder of Ileana Corrigan in police archives. Eddie Whittaker would take over leadership of the general's assets and he considers having been released by the court to be enough. I would be taken off the case. To solve the woman's murder and earn my fee, I had the same amount of time left the general had.

I was now convinced that the killer of Ileana Corrigan and the general's unborn great grandson lived in the general's house, an enemy within.

* * *

By two the next afternoon I had left Doc Medford and his dowdy nurse. Podkin had cracked a rib, a lower one on my left side. The doc also found a lot of bruising around my rib cage. He presented the crack as good news, saying it would hurt worse if it were broken. I doubted that, but in the end it was what it was. He wrapped it tight enough to make breathing harder. The upside being that I looked more svelte in my slacks than any time since I first got out of prison. Prison had kept me fit. I looked forward to exercise to work off the high carb foods the prison purchasing agents seemed to favor.

"Where you been boss?" Axel asked right off when I reached him on his cell phone. He and Buddha were back tailing Eddie Whittaker.

I told him about being abducted and worked over, that I had gotten away with a cracked rib and mushy face. He asked if I wanted him to come back and help. "No. I can manage. You two stay with Eddie." Then I asked if Eddie had done anything suspicious since they put the tail on him.

"No. Not really, boss. He goes to the gym, his broker's office, has lunch, and then plays golf or whatever. Like that. Usually eats supper with some doll. All in all, he's living the good life. Just a minute, boss … Buddha just reminded me to tell you about Eddie going by a biker bar down in Pedro, near the docks. He went in and came out in under ten minutes. Like he'd gone in looking for someone and that person hadn't been there."

Eddie could have been looking for Podkin.

"Let me know if he goes back. Where are you right now?"

"It's around four so Eddie's at play. He's over at the Skylinks course hitting golf balls on the driving range. You know, I gotta take up that game. You play, don't you boss?" I grunted. "Like I said, this guy lives a very casual lifestyle."

"Stay with him. If anything happens that looks suspicious, I wanna know about it. I'll keep my phone near me."

I checked in with Fidge by phone to let him know I was back at home.

"Brenda offered to fix you some of her homemade soup. You can rest up over here. She'll have you back in the game in a day or two."

I told him I didn't have a day or two and that I appreciated the offer—and I did. I promised we'd all get together when I had this wrapped up. The best guess said the general only had a few days left, and I had the same. That without the general I would not be on the case and, damn it, I wouldn't walk away with this half unraveled.

I felt like shit. Axel would be out until late. I expected he'd check in with me then. I went to bed, got up sometime after hard dark and made a soft-boiled egg, drank some cranberry juice, and then went back to sleep.

* * *

Before six, the sun started sliding into the room, doing its thing, the way cream softens black coffee. I'd had enough sleep, and wasting time wouldn't make it hurt less.

Axel winced when he saw me, which didn't make me feel any better. I understood because I had seen myself in the mirror. My face looked like uncooked beef Wellington with the puff pastry raw, and my eyeballs like one of those roadmaps printed off the Internet. The tissue around my left eye was purple and puffy, nearly shut. Axel had already made coffee and squeezed some fresh tomatoes in a juicer he had bought a few days ago. He sprinkled in some salt and ground pepper.

"I left out the dash of Tabasco," he said, "figuring you didn't want that in your mouth right now." The coffee was too hot. I drank the juice while I gave him more details on my time with Podkin and how I had escaped. He said nothing other than, "You shoulda burned his ass the way Clara crisps bacon." When I asked about Eddie, he said the general's grandson did nothing suspicious yesterday or last night. And, no, he had not returned to the biker bar. Then Axel left to do some shopping for us and for Clara so she'd make us another pie.

Ten minutes later, the front bell rang. Having no reason not to open the door, I did, and found my ex-wife standing in the doorway. She had never been to my condo and, if you had asked before I opened the door, she would have been the last person on the planet I'd expect to be standing on the other side.

"Matt, what happened?" She walked in without my saying come in, but I was about to say it. I spent some time filling her in. Then I showed her around. She loved the view from the terrace. She put a hand on my face, gently on my cheek and then the back of my neck. The look on her face told me she didn't like what she saw. But it was concern, not one of those hey, you're double-ugly looks. She said a few of my facial cuts and abrasions had not been cleaned properly. She took my hand. The next thing I knew I was sitting on the toilet with her using cotton balls and witch hazel and, I don't know what, to bathe some of my wounds. She had brought the stuff she was using with her. It figured that Fidge's wife had called her. She rubbed some ointment on several places, put a bandage on one, and said, "The others we'll leave open to the air."

Helen left after inviting me to her house on Sunday for breakfast. I didn't promise, but I told her I wanted to come. Today was Wednesday and I needed to cut some corners to bring this across the finish line while the general was still in the race. I needed to see him and give him a hang in there, I'm getting close talk. Even though I wasn't all that sure it was true. He wanted the answer that would come at the end of my investigation. I was counting on the general soldiering through till then.

About noon I heated up some of that chicken soup that comes ready to eat in the can. All you need do is warm it. I did. It tasted good, but I was longing for something to chew. I'm a meat and potatoes guy. I wanted to chomp on something, but my chomper wasn't ready. While I ate the soup, more like drank the soup, I opened the DNA report I had picked up at Chunky's the afternoon Podkin had diverted my attention. I had expected the report to be a routine thing. Investigators are always running checks or tests of some kind to confirm what they already knew. But Chunky's report didn't confirm anything I already knew. It didn't even fall within the shadow of anything I already knew.

Chapter 27

Slow traffic got me to the general's house later than I had hoped. I spent the first ten minutes calming Charles after he saw the condition of my kisser. I described it as one of those beefs private investigators sometimes get in and don't come out of as well as Sam Spade always did. Mostly, I watched his face. He had not seemed surprised to see me which he would have had he hired Podkin to keep me under wraps. Then he said, "I saw you through the window. You're not moving all that well." No verbal response was needed. I simply blew out some air and raised my eyebrows.

"The general is asleep," Charles said. "I'll be waking him in about an hour, when the cook has prepared his dinner. He's taking his meals alone now in his room. This morning, the doctor indicated he should use a wheelchair as much as possible. Fortunately, we've always had an elevator for workers to get back and forth to the upstairs. It's just outside his room."

"That's fine, Charles. I came to see you. Can we go someplace private?"

"We can use the study sir. The general doesn't go there anymore."

"No. Somewhere else, private."

"You certainly have my curiosity aroused, Mr. Kile. It's a bit irregular, but we can use my upstairs quarters at the end of the hall past Karen's suite."

When we got there he offered coffee or a soda. I accepted water, no ice; he had a glass with ice. We sat at his kitchen table that looked out toward the ocean. You couldn't see the beach. The view showed calm water far out to the horizon.

"Well, sir. Please take my curiosity down a notch or two. What is this about?"

"I'd like you to indulge me by finishing a brief sentence: Karen's father is?"

"What is this about?"

"Indulge me, Charles. Who is Karen's father?"

"Why, the general, Mr. Kile, everyone knows that."

"Her birth father, Charles. Who is Karen's birth father?"

"The general."

"No. General Whittaker did not sire Karen Whittaker, therefore her last name is not even Whittaker. I figure that only two people, not counting Karen's mother, know the answer, you and the general. Do I need to ask General Whittaker?"

"No, sir. You do not. I am Karen's father. The general's wife, Mary, and I … well, you know. She was a frisky woman. The general was in his fifties, I in my thirties. Her needs exceeded his. Due to my living here then as I do now, my sex drive could best be described as involuntary hibernation. It just happened that once. No. That's not true. It happened several times over a month or so. Then I put a stop to it. It was wrong. Mary always insisted the general was Karen's father, but I doubted it, sir. When DNA tests became available, I had them run. She is my daughter. How did you learn this, Mr. Kile?"

Charles had spent a good part of his life serving his daughter as if she were the mistress of the house.

"Charles, do you sometimes use the general's bathroom, the one between his bedroom and his private study?"

"Yes. Often when I am in the general's wing, it is closer and the general finds my doing so acceptable. Not regularly, but several times a week I would imagine. I asked how you learned the general was not—"

"The same as you. The general's DNA didn't match. Someone else's did. I figured you. Does Karen know?"

"No sir. I will tell her someday."

"After the general dies?"

"Yes, Mr. Kile, after the general dies. That is something I cannot imagine. I mean I am here. I talk to the doctors. I know. But the general always seemed indestructible, a man who would always be here. Always be in charge. Yet the reality is now undeniable. The general's deterioration is accelerating at a rapid pace."

"Would you have stayed with the general had Karen not been your daughter?"

Charles got up and walked to the window and looked out toward the ocean. "I don't know," he said with his back to me. Then he returned to sit with me again at the table. "I have wondered. It has been a distinct honor to be his friend and companion all these years. After my tryst with Mary, I felt so dishonest to be here. But with time that eased and finally passed."

"You said Karen doesn't know?"

He shook his head. "No sir. I saw no reason."

"Then there's the inheritance. Yours and your daughter's. If the general knew, he would likely remove you both from his will."

"I would expect so, sir. Karen has been loving and loyal to the general, as I have been. She is entitled, I believe. Don't you agree, Mr. Kile?"

"It is not my place to judge that. I leave that to you. My job is simply to determine who killed Ileana Corrigan. I don't have much time left, so what else can you tell me about that?"

"Nothing. I have been fully candid with you on that entire matter. I know nothing further."

"Have you ever heard the name, Ernest Podkin?"

"No, I have not. Who is he?"

"A biker. That's all I know. And I'd appreciate you not repeating that name to anyone."

"As you wish. You might ask Cliff, he rides a Harley and hangs out with those guys. Used to a lot. Less now, but he still does."

"I'll do that. Thanks for talking with me. I appreciate your honesty."

"Where do we go from here, sir? Will you need to tell the general? I realize I have a selfish interest on this, but the general would not take the news well. He is weak now. I see no reason to … change his memories at this point, sir."

"I think I agree. Then, I do work for the man which obligates me to tell him what I learn."

"What you learn about who killed his great grandson. You were hired to learn that, not who fathered his daughter."

"That's a point. I just don't know yet. If I decide I need to, I'll let you know first."

"Is there anything else, Mr. Kile?"

"One more thing. Did you kill the Corrigan woman?"

"Sir? Why would you think that? What reason could I have?"

"There was an attempt to frame Eddie. Had that held, he would have gone to prison. It is more than likely the general would have left his entire estate to your daughter, thinking she was his."

"I understand you must consider every angle, your job and the nature of being a detective, but I don't believe you think I did. Besides, while I could have arranged to frame Eddie in the manner it was done, why would I bribe Mr. and Mrs. Yarbrough to provide a defense to get Eddie released?"

"Yes. There is that, Charles. However, given your devotion to the general, it is possible you could not bring yourself to be the cause of him watching his grandson being convicted of murder. You could have used the Yarbroughs so you could shake down the general for the two million by selling him the alibi. That amount along with what the general is leaving you and Karen would set you both up without destroying the relationship between Eddie and the general."

"Being a detective can be a disgusting business, can't it, Mr. Kile?"

"Yes, Charles. At times like this, it can."

* * *

Cliff was in the garage changing spark plugs on the general's MG Roadster. It didn't get driven much anymore. Karen took it out once in a while, but the general loved the car.

"I can't imagine anyone getting their fists on you that much, Matt."

"You could if you knew my arms were tied, as well as my feet."

Cliff and I went over to the workbench and occupied two of the stools. "You okay for a beer?" he asked. I nodded, not knowing how it would go, but eager to find out. He brought them over, twisting the cap off mine before handing it to me.

"Ernest Podkin."

"How do you know Poddy?"

"Poddy?"

"Yeah. We used to call him that because he had bad breath. Poddy mouth. You know. Potty mouth. It stuck. Where do you know him from?"

I circled the air with my index finger pointing at my face.

"Poddy did that? I mean, he's tough but …" He left the rest unsaid.

"Are you two tight?"

"We know each other. He rides with the gang I once did. We always got along, but never close. It was a big gang. I can't imagine him doing that to you."

"Like I said, my arms were tied. So tell me about Mr. Podkin."

"Lifetime biker. Petty criminal. Hauls drugs up and down the coast. Strong arm work. Not a killer. Least not as I know. If he did this, he was hired by someone who wanted you worked over."

"That's right. Podkin told me so before I left him on a concrete floor down by the docks. He said he didn't know who. I believed him. The way he was set up to do it, well, it was the same way as some others."

"You say you left him on the floor in a place down in Pedro?" I nodded. "Tell me about the place. Describe it." I did, including the conveying belt of hooks running along the ceiling. "I know the place," Cliff said. "I don't know what those hooks were ever used for. The general had me drive him there after he bought it. He had me go in with him. I asked him what he was going to do with it. He said it was an investment. He liked the location and that eventually somebody would need the space and he'd turn a profit."

"How long ago was that?"

"More than a year, less than two." Then Cliff offered to help me find Podkin.

"Nothing would be gained. Podkin doesn't know anything further and I've evened the score for what he did. If I'm going to wrap this up for the general, I need to avoid being sidetracked by things that won't move the first down marker."

Cliff nodded. He understood. Everyone there did. The general was the only one who longed for this case to be solved. After eleven plus years the rest of them were willing to let it go. That would be particularly true for the one who killed Ileana Corrigan. That person had tried to slow me down until the general died, figuring I would then be paid something for my troubles and dismissed. What they didn't know is even if the general died, I wouldn't stop. I had the bit in my teeth and, since spending time with Podkin, I had skin in the game.

"What do you think of the general? Give it to me straight, Cliff. No party line."

"He's aces. I like the old dude. Apparently he was some top kick in the army. But I never knew him that way. My pa did and he swore by him. As for me, the general's my employer. That's it. But I like him. He's honest with you. He don't pull his punches when he's got something to say. Treats you like you're as good as him, which damn few of us are. Yeah. I'd cover his back."

"What's your read on Charles?"

"He's a bit harder to peg. I mean he's square. Honest. Hard working. Really cares about the general and his daughter. I'm not so sure he gives a hoot about Eddie."

"Have you heard that you're in the general's will?"

"I've heard."

"Where from?"

"I'd rather not say, Matt."

"Karen?"

Cliff looked at me for a minute with no expression. Then he nodded.

"One more thing, Cliff, what do you know about the bribing of Cory Jackson who was found dead in the surf a few nights ago?"

Cliff went on to tell me pretty much how it happened. The flashlight, the two grand on the front end with the promise of eight more. I had told the general about all that when we met and the general demanded a full battle report, as he called it. Cliff said the general told Charles and Karen and Eddie in a family meeting. That Karen had told him.

I left the Whittaker estate having learned that Karen's father was Charles, not the general. Actually, after Chunky's report I knew the general wasn't her poppy, but Chunky's report couldn't identify whose sperm had swum the channel. The DNA from facial tissue was not the general's. I figured Charles was a good candidate, because in part it explained his staying all these years. Then again, he saw the general as family and that might have been the only reason he needed. Karen's mother could have had one or a series of affairs during those years, such that she might not be certain of the identity of Karen's father. If Charles hadn't known, I would have gone to Karen's mother.

Everyone liked and respected the old man, but then they were all in his will. That also spoke to why Charles had not revealed himself to his daughter Karen, also perhaps why some of them were still hanging around.

Charlie Chan once said, "When money talks, no one is deaf."

Chapter 28

When I got home, Axel was there. "Buddha said he could handle covering Eddie the rest of the night. That I should come back and see what I could do for you. How 'bout something to eat? I'm hungry myself."

Axel offered me a choice of soups, but I held out for something to chew. He made some spaghetti with meat sauce, refusing to add meatballs or sausage. He also reminded me we still had half of Clara Birnbaum's apple pie in the fridge. While he cooked and while we ate, we talked through the various members of the general's family and what made each of them suspects.

"Charles could have a strong motive," I said. "With Eddie out of the way, his daughter would get the lion's share rather than the vulture scraps from the general's will."

"Two million plus would sure be enough to lay in winter groceries, boss."

His comment brought a smile since we had just heard that line in some old movie we had watched last weekend. Axel was right, most folks would be tickled to get two-and-a-half million. At least pleased enough to not murder to get more.

"So, you figure, in the end Charles couldn't let the general watch his grandson go to the chair. That led to a plan to save Eddie and pick up an extra two million through the shakedown of the general, for a total between Charles and his daughter of around six-and-a-half million."

"That sure ain't chump change, boss."

"I hear ya, Ax, but all this is a stack of hash with no real facts for bones."

I could only figure a few reasons why the real killer would not want Eddie convicted of the murder. In a complex plan, Eddie murdered his fiancée and arranged for his own arrest and release. Charles did it as a gesture to the general. Someone else killed Ileana, likely a jilted lover, who decided to take the risk of the case remaining open in order to extort two million from the general. That would add a payday to a murder of passion.

Axel ended up betting his chips on Clifford Branch, the chauffeur. "Boss, Cliff was a biker. He knew Podkin, so he could easily arrange to have you snatched. I'll bet there's plenty of guys in Cliff's old biker gang that would have murdered Eddie's lady for money. The shakedown of the general could have been about getting the dough to pay for the hit. And the alibi for Eddie was necessary to get the shakedown money from the general."

Axel had just presented what could be another reason why a killer would have needed to alibi Eddie. He needed to sell the alibi to the general to get the money to hire the killing of Ileana Corrigan and the bribing of Cory Jackson and Tommie Montoya.

Axel brought me back from my thoughts. "Cliff's in the will for a half a million. The shakedown was tide-him-over money while he waited for the general to croak. Those biker guys are always into some kind of crime so it fits. They're like the renegade gangs that rode in the old west."

In my mind, Cliff was incapable of putting together the complex plan of murder, a frame and an alibi. But Axel wasn't through nominating Cliff for the role of the murderer.

"Didn't you tell me that this Karen, the daughter, manipulated Cliff into attacking you down on the beach? If he's twisted around her finger, she could have got Cliff to arrange the murder through the bikers so that Eddie would take the fall and she'd get the big bucks. She could have promised him a chance to move into the mansion and live the fat life with her."

"But then why set up the phony alibi?" I reasoned. "No. If that was the case, Karen would only want to arrange the witnesses that got Eddie arrested. She'd want him convicted and sent up to clear her path to the general's will. If she also alibis Eddie then he stays in the catbird's seat in the will negating her reason for doing it to begin with."

"It's a real mess, boss. You got yourself a herd of suspects with no way to cut out the guilty one. Could Eddie and Karen be in it together? They split two million now for waiting around money, then split her share later. She's grown up with Eddie. She might not have been able to see him convicted of murder. That would explain why Karen would be interested in an alibi for Eddie."

"We shouldn't forget a solo performance by Eddie," I said. "He could have done it. It would have been a brilliant and diabolical plan to murder his fiancée to get out of a marriage he didn't want. Frame himself, while simultaneously crafting his alibi to get off for having committed it. He gets two million right away, minus expenses, and stays in the head chair when the will is read."

"Why, boss? I mean the guy's in line to inherit beaucoup millions. Why should he risk that with a murder? It'd make sense for him to just cool his jets and wait until the chips rolled his way."

"That seems logical, but let's say he found himself engaged to a woman he didn't want to marry. There's rumors that Ileana was a gold digger playing him for his money. That she had a sugar daddy on the side; the one who gave her the expensive jewelry found at the murder scene. Maybe Eddie didn't want a kid. He could've thought that he'd end up with the kid and she'd split with a divorce settlement. That's what happened to him. His mother left after his dad was killed in Desert Storm. That's why he was raised by the general. He didn't want a wife who didn't want her son, like his mother hadn't.

"If Eddie did it, this wasn't a sudden murder in a heated moment. It would have been cold and premeditated. And remember, this guy thinks he's smarter than the average bear, than all of the other bears, so he couldn't see himself getting caught."

"How's that spaghetti, boss? Chewing okay?"

"It works in small, easy bites, and tastes great, thanks for preparing it."

"In the morning, maybe we'll move you up to some scrambled eggs. Now back to the case. What about an old beau? Some dude who had the hots for Ileana and killed her when she dumped him for Eddie."

"I've thought about that. Back at the time of the murder, Fidge spoke to neighbors who had seen a couple of luxury cars visit her place, but never saw the drivers. He also found that expensive jewelry she couldn't afford on her own. That her folks couldn't have bought for her. Eddie claimed he didn't give it to her. If she had some well off fellas on the side that alone could have driven Eddie over the edge, or the lover she pushed aside to marry Eddie. That sugar daddy could be the person missing from my poker game."

"Huh, boss?"

"I keep having this feeling there's a player in this I haven't found. That could be him. Or I could be guessing another person exists because I'm not convinced any of the others did it. Let's get back to your idea of a jilted lover. That's certainly possible. He could have killed Ileana and framed Eddie for taking her away from him. But why would he wish to arrange an alibi for Eddie? No. He'd want Eddie to go up for it. That'd get him revenge and also close the homicide file."

"I don't know, boss. The shakedown makes the murder a paying proposition."

"Could be, with time to think and set it up. But a jilted lover is usually a sudden, angry murder. Not cold and calculated."

"Well, so which one did it?"

"We're not done yet. There's also the general."

"Why would the general kill Eddie's fiancée?"

"The general could have had his fill of unreliable women. His ex-wife, Karen's mother, Mary, was flaky. His son Ben's wife, Eddie's mother, had been no better, effectively selling Eddie to the general after Ben was killed in Desert Storm. Karen, his own daughter, is rather promiscuous, at least by the standards of the general's generation. He could have been of the opinion that Ileana had set herself up to get pregnant to trap Eddie into marriage. That way she'd get her hooks into the general's estate when Eddie inherits. That could have pushed him over the edge. And I can tell you, the general is more than capable of designing the entire strategy. He is a master tactician. He could have framed Eddie and arranged his alibi. Thereby protecting Eddie from what would undoubtedly be a failed marriage while also protecting his own estate which would go to Eddie."

"But, boss, the general got a phone call about the alibi demanding the two million clams. Then he got another call while he was driving home from the bank telling him to throw the money over the edge down to the beach."

"Only the general knew of those calls. They came in on his cell phone. He could have fabricated the whole bit about the calls. The general never reported the shakedown, so his cell phone was never examined. The general could have taken two million out of the bank and brought it home to put in his personal safe. Not thrown it over the edge at all."

"What about the general's health?"

"Ah. Today, sure, but this was done going on twelve years ago. The physical demands of the scheme were all activities he could handle then. And mentally, for him, the complex plan would have been a piece of cake."

"That's quite a yarn, boss. I buy the part about the killer setting up an alibi rather than getting the case closed by having Eddie convicted and sent up the river. Without that business about the alibi, there'd have been no shakedown. The best fit for that theory would be the general. He'd want to save his grandson. I don't see why the others would. They'd want him convicted so's the general might give them a bigger slice of his millions."

"Well, that's my dilemma."

"Have you been able to identify an old jealous boyfriend?"

"Ileana's parents don't recall one. Cliff had been friends with Ileana, nothing romantic, and he doesn't recall one. I think Cliff would have been more likely to know than her folks."

"I got a question for you, boss."

"Shoot."

"You made a strong point that the general had the knowhow to strategize it all out. And like I just said, the general had the best reason to alibi Eddie, but why in blazes does he hire you? I mean the killing was over eleven years ago. It's cold. Eddie's under no threat. Why does he want you raking through the coals?"

"That's the snag on the theory about the general. The only thing I can think of is the general wanted to find out if there were any loose ends. He figured if I worked the case and couldn't find the killer then he was home free. Of course, he knew he would die before he could be convicted anyway so he had no fear from the cops. It would have been more about someone challenging his will on the grounds of him not being in his right mind. Or perhaps to feel confident there was no basis for a claim by Mr. and Mrs. Corrigan for the murder of their daughter. That could explain two other unusual elements: The general provided in his will for a million dollars to Ileana's parents. Several months ago, the general gave the Corrigans a two-week all expenses paid cruise for their fiftieth anniversary. That could be guilt or compassion for the parents of a woman who had almost been his daughter-in-law. He could also have been creating a good relationship to discourage them from taking action against the estate on behalf of their dead daughter. I'm just guessing here, trying to stack it up every which way."

"The general would have had an accomplice. You said his health was good enough to pull this off back when it happened. But Cory Jackson was murdered a few days ago. The general couldn't have done that, could he?"

"No. He couldn't. Charles? Cliff? Either of them could have taken out Cory for the general. Then again, the police think the murder of Cory Jackson was unrelated to his claim of having seen Eddie kill the Corrigan woman. That could be the simple truth."

"You mentioned Karen could have boffed Cliff into doing her bidding. You said Cliff didn't have the brains to plan it. How about the doll, does she?"

"Eddie is a grandchild; Karen is a daughter. Most people would likely think she had the stronger claim. And yes, to answer your question. She had the brainpower to devise the plan and the proven skill to manipulate Cliff who could have performed the actual murder, bribed the witnesses, and hired Podkin to work me over. As you said, Cliff knows Podkin and a lot of other bikers with criminal records. If she did it that way, with Cliff carrying the water with all the contacts, nobody could directly finger her. If Cliff got arrested somehow and tried to cut a deal to testify against her, it would be his word against hers. In the end, that thinking brings us back to where we were before. Why would she arrange an alibi for Eddie? She would want him convicted. Otherwise, he still gets the bulk of the estate."

We could take it no farther. Axel went down to his condo and I decided to get ready for bed. First, I ate the last of Clara's apple pie. The soft, cool texture felt nice in my mouth and also tasted good.

I had no shortage of suspects and theories and they were all moving around in my head like tumbling cats caught in a clothes dryer.

Then something Axel had said replayed in my mind. "You gotta get one of them to rat on themselves. A man's tongue can work like a shovel to dig his own grave."

Chapter 29

Axel had set the coffee pot to come on in the morning before going downstairs to his condo. I had eased my way onto the couch to catch the late news before going to bed when the doorbell rang. I looked through the peephole to see Karen Whitaker.

I doubted Charles had told her about being her father. I couldn't figure what else would bring her here unless it was one of those I-don't-want-to-sleep-alone nights and she had flipped a coin with heads for me and tails for Cliff. I opened the door.

"Matt, I just learned about your having been beaten. Charles told me. Oh, golly, that looks really sore." She came in and closed the door behind her.

"It looks worse than it is. It only hurts when I move or breathe." We laughed together. I winced alone.

"Do you know who did it?"

I thought about asking her the same question. After all, she had already manipulated Cliff into attacking me. She could easily have arranged for a more serious effort by Podkin. If she had, she wouldn't tell me the truth, so I gave her the vanilla answer.

"Some biker thug. I got free. He ran off before I found out who put him up to it."

"You think it had something to do with what you're into for the general?"

"Yes."

She moved over to the couch and sat down. "Couldn't he have just done it on his own?"

"I suppose he could have, but ask me if I believe that. He wasn't demanding anything. He didn't take my wallet or steal my car. No. Someone hired him to work me over."

She crossed her legs, her pullover jersey drawing tight high across her upper thigh. "I see," she said. "I find it amazing how you can figure those angles." She then patted the cushion beside her. "Sit down with me, Matt. Maybe I can make it feel better."

"Actually, right now I'm more comfortable standing. I'm in no condition for any physical activity. It's difficult to even breathe without feeling it."

Unusual as it might seem, being impatient with a beautiful woman who had come to my room in the middle of the night, I didn't want to drag out her visit. She could have come out of concern for me, which was nice, but I'd had enough of that from enough people. Then again, the fact that the general would soon die could be accelerating the moves that might be coming from the various players in this family drama.

"Karen, is there some other reason you stopped by? I would love your company any other time, but I'm pretty whipped and I need to get started in the morning."

"Can I talk to you, Matt. I mean, really talk. My deepest concerns, my hopes, it won't take long." She turned toward me, the fabric's embrace of her legs more intense.

I needed to hear this, her reason for coming. "Go ahead," I said, my eyes on her gams, as I might describe her legs in one of my novels. My condition eliminated me as a participant, but not as an enthusiastic observer.

"Well, you know the general won't be with us much longer. I so wish I could change that, but the doctors say there is nothing further they can do." I nodded. "Well, you are aware that his will provides for all of us, with Eddie receiving the overwhelming majority."

Standing was now getting uncomfortable so I decided to try sitting with her on the couch. "You're gonna end up with two point five million." I slowly angled myself toward her the way we all do when talking to someone sitting beside us.

"Yes. But Eddie will receive close to fifteen million."

"That's the general's decision. Have you talked to him about your feeling it's not fair to you?"

"Not directly. Not in so many words. Still, you're right. He has made it clear that's how he wants it to be."

"You told me a few days ago that you had no thoughts about deserving more. That, given the way you were raised, over two million seemed like all the money in the world. You've certainly changed your mind rather quickly."

"I guess I deserve that, Matt. I've always tried to be bigger than, I don't know, being selfish. Truth is I've had these thoughts for some time. I've just kept them to myself."

I got up and went in the kitchen for a glass and two fingers of Irish. Karen said no to Irish, but asked if I had a Diet Coke. "No glass," she said, "I like the feel of the can against my lips." I brought our drinks in and sat down.

"So, as the general's death gets closer, your selfish thoughts have started demanding more consideration. Is that what you're saying?"

"Well, yes." She put the cold soda can against her lips, keeping it there a little longer than necessary to take her first drink.

"His will is pretty clear. There doesn't seem to be any way to change it without convincing the general to amend it." I sat back slowly and took a small drink of my own. The burn on the inside of my mouth was less than earlier. I swished it around before medicinally swallowing.

"There is a provision in the will—" She stopped speaking and looked at me, then looked down.

There it was. The reason she came by. "You mean the part about if Eddie predeceases the general. That part?"

"Yes, Matt." She moved closer and put her hand on my thigh, her face near enough for my battered lips to sense the warmth of her breath. "That part. We could be very rich together. Live a wonderful life of love and travel. Enjoy the best of everything."

"I've got enough for the way I like to live. The answer is no."

"You've killed before. For less than I'm offering."

"I won't do it. Even though everything inside me that beats and feels wants me to."

"But we could be together always."

"I won't kill for you and spend the rest of my life wondering when my turn will come. You need me now, but afterwards you won't."

"But I love you, Matt. I know it's sudden. It can happen that way. It's happened to me."

"No!" I slapped her in the face. Hard. I put my hand flat on the cushion beside me and squeezed, drawing it into a fist of fabric. I held my breath until the rat running around the pain wheel in my chest slowed to a canter.

She put her open hand on her cheek, then ran her index finger across her bottom lip, her mouth open slightly as her finger moved across it. "I guess I deserved that."

"No guess about it."

I looked at her hard. She looked down to the floor. Guilt made her do that. My bare feet weren't that attractive.

"You're an educated, beautiful woman who will soon inherit well over two million dollars. Get control of yourself."

Karen got up and walked to the glass slider and looked out toward the ocean.

"Why don't you get Cliff to do it? You've had him wrapped around your finger for years."

"I don't love Cliff. I'm in love with you. I want us to be together."

What that probably meant is she knew that Cliff couldn't figure out how to do it with a solid chance of getting away with it. And that Fidge would tie Cliff in knots during interrogation until he gave her up, whether or not he meant to.

"You're right, Matt. But I'm afraid. Without more money I just don't know. I put on a good front about being self-reliant, but at night I just get scared about being alone. The general has always been the strong man protecting me. I need you for that now. Aren't you ever afraid of being alone, of the dark?"

"The darkness is not frightening. Only the imagination of what might be there if the darkness was not. If I do as you ask, you'll be there, every night in the darkness. And I'll be wondering when I'll become excess baggage."

I got up and walked to the other side of the room. She followed.

"I know we haven't spent a lot of time together yet, but I love you. You love me don't you, Matt?"

"I'm in love with the idea of being in love with you."

"Go along with me on this, Matt. You'll never be sorry. We can be happy."

"No. I won't be your patsy."

I opened the door and glared at her until she walked out into the hallway.

I shut the door.

Chapter 30

I hadn't slept well last night, the pain in my cracked rib being the biggest hunk of the reason. I'd be lying if I didn't admit that Karen Whittaker's offer had lingered, chewing on the edge of my resolve. I had pegged her wrong and started wondering what else I had wrong.

I didn't like Eddie Whittaker, and frankly I didn't think anyone did. Not Charles, not Karen, not even his grandfather who loved him, but I don't think liked him. Not even the chauffeur Cliff cared much for him. Cliff had tried to be his friend, but Eddie had been born to eat filet while Cliff dined on canned ham. Eddie had hung out with Cliff only while he wanted to learn something Cliff could teach him. Then he tossed Cliff aside like a terminated tutor.

I remember having looked at the clock after two in the morning. That was the last time I had looked. I woke at nine-thirty to find hot coffee waiting with a note beside the pot: You didn't mention having an early appointment so I let you sleep. Axel.

I did a few easy twists and deep knee bends. Well they were more like shallow knee bends, but it did take out some of the stiffness. I buttered a muffin and poured a mug of coffee then went out on the patio. I had to get going, but first I had to figure out where my going would take me.

* * *

Axel called at eleven to say Eddie had just teed off to play a round of golf with three other guys. Axel had checked with the pro shop to learn they paid to play eighteen holes. That would keep Eddie in one place for at least four hours. We decided to meet at Mackie's for lunch. I wanted to hear more specifics about Eddie's movements.

The lunch gave me the opportunity to meet Axel's driver's ed teacher, Buddha Grunsky. I immediately knew the appropriateness of his name. Buddha stood about six feet, but had a matching width, a bald head and stern face with a soft, almost feminine voice. We took the table for six at the back, one that let Buddha move the table to give him more room. Mackie waved off his waitress and came over to take our order. I chose a beef dip. Axel had his usual, a bacon, lettuce and tomato with chunky peanut butter. Buddha said that both sandwiches sounded good so he ordered one of each. I motioned to Mackie to bring me the check. He nodded.

They asked me about being abducted and how I was feeling. I raised my head in case they had never before seen an author with a purple and yellow face.

"You don't look like you're moving much better than last night," Axel opined.

"And that'll likely be the case for a good while yet. Doc Medford's got me wrapped up like one of Mackie's deli sandwiches to go. I see the doc again next week and we'll go from there."

Mackie brought our food over. He carried mine and Axel's and had one of his nubile waitresses carry Buddha's two plates. She looked familiar. She should have, she was Axel's friend, Hillie. "Hello, Mr. Kile," she said. Axel introduced her to Buddha. When she stepped around the back of the booth to leave she leaned in and kissed Axel on the side of his forehead. My self-appointed staff man beamed like he finally had what he thought he never would, a family, recent and adopted, well, sort of, but a family. Then she circled back and took Buddha's soda glass to refill. Axel and I hadn't touched ours.

"Okay," I said, "tell me about Eddie's movements."

"Just what we've been reportin' boss. He eats, plays, goes to see his broker, and dates some great looking dolls." Axel and Buddha looked at each other and shook their grinning heads. If you can picture two high school boys talking about the lucky quarterback who gets all the cheerleaders, you have a good idea of the grins Axel and Buddha just shared. Buddha's grin was the first indication he had teeth.

"What about the biker bar?"

"It's down on Paseo Del Mar out near the point. But it weren't nothing. He went in, came out a few minutes later and left."

"Could he have stopped for a sandwich or a beer?"

"Wasn't in there long enough to even order it and have it brought, let alone eat it."

"Then what?"

"He left following the same route he had taken to get there."

Axel did the talking while Buddha ate, although the big one nodded his head now and then to evidence his agreement with whatever Axel said. A reasonable practice given that Buddha had two lunches to eat to our one.

"What route did he take?"

"Can't tell you exactly. We didn't write it down. He drove past Angels Gate Park and then angled onto Old something Road, then through some industrial area."

That's the area where Podkin took me to hang while he beat on me. "Did he stop anywhere?"

"No," Axel said.

Buddha spoke for the first time since his food arrived. He had finished his BL&T on toast and hadn't yet started on his beef dip. "He did slow, Ax. No stop sign or nothing, he just slowed. You know, that one block where the buildings sat back off the road."

This time Axel nodded his head. "That's right. He did. Both on the way out to the point and on the way back. Same place, right?" Buddha went back to nodding as he dipped the first end of his beef sandwich in the au jus. This sandwich came with coleslaw; his BL&T had come with fries. He had fat fingers, like bratwurst with fingernails.

"Can you find your way back to that building?"

Axel looked at Buddha who said, "I think so," while forking the last of his coleslaw out of a small bowl that disappeared inside his cupped hand. "Yeah. It might take a couple of minutes when we get over near there, but sure. We can find it."

"What makes that building important, boss? Eddie didn't even pull into the parking lot."

"From what you said, it might be the building where I was held. But then that neighborhood has lots of industrial buildings so the odds aren't good. Still, let's eliminate the possibility."

"Let's go," Axel said, rising from the chair. We had sat on one side and Buddha on the other. That seating arrangement seemed reasonable as that put two meals on each side of the table.

"Let Buddha finish eating." I motioned Mackie over by holding up my credit card. Axel sat back down.

I followed them in my car. They made a few wrong turns as we kept coming around the block and back to Old Fort Road. Then they turned onto W 22nd Street and slowed. After a couple of blocks they pulled to the curb. I pulled in behind them, across from the building where I had spent more time with Ernest Podkin than anyone should ever have to spend with the man. The lot was empty. I got out and walked up to the driver's door.

"Is that it? That one," I pointed.

"That's it, boss. That one there," he pointed at the same building I had. "The one with the green and white metal awning over the window."

"Thanks, guys." I started to turn.

"That's where you got worked over?"

"Yep. That's the place."

"That can't be no coincidence. Appears like Eddie's the man behind you getting snatched."

"That would be one explanation. Still, that building is owned by the general so Eddie could be looking at it in relation to some use for it. He might plan to sell or lease it out. Remember, he expects he'll soon be inheriting the general's assets which will include that building."

"Do you want we should keep the tail on him?"

"Absolutely. Now, you boys should be beating it over to the golf course so you can pick Eddie back up. Buddha, nice to meet you, I appreciate you helping us out, also teaching Axel how to drive. When he gets his license and can drive himself, my life will get easier."

"My pleasure, Mr. Kile. Anything else?"

"Yes. Axel, you need to get with Ms. Clara Birnbaum down the hall from you. She needs you to go to the store for her. She's going to bake us a banana cream pie, but only if she gets the fixings. If you don't get it done for her, she expects me to go."

"I already went for her the other day. I'll take care of Clara. She may have our banana cream ready some time today."

* * *

Two hours later, I had a plan. It hadn't taken full shape, but it had a clear overall theme. I called Axel and told him to get a hold of his graveyard man and give him the night off. "I want you and Buddha to stay with him and call me every hour tonight starting at eight to let me know Eddie's location. I expect to be relieving you myself."

Chapter 31

Axel called at eight to say he and Buddha were sitting outside Michael's, the Italian restaurant on east Second Street in the Naples area.

"Eddie went in with some doll. They've been in there long enough to know they're having dinner or doing some serious drinking."

"Okay, Axel. I'm heading your way. Oh, yeah, I'm driving Mackie's unmarked white van. Let me know if they leave before you hear from me. When I'm there, you and Buddha can take the rest of the night off. I'll fill you in later."

"Why you driving Mackie's van?"

"No time for questions."

"Okay, boss. Call me when you're in position. You sure you don't want to tell me what you're up to?"

"After it plays out and I've got something to tell."

The drive to the Naples area of Long Beach took me a hustling twenty minutes, without consideration of my rib cage. When I got near, I called Axel. They had a parking spot which gave them a good view of Eddie's car. I had Axel and Buddha pull out of their space and I pulled in. I took out my binoculars and settled back, watching the block leading up to the four-door black Lexus Eddie was driving tonight.

At nine-fifteen I recognized Eddie coming toward his car with a young lady with blond shoulder length hair walking to his inside, away from the roadway. She wore platform heels, and walked with her hand a tentacle around Eddie's bicep. She was what I once heard Axel call a one-and-a-quarter dame. Which Axel describes as a gal with one quarter too much makeup, one quarter too much jewelry, and one quarter too fancy a hairdo. She was attractive, but she fit Axel's definition.

I followed them back to some apartments off Wardlow where Eddie parked on a side street. She used a card key to get them through a side gate. With my binoculars I could see them walk down a center corridor through a landscaped area and around a building to the right. I slipped into Ernest Podkin's black leather jacket and his gray cap. I would have preferred the cap have a bigger front bill, but it didn't. I also had an extra-large shirt on with a small couch pillow under the shirt, inside the zipped up jacket. This closely compared to Podkin's build. In my hand I held a half a dozen cotton balls.

I waited.

At eleven, Eddie came around the corner of the building at the far right side of the landscaped courtyard area. I had turned the dome light off in Mackie's van. I shut the door gently and hurriedly walked toward the bushes to the side of the gate Eddie would come through to get back to where he had parked.

By the time I got in position, I had Poddy's hat pulled down partway on my forehead and the cotton balls lining my jawline between my teeth and my cheeks.

Eddie opened the metal gate, and closed it gently. I appreciated his having shut the gate quietly. With what I had in mind I didn't need to attract the attention of any apartment dwellers who might be up late. As he stepped away from the gate, he had his back to me. I took one step from the shadow and pressed the barrel of a fake gun into his back. He froze.

"Turn easy," I said with my voice deeper than natural.

"What do you want? Is this a robbery?"

"Not exactly. I'm going to keep this gun in my pocket so as to not attract attention, but my finger remains on the trigger. Get me?"

I sensed him going rigid. "What do you want?"

"Fifty thousand dollars."

"I'm sorry. I don't happen to have that much on me."

"You're a real smartass, Mr. Whittaker. Yeah. I know who you are and I know what you're gonna inherit. So let me tell you why I'm in your face."

He worked his hands down into his pants' front pockets. I had watched him walk. He had no gun. I stayed inside the shadow where the building blocked the floodlight.

"You can tell from my gang colors, I'm a buddy of Ernie Podkin. A few nights ago I come by his place, late. I see you coming out his door. No lights are on inside and Poddy ain't at the door seeing you off. I get suspicious and follow along behind you. From your license plate I learn your name. You're that big shot general's kid."

"Grandson."

"Pardon me, big shit. You're the general's grandkid. Anyways, I go back to Poddy's and wake 'im. He tells me some dude he couldn't see had coughed up a grand with a promise of more to do a job. He claims he didn't know the man, and I haven't told Poddy how I found out. Later, I tailed Poddy and see him snatch this guy out behind Russell's over on Atlantic. I made a note of the dude's license plate. I see Poddy shove the guy into a building on 22nd Street in Pedro. By midnight they ain't come out, neither one of 'em."

Eddie tries to say something; I stopped him.

"Shut up, Whittaker. You ain't heard nothin' yet. Later, I check the dude's license plate and learn he's some author by the name of Matthew Kile. To me, that adds up to some kind of ransom caper, but that don't check. No one else goes in the building where Poddy took Kile. No one comes out and Poddy wouldn't call for the ransom from the place he was holding the guy. The next day, I see a cop I know by reputation go in. Few minutes later, Poddy comes out, gets in his van and hauls ass. The cop comes out with this Kile guy who ain't walking all that well. I use my glasses and see Kile had been worked over. Poddy's pretty good at that. I figure that hooks you into a kidnapping and assault and battery. A little Google work tells me you had been arrested by that same cop a long time back about the murder of your fiancée. Now I figure all this ties. Okay. So, my silence will cost you fifty big ones. Now you can talk."

"You got nothing. You're stringing a lot of unrelated stuff together."

"Then don't pay me. I figure the papers will pay a nice fee for what I got. Complete with pictures. They're always interested in stuff about the general. And I got a little hassle with the fuzz that I can bargain off with the part I don't give the papers. I also read that your grandfather is close to croaking so he could get upset enough that it might mess up your inheritance. If he suspected you might have really offed your fiancée who the papers said was carrying the general's great grandson. Well, that's some nasty business, Mr. Whittaker, shame on you."

"You've got nothing that's worth anything to me."

"Okay. I musta screwed up somewhere. I got no interest in your pocket change. You're free to go. I'll make my deals with the media and the cops. Go on. Get out of here."

Eddie turned and walked down to the sidewalk and halfway to his car. Then he stopped. After standing still for about a full minute, he turns and walks back to me.

"I'd like to work out something. I don't want this to upset my grandfather. I just don't have fifty thousand. The general gives me an allowance. If you can wait until I get my inheritance, I can pay you then. The general won't live another week, according to the doctors."

"That don't help me now. What do you have on ya?"

Eddie pulls out his wallet. "Maybe two hundred." He takes out his bills and counts them. "For now, here take what I've got. Then you'll wait?"

"This here gives me some drinking and whoring money. But if I'm gonna wait, I want a hundred thou when your inheritance comes in."

"A hundred! No way. This is at best a nuisance item for me."

"Okay. Thanks for the walking around money. I'll make my deal elsewhere."

I turn and walk away from him. Behind me I hear a car door close from about where Eddie had parked. I walk past Mackie's van and keep on going. In the second block, Eddie pulls to the curb and leans toward his passenger window. I go over and squat down, keeping most of my face above where he could see. The world's best salespeople say there is a point where the next person who speaks loses. We look at each other. I stay quiet. After a minute, I stand up and start to walk away.

"Wait a minute," he says.

I go back to the car and lean on the sill again. "We got a deal or not, Eddie Whittaker?"

"Deal."

"One hundred thousand dollars you will pay me when your inheritance comes in. Right?"

"Right. Who else knows about me other than yourself?"

“Only one other person and he don’t know who you are or what I have. Right now he has a rifle pointed at you. He’ll be there again when you pay up. I also left an envelope with my girl. If anything goes wrong she’ll take it to the cops and the newspapers.”

“I don’t even know who you are.”

“I’m the guy with your balls in his fist.”

Chapter 32

After getting home from having braced Eddie Whittaker, I was met at the door by Axel. In the span of this case he had been promoted from houseman to houseman-case nanny.

After I ran tonight's events past him, Axel said, "Congratulations boss. It looks like Eddie's the guy the general hired you to find. The no-good bastard rubbed out the Corrigan dame and his own baby."

"It sure looks that way, Axel, but it's not conclusive. Eddie could have been offering to pay the bribe to keep the general from learning he was behind my being abducted and beaten. He wouldn't want the general to know that. It doesn't establish that he killed his fiancée or bribed Cory Jackson, Tommie Montoya, and threatened the Yarbroughs, but the general might be suspicious enough to change his will."

"Now wait a minute, boss. You got Eddie connected to Podkin who said the way he was paid was the same way the stiff Cory Jackson got paid and that gas station jockey. How 'bout them apples?"

"Eddie heard all those detail from his grandfather who heard it from me. They all know, even Cliff. No, it only means Eddie knew how Jackson and Montoya were bribed, not that he had bribed them. By doing it that same way, he made his using of Podkin look like the same guy who had arranged the shakedown alibi. And yeah, that could've been Eddie, but not necessarily."

Axel just shook his head.

"Hey, we got any of that rocky road ice cream left?"

"Nearly the whole carton, boss." We headed for the kitchen. While he got out bowls, he said, "Who else you got in mind if not Eddie?"

"A few days ago you and I brainstormed that it could have been Eddie, but also that it could have been Karen, or Charles, or even Cliff at Karen's direction, maybe even the general himself. All of that's still true. All we have is proof that Eddie hired Podkin to work me over. The rest of it is supposition, but not probative."

"You got Cory Jackson's story."

"No. I got that explanation from Cory's half brother, Quirt Brown, who heard it from Cory, and Cory's dead. That's all hearsay now, and it'd likely be ruled inadmissible. The only thing we have Eddie on is his having paid to have me beaten and even for that we'd be better off to have Podkin testify and he's God knows where. May I remind you that the two-hundred grand fee you keep talking about will not be earned unless someone is arrested for the murder of Ileana Corrigan. No one could be arrested off what we have. Not even close."

"So what do we do now, boss?"

"Rinse out our ice cream bowls."

"Boss. You know what I mean."

"I need to sleep on that. I'm not certain yet."

An hour after going to bed I woke up abruptly. The brain is a strange thing. How it makes decisions. The way unresolved things marinate on your mind until the simple core of complex things suddenly slap you across the face. The Corrigan killing was way short on facts, always had been. We all knew that. Over time memories had faded, one supposed witness had been killed, and even when the murder occurred eleven years ago there had been a dearth of clues. I would never find the answer the general wanted through a dogged pursuit of evidence that didn't exist. It would take sneaky doings. And right then, sitting up in bed, the sneaky doings came into focus. A plan rose from my mind mud. Not a guaranteed, slam dunk kind of plan, but one with a reasonable chance. I had to get these people to tell me what they hadn't yet told me. I needed to crawl into the crevices where the things that frightened them hid from the light.

Chapter 33

I got up at first light, slowly, but up. With a cup of coffee in hand, I called Cliff Branch, the chauffeur.

"Cliff, I need you to do something critical to help me solve this case and it must stay between you and me. I promise you I can square your doing it with the general."

"I've been told to cooperate with you fully, Matt. What do you want?"

* * *

Two hours later, I called Charles. "How's the general doing? I'd like to see him as soon as it works for him."

"Good morning, Mr. Kile. Let's see, it's eleven now, so he's been awake about an hour reading the morning paper in his study. He should be ready to see you by noon. No. Make it half past. Is that okay for you?"

"I'll make it okay. And, Charles, don't bring me an Irish if it's going to encourage the general to have one as well."

"That's no problem, sir. The general hasn't had another drink since the last one he shared with you. He told me what you said and he agreed. I thank you for convincing him."

"See you at twelve-thirty."

* * *

I got there on time and Charles led me upstairs to the general's small study off his bedroom. The noon sun filled the room, having invited itself in through the hexagon-shaped window high on the opposite wall. A wheelchair sat to the side of the room facing the wall, equipped with a portable oxygen tank and a line that would feed the hyped air to his nose. He wasn't using it, choosing instead to struggle a bit when taking breaths.

"Good morning, General. Did you sleep well?"

"Hello, Matt. As good as could be expected. Look, I know you don't need pressure from me, but the truth is I want you to earn the fee I agreed to. That means you don't have much time."

"I understand, sir. That's why I'm here."

"Do you know who killed Ileana and my great grandson?"

"I'm closing in, but, no, General. Not this morning, at least not as yet this morning."

"So?"

The door opened after a light knock. As I expected, it was Charles bringing me an Irish on cracked ice with a lemon wedge. "It's one o'clock, Mr. Kile, after lunch, so I thought you and the general would enjoy your having this." He leaned down far enough for me to take it from the tray. He put a paper coaster on the side table.

"Before we talk about why you came, Matt, let me give you this, there are two originals. I have signed them both. You will need to do the same." Noticing my confusion, the general explained further. "When I hired you and we agreed to your success fee, well, to say it plainly, I didn't expect I would die as soon as it now appears I will. Thus the terms of our agreement were not reasonable."

"General?"

"We agreed your fee would be earned when someone was arrested for killing Ileana. You have worked diligently in that effort. And, make no mistake, I still expect results, but the arrest requirement, well, it now seems inappropriate. This new agreement stipulates you are to be paid upon either that arrest or my statement that I consider your services satisfactorily completed and your fee earned."

"Thank you, General. You are most generous."

"I can't take it with me, and there's plenty left for the others. If you solve this to my satisfaction you will have done me a great service."

I took a pen and signed both copies. The general then rang his bell and Charles came in to witness both copies of the document and to take one with him.

"Now, Matt, why did you wish to see me this morning?"

"General, did you mean what you said about my not holding back on what I do or how I do it because you might be listening?"

"I mean everything I say, Matt, or I wouldn't say it. Time is my enemy and it is gaining fast. Forget nicely. Get it done."

"Charles tells me Eddie is still at home and if he tries to leave, Charles will let him know I would like to meet with him in the study. You'll want to keep listening until Charles tells you I've left."

"I see." The general's face went pale, even paler than from his ever-weakening circulation. "Is there anything else, Matt?"

"Yes. Curiosity, I guess, but you told me that Charles was with you on your general staff. That was how you two first met. You also mentioned he left you for a few years to take another assignment with the army. Then he returned and was your adjutant, or whatever the correct title was during your years on the joint chiefs. What did he do during the years he left your staff?"

"He always wanted to do intelligence work. I arranged for him to do some cloak-and-dagger stuff for the Department of Defense. After a few years he'd had enough." The general chuckled, and then coughed. "Like so many young men, he had imagined that to be romantic and adventurous. He found it quite different fighting an enemy you got to see up close, in unfamiliar terrain that often ended in assignments that turn most men's stomachs. It is not as clean and detached as eyeing a man through a sight and pulling the trigger."

Chapter 34

Eddie walked into the study where I sat in one of the overstuffed leather chairs near the glass door out to the patio. Charles closed the door behind him.

"Hello, Mr. Kile. Charles told me you wished to see me." He sat across from me.

"You grandfather's attorney, Reginald Franklin, has given me a copy of the general's will."

"That fat fuck, excuse me, but he can't even see his dick without a handheld mirror."

"You really are a little prick, you know. Your grandfather is dying and Mr. Franklin is doing more to help the general than you, who will receive the lion's share of the general's estate. Don't you think it's time for you to grow into the position and responsibility you are about to inherit?"

"I don't see that as any of your business, Kile."

"I think anyone who wastes talent and opportunity is everyone's business, or maybe just everyone's disappointment. I'm rather fond of your grandfather, and I'd like him, just once before he leaves us, to see you as a level-headed responsible adult."

"Oh, can the sob story. You don't give a shit one way or the other." He stood up. "Your only interest in any of us is to get somebody arrested so you can grab your fat fee."

I stood and reached out pushing him hard against his chest. The push hurt my rib area, but I liked doing it just the same. Eddie fell back into the leather chair across from where I had been sitting. He started to get back up. "Get up again and I'll close my fist the next time."

He took his hands off the arms of the chair.

"You're an educated guy, Eddie. A smart guy, but you got no style."

"I have style."

"A smart mouth isn't style. Treating everyone with disrespect may be consistent, but it's not style. You're a punk in rich man's clothes and an empty suit isn't style either."

"Is there a reason for this meeting, Kile, other than breaking my balls?"

"What was your interest in the industrial building in San Pedro on 22nd Street? You drove by there twice the other day."

"How did you know I did that?"

"Answer the question."

"It's a family holding. I'm trying to get familiar with all of our assets."

"In a bit of a hurry, aren't you?"

"It seems like we are always at odds, Kile."

"It seems like you're always more interested in the general's assets than in the general."

"Are we through here?"

"We haven't even started. You stay where you are. I've got some things I want you to hear." I took the tape recorder out of my satchel, put in the first tape and played it. The tape being Quirt Brown telling the story of how his half brother Cory Jackson had been bribed to testify about watching Eddie Whittaker kill Ileana Corrigan.

When it finished, Eddie said, "Old business, Kile. We all know Cory Jackson lied when he claimed he saw me."

"Old business? You knew about how Cory Jackson was bribed?"

"Not that part. Just that he had to have been. The person who bribed him would have been the killer who wanted me convicted. That tape would be hearsay since Cory Jackson's been murdered and the telling on your tape is second hand."

"Who do you figure bribed Cory Jackson?"

"I have no clue," Eddie said with a flip of a soft wrist. "I gave up trying to figure that mess out years ago. That's your job."

"I have another tape for your listening enjoyment." I put on the tape of Tommie Montoya telling his story of a flashlight being shined in his eyes when he opened the door to the ladies' bathroom at the gas station where he worked. Where he had been bribed to tell the cops he sold you gasoline shortly after Ileana was murdered.

When it finished, Eddie said the same thing. "Everyone has known that part of it too, except for the how. Same hearsay rule will likely make it inadmissible. This is all a waste, Kile. We all knew about that. You told the general. The general told us. All these tapes do is let us hear these claims first hand."

"I agree, the Quirt Brown tape would in all likelihood be inadmissible, but Montoya is still alive and I made this tape with his knowledge and consent. Still, we'll leave the admissibility to be resolved by the legal people."

"Okay, but so what. All it proves is that Montoya admits he lied to the district attorney. Beyond that, it proves I wasn't nearby. If you're trying to pin the murder on me, that tape helps me, not you."

"No. This tape does not prove you weren't nearby. It only proves that Montoya lied about seeing you nearby."

Eddie stood up, this time turning quickly to avoid my reach. "I've wasted enough time with your silly evidence of nothing. I'm leaving."

I stood up across from him. "You're staying. Sit back down. I've got one more tape for you to hear, and you'll want to hear this one."

"So, now I get to listen to Mr. and Mrs. Yarbrough talking about being bribed to confirm my being in Split Pea Anderson's at the time my Ileana was murdered? Same old, same old, Kile."

"This is one you don't know about, Eddie. I think you'll find it fascinating."

Eddie looked disgusted, but he sat back down, crossing his legs, curiosity leaking from his pores. I put in the tape of him and me talking outside the apartment building where his date lived.

It had played only a few seconds when he sat upright. "Where did you get that?"

"That was me you were talking with. I taped my own conversation with you. I think you should hear it all. Then we'll talk some more."

He had been there, but I wanted him to hear just how clearly he had confirmed hiring Podkin to kidnap and batter me. I knew the general was also listening. It would be tough for him to hear, but the general personified toughness and he needed a straight shot of what his grandson had grown into. How Eddie had agreed to pay a bribe to keep the police and his grandfather from hearing the tape. The charges against him through this tape were serious, but they didn't establish murder or even connect Eddie to the Ileana Corrigan homicide.

"Kile, you've got me on paying Podkin and being responsible for your getting worked over. If you turn it over to the cops, my attorney will fight it on the grounds that I incriminated myself without my knowledge as I didn't know you were taping our conversation. Now, I know you don't have anything that ties me to Ileana's murder. You can't. So, can I leave without you doing the fight club routine again?"

We sat staring at each other for several minutes.

"Get out of here."

Chapter 35

Charles came in after Eddie left and offered to bring me an Irish or something to eat. The kitchen staff had just made a batch of roast beef sandwiches for the crew of the outside landscaping service. Their men had been working to thin and shape a group of trees in the front yard arranged in a quincunx.

"That would be nice, Charles. I'll take both. And please join me. I need to kick some things around and I'd like your thinking. Can you do that?"

"Give me fifteen minutes. I'll let the kitchen know to make up a tray while I go check on the general. I'll come back with our lunch." I nodded and Charles left the study, closing the door.

Fifteen minutes later, Charles reopened the door to the study and held it so the maid could carry in a tray that held two plates with sandwiches and potato salad, two glasses of water, my usual and a glass of beer for Charles.

Through lunch we spoke of the general's condition, and of Christmas approaching without the shopping being finished, an annual state of affairs for most Americans. Also of the status of the Los Angeles Dodgers and the excitement their new owners had brought to their fan base.

When we finished, Charles wiped his mouth with his napkin. "Well, Mr. Kile, how can I be of help?"

"Charles, we've become friends and I'd like to talk with you about how this case got solved." His eyes went wide when he heard me say, *solved*. "That's right; I've found the killer of Eddie's fiancée and his child. I have an accessory to the murder held incommunicado. When I leave here I will go to the police. I fully expect they will return to arrest Karen."

"What?"

"I'm sorry, Charles. Karen, in concert with Cliff, who this morning has made a deal to avoid prosecution, killed Ileana. She is also guilty of trying to hire me to kill Eddie. These efforts were designed to move her to the top spot in the general's will."

"That explains why Cliff didn't come to work this morning and isn't answering his phone."

"Cliff has given sworn testimony as to how he helped Karen kill Ileana. At her direction, he bribed Cory Jackson and Tommie Montoya to create witnesses against Eddie. She wanted Eddie convicted of murder and discredited in the general's eyes, expecting the general would denounce Eddie so she would inherit the bulk of the estate. All that occurred eleven years ago. Just recently he helped her again by killing Cory Jackson. This eliminated the only person who claimed to witness the murder. Cliff hired one of his biker buddies to abduct and beat me. Their plan, to keep me out of commission until the general died, knowing that once the general passed away, I would be paid some nominal amount and dismissed. At that point, she would have gotten away with murder and become extremely wealthy. She promised Cliff that he would live that life with her. After we talked with him, he understood that Karen has no intention of marrying him. Instead, she would count on his remaining quiet to avoid his own arrest for murder."

"But given what you said, she would not have constructed an alibi for Eddie. She would have wanted him convicted."

"That was the burr under her saddle. She loved the general and had no desire to watch him suffer while his grandson was being convicted of murder. She saw Eddie as the weak man he is, and expected he would become a sniveling coward once arrested, begging the general to save him. That the general would be ashamed of him and either cut him out of his will or give the two of them equal shares. She would have been satisfied with that. I think she also loves Eddie. After all, they are family."

"Why would Cliff confess to this? "

"After the Yarbroughs told their story to the police about their dog being shot, the police reopened the case. Cliff was a sharpshooter in the military. He knew Podkin who abducted me. He likely had biker friends who would kill Ileana. I had to tell the police about Karen offering me a lavish life if I would kill Eddie. They kept pressing Cliff until he made a deal to save himself by giving them a more sensational killer, Karen. "

Charles just sat there in a slouch, as if someone had magically removed the largest bones from his body. After more than a minute, he muttered, "I don't believe it. No. I just don't believe it. She couldn't have done it."

"You know the saying, follow the money. The world sees her as the general's daughter, while Eddie is a grandson. She became jealous, insanely jealous. She believed she was entitled. I will have to testify that she offered me a wealthy life with her if I would kill Eddie before the general died. I'm sorry, Charles. With Cliff and my testimony, it's open and shut as they say. All I need do is call Sergeant Fidgery. He has already heard Cliff's confession. It's in motion. She will be in custody before the sun goes down. Again, I'm sorry, Charles. I know what this means to you. But this can't be swept under the table."

"She couldn't have done it, Mr. Kile."

"I didn't want to believe it myself. There is no evidence to the contrary. Nothing."

Charles remained slumped in his chair, his bones still missing. "I did it," he mumbled. Then he looked up. "I killed Ileana. I bribed the witnesses. I did all of it, except for whomever hired Podkin to detain you. My guess is Eddie did that. He believed you were trying to prove he had been guilty, that you wanted to help Karen that way. The key Podkin had to get into the building on 22nd had to come from one of us. No one else would have access."

"If you did kill Ileana, you would not have provided Eddie an alibi. You would have only framed him."

"Like you said about Karen, I couldn't bring myself to let Eddie be convicted. Oh, I didn't give a moment's concern to Eddie. I love the general and could not bring about the death or life imprisonment of his grandson. I couldn't let him lose all three, his son, Ben, his grandson, and his great grandson. I gambled that, once arrested, Eddie would come apart. The general would see him for what he was and give Karen an appropriate portion of his estate. In the worst case, what the general was leaving me, the two million I had that he paid for the alibi, and the two and a half million he was leaving Karen, even without an adjustment, would take care of us well enough. He has talked with me many times about doing that, and it would not have taken much for him to make that decision. Had Eddie fallen apart as I expected, the general, well, he has never had any tolerance for weakness in men. But Eddie held up better than I expected and that did not transpire."

"I understand your reason for confessing. But, it's no sale. Sergeant Fidgery will come for Karen as soon as I call him. Are you able to continue with your duties? Care for the general, I mean. If not, I'll arrange for someone right away."

I had Axel on standby. He had spent part of the morning getting groceries for Clara Birnbaum. Buddha was on standby to bring him if I called.

Charles's cell phone rang. He answered it. After a brief pause, Charles said, "Right away, General." Then he turned to me. "The general, sir, has instructed me to bring Eddie and Karen to the study. I suggested we come to him, but he insisted we always use the study for family business. He has asked me to attend and wishes that you stay. He is coming down in his chair and said he can handle it with the elevator."

I nodded.

"Mr. Kile, this is not over. I will make a full confession and I can provide support including the whereabouts of the two million the general paid me for the alibi. Karen will be released."

"It's with the cops now," I said, "and the district attorney."

"If there is nothing else at the moment, Mr. Kile, I should go and get Eddie and Karen to head down here." Charles bowed slightly, and left.

I wasn't sure, hell, I had no idea why the general wanted this meeting. The one thing I knew that Charles didn't was that the general had heard my conversation with him and also with Eddie. I assumed the general, used to being in command, could not see this play out with him on the sidelines.

We would soon know.

Chapter 36

Karen came in first and walked over to me clearly unsure of herself after my having tossed her fanny out of my condo the last time we were together. "What's going on, Matt?"

"I have no idea. Your father has asked us all to assemble. He's on his way down. Given his health, I assume he has something final he wishes to say to you all. He asked that I stay."

Eddie came in and when Karen saw his confused expression, she shrugged, adding, "The general wants to talk with us all. That's all we know."

Charles came in a moment later, leaving the double doors to the study open wide. A minute or so later, the general wheeled through the open doors. Charles walked over to him. When he got close, the general took his hand out from under his lap blanket. In it he held his Welrod

British pistol. The one reportedly stolen years ago. He raised it and without hesitation shot Charles in the chest.

The general had heard Charles confess and believed him as I did. It was too late for me to do anything, for anyone to do anything. It happened too quickly, too unexpectedly. I draped a napkin over my hand, went to him and took the Welrod with my fingers. I put the British assassin's pistol on the table; the smell of the firing still flavoring the air.

The general wheeled himself around Charles's body and positioned himself so we were looking at him and not Charles.

He looked directly at Eddie. "Charles killed Ileana and your son, my great grandson. He deserved to die and I wanted to be certain the sentence was carried out in my lifetime. He got swift, certain justice. We need more of that."

"But," Karen said, "but how do we know?"

"It's true," I said. "It all fits. Charles killed them. He spoke to Jackson, Montoya and the Yarbroughs using his own voice, none of them knew him. He disguised his voice to that of a woman when he called the general to sell the alibi, and the second call telling him to throw the satchel with the extortion money over the cliff." I looked at the general. He nodded.

"But," Karen said, waving her arms, "that doesn't prove Charles was the killer."

"Karen, I'm sorry to be blunt. There isn't enough time to do otherwise. Charles was your father. Your birth father anyway. He felt you were entitled to more of the estate.

You lived as the general's daughter and treated him with respect and dignity. To the contrary, Eddie did nothing to show love for his grandfather. Before you condemn the general, you should recall that you offered me a chance to do something similar. Your reason was greed. The general's reason was justice."

"I always suspected it was one of us," Eddie said. "That ate at me. But given the friction between us, Mr. Kile, why would you not conclude I was the killer?"

"I was investigating a murder, not judging a popularity contest. You don't have the stomach for murder. Now before you feel insulted, don't be. Not having the stomach to kill for any reason is not something to be ashamed of."

"But why not me?" Karen asked. "I mean, after I asked you—" She stopped, letting her words hang up in her throat.

"If you had killed Ileana, you could have simply killed Eddie as well, but you couldn't kill Eddie, he was family, at least you thought it was. You would have expected Eddie to come apart after being arrested, and humiliate himself in front of the general who would then amend his will. That is exactly what Charles anticipated. But Eddie has more inside than any of us gave him credit for having, and held it together through that ordeal. Later, with the general dying and his will not changed, time was running out and you became desperate enough to approach me. As for Cliff, had he helped you kill Ileana, your relationship with him could not have lingered on the same level it has for these past eleven years. And, had he killed for you before, you would have used him to kill Eddie, not come to me. You're guilty of nothing more than greed poisoning you into inviting me to murder Eddie. In the end, you wouldn't have gone through with it. You couldn't kill Eddie, but Charles had several years of covert action behind enemy lines." Before I finished, Karen had begun nodding.

"Mr. Kile," Eddie said, "if Charles killed Ileana, why would he frame me and also provide an alibi for my release? The frame alone would have gotten me out of the way."

"Charles saw himself in a difficult position. All Karen's life, he had given up knowing her as his daughter for one purpose, to afford her the opportunity to share in the general's estate. He dedicated himself to the belief she was entitled. His conflict came from his concurrent devotion to the general. He could not bring himself to be the cause of you going to prison for life or possibly being put to death. Juries can be incensed when unborn children are murdered. So, Charles crafted a solution that adequately balanced the things he held dear. He expected you would fall apart upon being arrested. And the general, after seeing you crying and begging, would reconsider the division of his estate. The alibi would save you, but you would be humiliated and discredited."

Eddie stood up, lowered his head and stayed quiet, then spoke calmly. "Mr. Kile, I see no reason for our calling the police. Nothing will be changed for the general, only the rest of us. The general will never see a prison. Likely never even a courtroom. If you agree, what can we do?"

"Karen, do you agree with what Eddie just said? I understand this is all very confusing and difficult for you, not to mention sudden."

She sat still for what seemed longer than it was. Then she nodded, at first almost unnoticeably, then stronger. "Yes, nothing will be accomplished by bringing the police in. I was nearly as guilty as Char—my father. How should we handle it?"

I disassembled the Welrod and wrapped in a newspaper and handed it to Eddie. "Drive over the Terminal Island Bridge and toss this piece by piece. Stop in an empty lot several miles off the route you drive and burn the newspaper. Then come back immediately. We call the police when you return. Karen, you and Eddie were in here with the general. The shot came from outside, through the opened door. I arrived fifteen minutes later. After I helped settle things, I spent some time looking around outside. Then we called the police. That'll explain the passage of time."

"Why can't we just say you were here with us the whole time?"

"Because of my police background, Sergeant Fidgery would expect me to have behaved in a certain manner. I would have taken flight outside immediately, before the shooter could get away without being seen. No. My skills cannot have been here. You two were shocked. Stunned. Dumbfounded. You did nothing. You just froze. I arrived after the murder of the general's longtime friend and loyal staff man."

The general spoke for the first time. “This isn’t necessary. Call the police. I will confess.”

“General. No. You don’t want to saddle Eddie and Karen with having to deal with this. You will never be tried, and never imprisoned. Truth is, you simply don’t have enough time left for any real legal proceeding. You don’t want this hanging over them forever. Scandal sheet gossip, talk shows, my guess is even a made-for-TV movie. There could be legal challenges to your will, who knows. Don’t make this your legacy to them. If you insist on confessing, the fact that Karen is not your daughter will come out. After that she will always be known as the daughter of the man who killed General Whittaker’s great grandson. You don’t want that for her.”

I explained that Cliff had been absent at my instruction. That he had remained loyal to the family and his not being around should in no way be held against him. I also advised them to not share what really happened with Cliff. It will provide no benefit, and each person who knows stretches the rubber band closer to the breaking point.

Eddie walked over to the general. “Grandfather, Mr. Kile is right. We need to get moving. Do it his way.” The general looked up and said, “Okay, Eddie.”

“And, Grandfather,” Eddie said, “Karen is your daughter. That is how she was raised. It is time for all this to stop poisoning this family. Please contact Reginald Franklin and have him revise your will to provide equal portions for Karen and myself. Charles, of course, should no longer be included, but Cliff should and also Ileana’s parents, just as you have them now. Have Franklin bring your new will here immediately for your signature." The general started to speak, but Eddie put his hand on the general's shoulder. "Grandfather, your will has caused too much pain, too many suspicions among us all. I'm sorry for the way I have acted. It's time I grow up, past time. I want you to do this."

"We need to get moving, folks," I said. "Time is an important element in these things." I turned to face Eddie. "Pick up Charles and put him on the couch. The police won't like you having moved the body. You didn't know any better. You acted from caring. That's part of why I couldn't have been here. I would have prevented you from moving him. And remember, all of you, Charles was facing the open door to the patio when he was shot."

Then I stepped closer to Karen. "Take the general upstairs. I want him to shower. Scrub his hair. Clean his knuckles and under his fingernails, his ears and inside his nostrils. Everything he is wearing is to be immediately put in the washing machine with the hottest water possible, including his lap blanket, even his slippers. Clean his glasses, very well. Soak them while he is in the shower. When he's out, put his wheelchair in the shower and wash it, including the leather seat and back. Have him put on different clothes and come back downstairs. By that time Eddie should be back. Come on now. We've got no more than an hour. I came fifteen minutes after the shot and spent about a half an hour outside, then we called the police. Let's get a move on. Now! Oh. Karen, get the doors and windows open down here. We can't smell it right now, but the shot fired in here was supposed to have been fired from outside. Get this place aired. Close it up when you come downstairs. Okay. Scat."

Eddie moved Charles onto the couch. Then Eddie took the wrapped gun from me and left for the garage in a jog. Karen pushed the general's wheelchair out the door toward the elevator. With them gone from the room, I went out the glass door to do the things I would do if looking around for the shooter or anything left behind. I made sure my footprints were in the garden and across the lawn. I went out into the driveway and along the side of the house noticing the things there sufficiently to be able to discuss where I had looked.

***

Karen brought the general back downstairs a few minutes before Eddie got back. When they returned the general was in his wheelchair with the tube from the oxygen tank aiding his breathing. They had swapped out the seat and back cushion of the wheelchair from the leather one they had scrubbed to a fabric covered set he used in the winter months. He handed me an envelope. "Your fee, Matt, including a nice bonus. You have served my family well."

We went back over the facts of how we would play it. I cautioned them to put it in their own words so it wouldn't sound rehearsed. We moved the time of the shooting up so that only about forty minutes had passed before I called Fidge to report the murder of the general's devoted friend, Charles Bickers.

Someday I will tell Fidge what really went down this day at the home of General Whittaker, after the general has died, in a few days.

This wasn't perfect justice. Not in an antiseptic textbook fashion anyway. But like I said earlier, I remain more interested in getting things as close to right as possible than I am in how that gets accomplished. And the hell with the details.

THE END

Thank you for reading

The Original Alibi, a Matt Kile Mystery

by David Bishop

Note to Readers

It is for you that I write so I would love to hear from you now that you have finishing reading the story. I can be reached by email at david@davidbishopbooks.com, please no attachments. For those of you who write or who aspire to write I encourage you to write, rewrite, and write again until your prose live on the pages the way it lives in your mind. I will reply to all emails that do not contain an attachment. And with your email address, I will send you announcements for my upcoming novels. Thank you for reading this story. I'd love to hear from you.

With appreciation,
David Bishop

P.S. I have one more writing project in mind for release this year. A single short story titled, *Money & Muder, a Matt Kile Mystery*, short story. I will also be working on another mystery for release in the first half of 2013, titled *Death of a Bankster, a Maddie Richards Mystery. Death of a Bankster* is a working title, but at this point it appears firm. To stay current on these endeavors and other announcements, please visit my website from time to time or stay in touch with me through email, Facebook or Twitter.

With appreciation,

David Bishop

Who Murdered Garson Talmadge

An Excerpt:

The Original Alibi was the second Matt Kile Mystery. For those of you who have yet to read *Who Murdered Garson Talmadge*, the mystery that established Matt Kile as one of America's leading fictional detectives, I have provided an excerpt beginning on the next page. Enjoy and please do let me know your thoughts on my mysteries.

david@davidbishopbooks.com

Who Murdered Garson Talmadge

Prologue

It's funny the way a kiss stays with you. How it lingers. How you can feel it long after it ends. I understand what amputees mean when they speak of phantom limbs. It's there, but it isn't. You know it isn't. But you feel it's still with you. While I was in prison, my wife divorced me; I thought she was with me, but she wasn't. She said I destroyed our marriage in a moment of rage in a search for some kind of perverted justice. I didn't think it was perverted, but I didn't blame her for the divorce.

But enough sad stuff. Yesterday I left the smells and perversions of men and, wearing the same clothes I had worn the last day of my trial, reentered the world of three-dimensional women, and meals you choose for yourself; things I used to take for granted, but don't any longer. My old suit fit looser and had a musty smell, but nothing could be bad on a con's first day of freedom. I tilted my head back and inhaled. Free air smelled different, felt different tossing my hair and puffing my shirt.

I had no excuses. I had been guilty. I knew that. The jury knew that. The city knew that. The whole damn country knew. I had shot the guy in front of the TV cameras, emptied my gun into him. He had raped and killed a woman, then killed her three children for having walked in during his deed. The homicide team of Kile and Fidgery had found the evidence that linked the man I killed to the crime. Sergeant Matthew Kile, that was me, still is me, only now there's no *Sergeant* in front of my name, and my then partner, Detective Terrence Fidgery. We arrested the scum and he readily confessed.

The judge ruled our search illegal and all that followed bad fruit, which included the thug's confession. Cute words for giving a rapist-killer a get-out-of-jail-free card. In chambers the judge had wrung his hands while saying, "I have to let him walk." Judges talk about their rules of evidence as though they had replaced the rules about right and wrong. Justice isn't about guilt and innocence, not anymore. Over time, criminal trials had become a game for wins and losses between district attorneys and the mouthpieces for the accused. Heavy wins get defense attorneys bigger fees. For district attorneys, wins mean advancement into higher office and maybe even a political career. They should take the robes away from the judges and make them wear striped shirts like referees in other sports.

On the courthouse steps, the news hounds had surrounded the rapist-killer like he was a movie star. Fame or infamy can make you a celebrity, and America treats celebrity like virtue.

I still see the woman's husband, the father of the dead children, stepping out from the crowd, standing there looking at the man who had murdered his family, palpable fury filling his eyes. His body pulsing from the strain of controlled rage that was fraying around the edges, ready to explode. The justice system had failed him, and, because we all rely on it, failed us all. Because I had been the arresting officer, I had also failed him.

The thug spit on the father and punched him, knocking him down onto the dirty-white marble stairs; he rolled all the way to the bottom, stopping on the sidewalk. The police arrested the man we all knew to be a murderer, charging him with assault and battery.

The thug laughed. “I’ll plead to assault,” he boasted. “Is this a great country or what?”

At that moment, without a conscious decision to do so, I drew my service revolver and fired until my gun emptied. The lowlife went down. The sentence he deserved, delivered.

The district attorney tried me for murder-two. The same judge who had let the thug walk gave me seven years. Three months after my incarceration, the surviving husband and father, a wealthy business owner, funded a public opinion poll that showed more than eighty percent of the people felt the judge was wrong, with an excess of two-thirds thinking I did right. All I knew was the world was better off without that piece of shit, and people who would have been damaged in the future, had this guy lived, would now be safe. That was enough; it had to be.

A big reward offered by the husband/father eventually found a witness who had bought a woman’s Rolex from the man I killed. The Rolex had belonged to the murdered woman. Eventually, the father convinced the governor to grant me what is technically known in California as a Certificate of Rehabilitation and Pardon. My time served, four years.

While in prison I had started writing mysteries, something I had always wanted to do, I finally had the time to do. During my second year inside, I secured a literary agent and a publisher. I guessed, they figured that stories written by a former homicide cop and convicted murderer would sell.

My literary agent had wanted to meet me at the gate, but I said no. After walking far enough to put the prison out of sight, I paid a cabbie part of the modest advance on my first novel to drive me to Long Beach, California, telling the hack not to talk to me during the drive. He probably thought that a bit odd, but that was his concern, not mine. If I had wanted to gab, I would have let my literary agent meet me. This trip was about looking out a window without bars, about being able to close my eyes without first checking to see who was nearby. In short, I wanted to quietly absorb the subtleties of freedom regained.

Chapter 1

Six Years Later:

I was about to walk out my door to have breakfast with the tempting Clarice Talmadge and her septuagenarian husband, Garson Talmadge, without knowing Garson would be skipping breakfasts forever, not to mention lunches and dinners. The Talmadges lived on my floor, at the end of the hall in a twenty-five hundred square foot condo on the corner with a balcony overlooking the white sand shoreline of Long Beach, California. Then my phone rang. It was Clarice, but she hadn't called to ask how I liked my eggs. The cops were with her and they hadn't been invited for breakfast.

A uniformed officer halted me at the door to the Talmadge condo. "My name's Matt Kile," I said, "I was asked to come down—"

The saxophone voice of Detective Sergeant Terrence Fidgery interrupted, "Let 'im in."

For seven years before my incarceration Fidge and I had worked homicides together for the Long Beach police department. Fidge was a solid detective, content with his work, a man who appeared to need nothing else. Well, perhaps a diet-and-exercise program, but Fidge was a man who would do anything to stay in shape except eat right, exercise, and drink less beer. I left the force ten years ago but stayed in touch with Fidge and his wife, Brenda, whose pot always held enough for one more plate. I often sought out Fidge for his take on the first draft of my mystery novels.

The master bedroom where Garson Talmadge slept alone was immediately inside to the right. His door loitered partially open. I could see Garson on the bed, his arm in an uncomfortable position he could no longer feel. Clarice stood in the middle of the living room, clutching her little Chihuahua to her bosom, her wet eyes pleading for help. I envied the pooch. I put my open palm straight out toward her so she would not come to me, then my finger to my lips signaling her to stay quiet.

"I'll be with you in a minute Matthew," Fidge hollered from somewhere deeper into the condo.

I waited in the foyer while the police photographer finished shooting Garson's bedroom. A liquid had been spilled or thrown against the bedroom door. I touched the wet carpet and smelled my fingers. Coffee. With cream, I thought. The photographer came out of Garson's bedroom. I couldn't place his name, but I'd seen him around. We exchanged nods as we passed in the doorway.

Sometimes you strain so hard listening for the quietest of sounds that you don't hear the loudest. The shot that had hit my neighbor just above the bridge of his nose had come so fast that before he consciously heard it, he had stopped hearing everything.

The edge of Garson's bedcovers was pulled back exposing a foot too white to be a living foot. A modest amount of dried blood soaked Garson's pillowcase, and stippling surrounded the entry wound. My elderly neighbor had taken it from up close.

I started toward the bed, heard a crunching sound and stopped. The gold carpeting between the door and the bed had been sprinkled with what looked to be cornflakes. I stood still and looked around. A man's billfold sat on the dresser in front of the mirror, the corners of a wad of cash edging out where the wallet folded over. Five boxes of cornflakes stood at attention along the wall at the end of the dresser, the flaps on the end box erect in a mock salute. At the end of the row of boxes a bottle of Seagram's Seven Crown played bookend to the cornflakes.

A hissing sound led my eyes to the sliding door entry to their ocean-facing balcony. The slider was open two inches with the air fighting its way inside like folks at the door to a popular after-hour's club. The room was cold enough that I would have closed the door, but not in a crime scene. I pulled the sleeve of my sweater down over my fingertips, reached as high as my six-three frame allowed and opened the slider far enough to stick my head outside. Halfway between the door and the railing, a zigzag print from the sole of a large deck shoe smudged the dewy balcony. The sole print testified that the step had been taken toward the condo. I pushed the slider back to its original two inches. Moving carefully to avoid the cornflakes, I went into the walk-in closet. There were no shoes with that sole pattern, and no shoes of any kind under or beside the bed. Garson had always struck me as an everything-in-its-place kind of guy. His room proved it. Whatever he had worn had been hung up or dropped in a hamper. He would not have wanted to see the jagged out-of-place blood stain that defaced his pillow.

Sergeant Fidgery came through the doorway, his posture slouched, his stride short. "Hey, Matthew, I just finished your latest, *The Blackmail Club,* it's your best yet."

"Thanks, Fidge. As always, your technical tips helped. Where's your new partner?"

"What's with the new? You know George has been with me since, well, since that stupid stunt you pulled on the courthouse steps ten years ago."

"Anybody since me will always seem new. So, then, where's George?"

"Sick," Fidge said. "I'm soloing. That's why I approved your coming down here. I need you to remember how to behave in a crime scene."

"By the way, happy birthday old man. Sorry I didn't make the party last weekend. Forty-seven, right?"

"Forty-seven," Fidge said sarcastically. "We go through this every year. I'm forty-seven, you're forty-six, but only for a few months, then you'll be forty-seven like me. Brenda said to tell you she hasn't forgiven you for missing the party."

"You know I would've been there if I could. My agent scheduled a book signing way over in the San Fernando Valley without checking the date with me. She won't do that again."

"No sweat, Matthew. I'm just yanking your chain. Brenda understands."

"Thanks. Look, I stepped on the cornflakes before I saw them. They blended with the carpeting. It looks like the flakes had been walked on before I got here. You?"

"Who the hell expects cornflakes on gold carpet?" Fidge asked. "Christ, on any color carpet." Fidge put a steadying hand on my shoulder, crossed one knee with his opposite ankle and looked at his sole, then the other. Neither of us saw anything on the soles of his shoes.

"Did Clarice walk on them?" I asked.

"Says so. Says she got up, threw a load of clothes in the washer, put the coffee on, showered and slipped into what she called 'a little thing,' and then came in here to wake her old man."

"What about the uniform at the door," I asked, "did he come in too?"

"I cursed when I stepped on the flakes," Fidge said, shaking his head. "A bit too loudly, I guess. Officer Cardiff came running. Now stop poking around, Matthew. I let the wife call you because she said she had been with you last night and that you might have a key to this place, not so's you could play detective. Tell me about her, and keep your voice down."

"What can I say? She's got her own teeth, great hair, and this and that."

"Yeah. Right off I noticed her this and that. Also the 'little thing' she put over her this and that when she got up this morning; it's hanging behind her bathroom door. You ought to take a look. Then maybe you've already seen it, with her in it." He looked at me from the corner of his eye, and then added, "I haven't heard you deny she was with you so tell me about her visit."

"Clarice came down during the night. Said she thought someone would try to kill her husband. I didn't take her seriously, but she had been right."

"What time did she get there?"

"It was dark, had been for a while. I had been zonked. I went to bed around ten. Midnight would be a good guess."

"What did she say? I want all of it and I want it exactly. Everything."

"Page one: The doorbell woke me a few minutes after midnight. I found Mrs. Talmadge leaning on my door jamb wearing a man's white button-down shirt, a strategic gap formed by the mismatching of a southern buttonhole with a northern button. Her blond hair teased her shoulders. She had on a pair of shiny gold sandals, her toenails painted red to match the bloody mary she held, a celery stalk stood tall in the short glass."

"Knock it off, Matthew; this isn't one of your novels. You know what I want. Give."

I nodded. "Her opening line was 'something bad is gonna happen.' She brushed past me, her sandals slipping as she stepped down into my sunken living room, her shirttail failing to fully cover her backside. Oops. I forgot. You said no descriptions. I asked her what she was talking about. She said, 'somebody's going to kill Tally.' That's her pet name for her dead husband."

"Then what did she do?" Fidge asked.

"She took a big drink, chomped the end off the celery stick that had poked her in the cheek, and oozed her bottom over the arm of my leather chair, creating two small miracles. She didn't spill a drop, and her face showed no reaction when her bare bottom settled onto the cool leather."

Fidge screwed up his face.

"Okay. Okay, just the facts, Sergeant. I asked why she thought that. She said, 'Three days ago, I answered the phone. Some guy with a raspy voice asked for Gar. Only he made it sound like jar. I told him there's no jar here and hung up.'"

"Was her dead husband there?"

"No. But her live husband was." Fidge gave me the finger. I ignored his bad manners and continued. "She said her husband, sitting at the table drinking coffee, turned white when she mentioned *Gar*. To illustrate the color she held up her short white shirttail, her unblemished skin imitating melted milk chocolate. She had no tan line. I know you said to can the descriptions, but I figured you'd like that one."

"What did her husband say?"

"He told her that some former business acquaintances in Europe used to call him Gar. Then he told her to hang up when they called back."

Fidge put one hand in the air like he had been busted back to directing traffic. "When? Not if?"

"I asked her that too. She definitely said, 'when they called back.' And, before you ask, she said there were no more such calls, at least not while she was at home. She got in Garson's face about that call again the next morning, and they again fought."

"How well did you know this guy?"

"Not all that well," I said. "I went out to dinner two or three times with the Talmadges. Garson was a bon vivant. He and I played poker with a few men in the building, maybe four times."

"Did the Talmadges go to dinner with you or did you go with them?"

"What's the difference?"

"Who invited whom?"

"I don't recall."

"Who drove? That's usually the person who extended the invitation."

"That I remember. Clarice. She gets motion sickness in a car. She found it didn't happen when she drove. Garson said it had something to do with her vision and hearing senses getting the same stimulus."

"When I was a kid," Fidge said, "my uncle always drove for the same reason. You mentioned you played poker with the deceased and a few other men in the building. The wife's about thirty-five and a real looker. The dead guy's around eighty. Was she also playing with some of the other men in the building, and I don't mean poker?"

I ran my hand through my hair, wrinkled my lips, and then said, "Yeah."

"You?"

"I expect it'll come out, so here it is. One afternoon, two days before they moved in last spring, Clarice knocked on my door. I had seen her and Garson in the building earlier, but hadn't been introduced. She said … no, she didn't say, I assumed she and Garson were father and daughter."

"But she didn't say otherwise, right?"

"She didn't say otherwise. Before she left we did the deed, you know. Then I found out they were married. It's rumored several other fellows in the building have also taken turns. I don't know any names, but I suspect you'll find wives eager to spill their suspicions."

"Someday," Fidge said, "I need to give you my sex-without-deep-feelings-is-worthless speech. I just don't have time right now."

"Oh, too bad, I've been so looking forward to that one. But it's a load of bull. Sex for pure lust is not worthless. Not all of us are fortunate enough to have someone we love deeply in our lives every time we get a case of the galloping hornies."

"You've obviously given this a lot of thought, Matthew. But may I bring you back to why we're together this morning?"

"You brought it up." I sighed. "Go ahead."

"What do you know about Garson Talmadge's background?"

"Less than I know about his eating habits. During one of the dinners, Garson said he came from Europe, but shied from anything beyond generalities. I can tell you he spoke some words with the softer consonants common to the French. Once when the poker talk came around to Iraq, Garson pronounced 'Allah' with the back of his tongue raised to touch his soft palate as is done with Arabic."

The sun broke through the clouds to reflect off the ocean and brighten Garson's bedroom. We moved a bit to avoid the glare. Fidge walked over to look at a desk along the bedroom wall which held a computer setup and also a typewriter.

"Don't see many people with a typewriter these days." Then he asked, "What else happened while she was at your place?"

"She took another bite from the celery stalk. A drip of bloody mary fell onto her skin to slalom down her abundant cleavage until blossoming into a pink splotch on her white shirt."

"Knock off the colorful bullshit, Matthew."

"You know, you're the only person since my mother who regularly calls me Matthew. Brings back memories. I like it."

"I told you to knock it off."

"Sorry. It's the novelist in me; I think that way now. Clarice said the next morning when Garson went into the bathroom, she saw a bunch of passports in an attaché case he'd left open on his bed. They all had his picture, but different names. She didn't remember any of the names, but from the way she told it he had enough to start his own phonebook."

"I understand they fought a lot?"

"According to her, yeah," I said, "at least since that call asking for Gar. She also heard him on the phone speaking some language she didn't understand. She said it wasn't French. That she didn't speak French, but had taken French in high school so she recognizes it. After the 'Gar' call, she said her husband stopped leaving their condo except to go to the workout room and spa area in the building. The only time he left the building was the prior week to keep an appointment with his attorney."

"What else?" Fidge widened his stance, taking care not to step on more of the cornflakes.

"Did I mention her fingernails were painted to match her toenails?"

Fidge flipped me off again, then asked, "What time did she leave?"

"I didn't look."

"Guess."

"I'd put it at close to four in the morning. And, yes, the skin on her fanny made a popping sound when she pulled free of the leather chair."

"She stayed nearly four hours? Just what were you two doing?"

"We talked. All right? Her life. Well, her life some. Mostly mine, I guess."

"And you spilled your guts, right?"

"Some stuff. Yeah. I guess. The woman knows how to get a man talking."

"I'll bet she can. Her naked under a man's white shirt enhanced by mismatched buttons and buttonholes. I suppose you told her your wife got a divorce after you went to prison?"

"Yeah."

"And that she had been mad enough to file ever since you shot her father's prize hunting dog? You tell her that too?"

"That damn dog was hunting me, Fidge, charged me in the study, saliva hanging from its teeth. For heaven's sake, you had to be there. That animal took down game with that mouth. What would you have done?"

Fidge laughed. "I'd have brought along Milk Bone when I visited the in-laws."

"Ha. Ha. Like you said, my marriage was kaput by then anyway. My arrest just gave her an easy explanation for it."

"So you sort of moved up her timetable."

"Shooting that damn dog was self-defense. Hey, you got a murder here. Shouldn't you be doing something more important than critiquing my fucked-up personal life?"

"You're right; I'm here about the murdered man, not the murdered dog. But, like we say in the crime-fighting business, you having shot the dog, then the guy outside the courthouse established your pattern of behavior. Now, you were telling me about you and Clarice and your four hours in paradise."

"I can't really tell you what we talked about. It was late. You know, you get sort of groggy, the mindless talk comes and the time goes."

Again his silent finger preceded his question. "What about the key?"

"I don't know why she said that."

"That don't answer my question, Matthew. She said you were her old man's only friend in the building. Says she figured her husband might have given you a key for emergencies or whatever. Sounds awfully convenient for when you wanted to visit with his wife."

"Okay. Here it is direct. I do not and never did have a key to the condo of Garson and Clarice Talmadge. Is that plain enough, Sergeant Fidgery?"

"Don't get hot, Matthew. You know how this works."

"I wasn't dodging your question. As for emergencies, hell, the building supervisor lets people in then. He's got keys to every unit."

"Okay. I'll check with the super."

"How do you size this up?"

The sergeant stepped closer. "The wife's a pastry on legs, but her deck is missing a few cards. She plugs her old man, and then leaves the front door dead bolted from the inside." Fidge gestured toward a .22 revolver on the bed. "Says that there's her husband's gun, it's loaded with longs. Only one shot's been fired. I expect ballistics will show the missing long is in the old guy's brain. Says the red scarf draped over the gun handle is hers, so's that pretty little pink pillow with the ugly little black hole. Her dog sleeps on it, or used to."

"Why the pillow?" I asked. "A .22's pretty quiet. An expert would know that."

"She ain't no expert."

"Come on, Fidge." I shook my head. "Clarice isn't the kind to kill a man unless it's with loving."

"And just what kind is she, Mr. Writer?"

"The divorcing kind. She'd move on and find a new rich guy. Think of it as legal prostitution with fewer customers and better working conditions, with a topnotch severance package as a bonus."

Fidge grinned. "Maybe you should write one of them columns for the lovelorn."

I imitated his finger, using my own. "What's the story on the cornflakes?" I asked.

"Says her husband's a light sleeper. That he sprinkled the flakes on the floor so no one could sneak into his room. How's that for nutso?"

Clarice's voice shrilled from the living room. "I didn't do it, Matt. Honest to God, I didn't do it." Her chihuahua whimpered, perhaps in agreement.

I had never before heard the dog make a sound. Garson had refused to buy the condo unless his wife could keep her dog. She proved to the condo association that Asta had been trained to always stay quiet indoors and, after Garson paid a large nonrefundable deposit, Asta became the only pet in a building posted: no pets.

I looked at my old partner. "Just what points this at her?"

Fidge started with a facial expression that screamed I've already told you. He summarized: "The deadbolt. No forced entry. Nothing's missing. The neighbors have heard lots of screaming. The gun was in the house. The scarf and pillow are hers."

"That won't get you a conviction."

"That's just the part I'm telling ya. We got more and we're still in the first inning."

"What else have you that ties to her?"

"I'm not paid to report to you, Matthew. But I'll tell you this, when the wife used her scarf and her dog's pillow she moved it up to premeditated."

"Maybe Garson did himself in?" I said.

"Usually they leave a note, and suicides don't often worry about fingerprints and keeping their work quiet, not to mention the awkwardness of plugging themselves in the front of the skull."

Fidge shrugged after discrediting suicide. I agreed with him. This wasn't suicide. Still, I hadn't seen Fidge shrug that way in years, but habits become habits by lasting over time. This Fidgery shrug meant, *open and shut.*

"I'm not going to tell you again, Matthew, get outta here. The medical examiner could be here any minute."

"I'm going." I used the back of my hand to pat the sergeant on the breast pocket of his dark-blue suit coat. "She can phone her attorney after you get her downtown, right?"

"Sure."

"Who called this in?"

"Her."

"What about the coffee?" I asked.

Fidge coughed into his fist. "Says she dropped the cup when she saw the hole in her sugar daddy's noggin."

I left my ex-partner in Garson's bedroom and went to Clarice in the living room. "I'll come see you once you're permitted to have visitors."

She shifted Asta from one arm to the other while blotting her eyes with the soft pads of her straightened fingers, the way women do to avoid smudging their eye makeup.

"Please take Asta," she pleaded. "There's no one else I can ask. I got her a continental clip three days ago. She won't need another grooming for weeks. I'll be home before that."

I had once thought about getting a dog, but figured on one I could name Wolf or King. Then, after the incident with my father-in-law's mad creature, I repressed the whole idea of a dog.

"I need another minute in the victim's room," Fidge said, leaning out of the doorway of Garson's bedroom. "When I come out, I want a decision on that dog. It's you or the catcher."

"What'll I do with a little dog like that?" I asked looking at Clarice.

"She won't be any trouble." Clarice's eyes went all funny. "Please, Matt."

I had always envied the way Sam Spade could stand up to the femme fatales who tried to play him. I had given that skill to my fictional detective, but no one had given it to me.

"All right," I said, hoping I sounded less defeated than I felt. "Asta can stay with me."

"Are you sure?" she asked.

"I'm sure of almost nothing. But, yes, Asta can stay with me." I put my fingers against her lips and headed for her bedroom where I found no deck shoes with zigzag soles. I quickly looked in the bathroom, the kitchen, and the laundry room and found no zigzags there either. Fidge had likely already done this. He was a solid detective so he would have seen the shoe print on the deck and the partially open glass door in Garson's bedroom.

Back in the living room, I asked, "When did Garson start with the cornflakes?"

"Tally went all crazy after that call. He started carrying his gun around in his waistband, sleeping with it on the night stand. He kept insisting I go get six boxes of cornflakes. We fought about that. We fought about everything, about nothing. Day before yesterday, I stopped at the post office to mail a few house bills and something Tally wanted mailed to his attorney. On the way back I bought the damn cornflakes. Guess what? We still fought." She leaned closer and whispered. "He scared me real bad. I wish I hadn't—"

I grabbed her shoulders. "Save it for your attorney, you have no legal privilege over what you tell me." But she kept talking anyway.

"Damn it, I didn't shoot him. I was trying to say I wish I hadn't gotten mad at him so much those last few days." She stood clutching the dog, breathing slowly. Her eyes shut. Then she put down Asta and said, "Go with Uncle Matt."

The hair ball leaped into my arms.

"She'll sleep on the foot of your bed. You'll need to get her a new pillow. Her pink one has a … hole in it. Take a few of her toys. She'll be fine."

Fidge again filled the bedroom doorway, "Just the mutt."

"But Asta needs her toys. She—"

"Lady. Just the mutt or we call the pound. None of this is up for negotiation."

I put my fingers under Clarice's chin, raising her head. "Get your mind off this damn dog. You're in a real mess. Do what Sergeant Fidgery tells you, but don't talk about this to anyone until you get an attorney. A criminal attorney. A good one."

Fidge came out of the bedroom wearing a grin wider than his flat nose. "I hope you and Asta will live happily ever after." His eyes sort of twinkled, which is hard to imagine on the face genetics had passed down to Fidge.

"Now," he said, "for the last time, Matthew, get lost."

I lowered the dog to stop it from licking me on the mouth and walked out with Asta scrambling up my front, watching Clarice over my shoulder.

Chapter 2

Like yesterday, today started way too early. After a shower, three cups of coffee, a scan of the sports section, and solving four words in the crossword puzzle, I pulled my Chrysler 300 out of my building's underground parking and pointed it toward town. The veil of salty wetness that had sneaked in while the city slept still coated everything that had spent the night outdoors. I turned on the windshield wipers, hit the defroster button, and headed for the city jail. Clarice had been temporarily held at the smaller Long Beach jail inside the police department. After her arraignment, she had been moved to the larger main jail on Pacific Avenue near Twentieth Street.

Last spring, my ex-wife and I started sharing dinners, movies, and what was now her bed a few nights a week. We still cared, but she couldn't get past the anger and betrayal she felt over my having gunned down the thug outside the courthouse. After nearly a month of our running in place, I put a stop to the experiment. The ending of most relationships digs an emotional hole that refills with emptiness. Ours was no exception.

Hemingway had said something like the best way to get over a woman is to get a new one. I hadn't decided whether to take Hemingway's advice or to write a novel, use her name, and have her killed—heinously. For a few weeks after I pulled the plug on our mutual effort, I considered both, a sort of double exorcism.

Then I met Clarice, who was bright and funny as well as passionate. The only problem, Clarice was married. I hadn't known that, and I hadn't bothered asking. My libido was screaming, "Any port in a storm," and Clarice was a dock slip built to hold a good sized yacht so I powered on in.

* * *

The Long Beach jail, one of California's largest, booked about eighteen thousand inmates annually. That seems like a huge number of bookings, but then Long Beach was California's sixth largest city, and America's thirty-eighth biggest with a population around half a million. To most people Long Beach doesn't seem that big, probably because it butts up to Los Angeles without an obvious border crossing.

The chairs of the Long Beach jailhouse were all occupied with people jabbering in multiple languages. I figured all of them were talking about seeing a loved one and cursing someone else for the poor choices made by the loser they had come to visit. The air felt tight from the fear which grips everyone in a jail, even those working hard at showing tough. The mothers who had brought babies were trying to keep them from crying. But the babies had it right; a jail was a place that could make anyone cry.

For now, Clarice's world was the place writers had given names like stir, the slammer, the joint, the pokie, and a thousand others. But not the big house, that name referred to prison not a jail. Whatever the name, except in the movies, escapes were rare. Once you went in, you stayed in until they let you walk out or they carried you out.

Eventually I was called through a heavy door and left to walk behind a row of uncomfortable looking chairs. Visitation was limited to fifteen minutes. I chose the first place to sit where the chairs to each side of me were not occupied by other visitors. A moment later, Clarice entered through a door like the one I had come through, only her door was on the inmate side of the glass partition. Her entrance started the clock on our fifteen minutes. She walked toward me behind a row of chairs on her side, forced a smile, not much of one, and sat down.

We were separated by a pane of glass as thick as old coke bottles. I picked up the dirty phone on my side. She picked up the dirty phone on her side. She put the flat of her other hand on the unbreakable glass, the pads of her fingers turning white from the pressure. I covered her hand with my own, the insulation of the cold glass denying me the heat from her fingers.

She ignored the tide of tears spilling through her black lashes. "The prosecutor convinced the judge I was a flight risk. He denied bail. They photographed and fingerprinted me, then some dyke with a mustache long enough to curl felt me up during a strip search. After that I got shoved in the shower."

By the time Clarice finished, her voice had raised several decibels. The visiting room guard walked over and leaned down next to her. I couldn't see his face, but a good guess went something like: behave yourself or this visit's over and that gorgeous fanny of yours goes back in lockup.

She lowered her head and nodded. The guard stepped back. I gave her a minute to compose herself.

I had called ahead to get the official words. Clarice Talmadge had been charged with capital murder, also known as first degree murder with special circumstances, under California Penal Code 187 (a). The fancy title meant that if she was found guilty of having murdered her husband for financial gain, one of more than twenty different situations which constitute capital murder in California, she would face either the death penalty or life imprisonment without a possibility of parole.

Clarice jerked her hand up to swipe at a running tear. Then let her hand freefall onto her lap. Her face looked whiter than I had ever seen it, probably due to the shower and no makeup. Still, the woman was lovely. The jailhouse orange jumpsuit brought the emerald out of her bluish-green eyes. Her naturally creamy skin made me wonder why she ever bothered with makeup. Even her lips had a natural hot-pink hue. Her tongue had to enjoy keeping them moist.

She brought the phone back up to her ear.

"Asta's a strange name for a dog." I said, hoping to pull her out of her funk.

Her unpainted lips thinned and trembled. "How is my baby? Is she okay?"

"She's fine. Slept on the foot of my bed just like you said she would. We're getting along swell. I got the food and snacks you told me about. No problem. Where'd you come up with the name Asta?"

Clarice's head and shoulders swiveled to her left as a heavyset Hispanic inmate moved toward her, then quickly spun to the right to confirm the big woman had continued on by. Caught up in her jailhouse vigilance, I also watched the large woman until she sat in a chair two cubicles beyond Clarice.

"Tally bought Asta for me," Clarice said, returning from the distraction. "He named her after a dog owned by some guy named Nick Charles. I told him this Charles must be one of his friends I never met. Tally just smiled. He likes his private jokes. Then he said something about my being too young to understand."

"I don't think the police are going to be looking too hard for anyone else to pin this on." It was a hard message, but one she needed to hear. She took it without reaction.

"After we met," she said, as if she had not heard my harsh message, "I researched you in the online archives. You don't know it, but I'm hot searching stuff on that Internet." She moved the phone to her other hand, the aluminum wrapped cord draping across her mouth like surreal braces. "I read all I could find about your career as a cop."

"Then you know I went to prison and why."

"I know, and I agree with the majority of the people in the poll. I'm glad you shot the bastard. He deserved it."

"I appreciate that. In any event, I doubt I would have lasted much longer as a cop."

"Why?"

"The easy answer is the department thought I had too much Mike Hammer in me, while I thought the department had too much Casper Milquetoast. In my novels, I define and dole out justice the way it feels right to me. My readers must agree that justice isn't always best found in a courtroom. They keep buying my books."

"So your departmental papers show, terminated: too much Mike Hammer?"

"Well, they glossed it over as insubordination. I never have been any good at letting someone play smart when they're talking stupid, just because they're the boss."

Clarice moved in her chair, my gaze moved with her. She said, "One of the articles mentioned you're also a private detective."

"True. After my pardon they couldn't deny me a PI's license. Investigative work was my profession, but the law wouldn't allow me a permit to carry a weapon. I'm not sure why I got the private license. Maybe I thought it would add to my mystique as a crime novelist."

"Maybe because it lets you feel in some way you're still a detective." She grinned for the first time since I arrived, and then said, "The job that made you happier than being a novelist."

When they were being nice, the biddies in our building referred to Clarice as the airhead on the fourth floor, but my instincts told me Clarice was Phi Beta Kappa in street savvy.

"Me thinks the lady has brains as well as beauty."

"My mother was a lady. I think of myself as a woman. There is a difference you know?"

"No. I didn't know. As a writer, I'm naturally curious."

"When a lady sees a man who attracts her she thinks of herself as a flirt. When a woman does she thinks of herself as a prick teaser."

"I like it. May I use it?"

"Of course, but it requires you recognize one from the other."

"I'll do my best. Now, our time is limited so let's get back to your situation."

"You said the cops won't look much beyond me, so I need you to find out who killed Tally."

"Except in the pages of my books, I haven't worked a case in a lot a years. You don't want me. At best, I'm a rusty ex-detective."

"I've know a few smart men, Matt, even a couple of honest ones. But you're both. That's rare and it's just what I need."

"Don't make me out to be holy, you know my record."

"You plugging that guy shows you cared about the victim and about justice. That you're passionate about what you believe in. I need you to believe in me."

"I don't know." I kept shaking my head long after I finished saying it. "I just don't think I'm the man for this job."

"You are exactly the man for the job. You were with me. And you know I couldn't kill Tally … You know that, don't you Matt?"

Sam Spade would easily know whether or not Clarice was working me, but I couldn't tell. In the end it mattered little, I had always had difficulty re-corking an opened curiosity.

"No promises," I said. "I'll think on it. But, as long as I'm here, I do have a question about last night."

I saw that the always perfect polish on her fingernails was now chipped when she turned the back of her hand toward me and wiggled her fingers. "Bring it on."

"When you got home from my place, did you look in on Garson?"

"No. His door was shut. He usually went to bed before me. He'd close his door when he turned off his TV. Unless he called out, I would never go in after he shut his door … Why do you ask?"

"It would have told us whether he had been killed while you were with me or not." Her expression told me she understood.

"I expect," she said, "the autopsy will show Tally died while I was with you."

"That will show a range of time, a range that will likely cover part of the time you were with me and some time you weren't. But we don't have the autopsy yet."

She didn't say anything, just looked down and pursed her lips.

"You handling this place okay?"

She shrugged. "It's nasty and that's just the surface. Look at these outfits. How's a girl gonna look good in this ugly thing?" She tugged hard enough to billow the loose-fitting orange material over her bust, then glanced toward the door and the guard.

"You'd look good in anything," I said, meaning it, "but this is not a place for looking sensuous. Let your hair go. Don't bathe unless they insist, but cooperate when they do."

"No sweat, Matt. I hold a brown belt in karate. If any of the lesbos in this place put a hand on me, they'll wish they hadn't."

"Also, this is not a place to get in a fight. Walk and talk with confidence, not cockiness. Stay to yourself, but don't act like a victim or like you're too good for the rest of 'em."

She smiled for the second time. "Seeing we're talking outfits here, I see you wore your trench coat. That ought to help you get into your detective persona."

The trench coat may have been a little over the top into my novelist side, but I wasn't about to confess that to Clarice. "Morning fog," I said. "Wet. Now, did you get an attorney?"

"I called Henry Blackton." She stroked her fingers on the glass the way she might to tickle the open palm of my hand. "He was Tally's lawyer for all his U.S. business deals."

"You need a criminal mouthpiece, not a corporate attorney."

"That's what Blackton told me. He sent over Brad Fisher who went with me to the arraignment. I gave Fisher your name and told him you'd help. Was that okay? Do you know Fisher?"

"Only by reputation, which says he's a topnotch criminal lawyer. No promises, but I'll talk with him."

About the Author

David Bishop enjoyed a varied career as an entrepreneur during which he wrote many technical articles for financial and legal journals, as well as a nonfiction business book published in three languages. Eventually, he began using his abilities as an analyst to craft the twists and turns and salting of clues so essential to fine mystery writing. David has several mystery, suspense and thriller stories available for your pleasure reading. For more information on David and his other novels please visit his web site. He would appreciate hearing your thoughts on this mystery or any of his novels.

www.davidbishopbooks.com
david@davidbishopbooks.com
https://www.facebook.com/davidbishopbooks
https://www.twitter.com/@davidbishop7

#1 Amazon Bestselling Author
750,000 books in circulation

DAVID BISHOP

Author of 'The Woman'

A MATT KILE MYSTERY – BOOK THREE

MONEY & MURDER

A SHORT STORY

28425682R00188

Made in the USA
Columbia, SC
10 October 2018